Woman Of
The Mists

Lynn Sholes

WOMAN OF THE MISTS

Published by Stone Creek Books
Oakland Park, Florida

Originally published by Diamond Books

Cover art by Joe Moore

ISBN-13: 978-0692527979:

DEDICATION

This book is dedicated to Madison, my father, and Gail, my mother, because they always believed it; to Ashleigh, Mac, and Alexis, my children, who put up with it; to Gypsy, my friend and mentor; to Penny, my friend, who listened to it; and to Sandi, who shared a shirt, a toy G.I. Joe figure, an urn, and headaches.

Prologue

TWO THOUSAND FIVE HUNDRED YEARS AGO there lived a nation of people who have vanished from the face of the earth. The only thing known of them is what archaeologists have found under the rich, black South Florida muck. Their distant ancestors had lived beside the great ice age mammals and had witnessed the cataclysmic changes that wiped out the giant animals that had fed them for so long. They survived, carving out a complicated culture that listened to the lessons learned through the generations.

In the early 1990s the Army Corps of Engineers dug a ditch on the perimeter of the Everglades, slicing through the southern edge of a tree island, a hammock that humped out of the thin lens of water that slowly flows across the tip of the peninsula. The operator of the backhoe jumped from his machine when he saw human bones falling from the bucket.

The medical examiner was called to investigate, and he determined that the remains were those of the Indians who had once lived in the area. The ditch was abandoned, and archaeologists were called in.

On this piece of land that was dotted with strangler figs, a characteristic of Indian sites, the archaeological team found a massive burial component, habitation mound, and ceremonial complex.

The group was made up of mainly amateur volunteers, led by a couple of professional archaeologists. For years it had been assumed that the small inland camps, located on the hammocks, were only short-term hunting camps. But more recent data indicated that many of these sites were actually large habitation sites, where all types of village-related activities took place. Archaeologists began to take another look at the people who had long ago occupied this land.

Perspiration dripping from their brows as they worked under the hot Florida sun, they sat steadily beside individual pits, which were linked together to form a trench that crossed what they believed was the habitation area.

Eyeballing the level-line against the meter stick, one of the volunteers measured the depth of pit 4 North, making sure that the floor of the pit remained level. Working next to her, in 5 North, one of the archaeologists lay on her belly, looking down into the one-meter square pit. Gingerly, with a bamboo skewer, she scratched away small clogs of soil, exposing parts of an alligator's skeleton. The midden, or garbage heap, revealed the diet of the inhabitants.

After sifting the spoil through wire screens, they picked out and bagged the sharp snake vertebrae that poked their fingertips. They collected the bones of turtles, fish, and birds, as well as the remains of deer, rats, lizards, alligators, raccoons, and other small mammals. Each bag was labeled with the site, date, pit number, and depth at which the articles had been found. Potsherds, drilled sharks' teeth, and other worked bone or shell artifacts were bagged separately. Later, in the lab, everything would be identified, sorted, and cataloged.

Tools and intricately carved bone stimulated conversations about their possible uses. A miniature shell hoe, officially tagged as a tool, suggested a toy, and suddenly to all who were working, the extinct people seemed quite real.

In pit 7 North, there was an abundance of shells the Indians had brought back from one of their trips to the ocean. The volunteers quickly dubbed it the "raw bar."

Another team worked the burial site. Not many grave goods had been interred with the dead, but the bones spoke loud and clear. Their teeth were worn down nearly to the roots. A few of the characteristic shovel-shaped incisors were found, inspected, and commented on by the group. Some molars had worn-away crescents at the gum line from years of leather working. There was very little evidence of dental caries.

Most of the people had been relatively short and robust. The graves were filled with bodies of all ages, the geriatric population as well as the newborn. Some pieces of skull showed pitting, which might have been a result of a childhood disease, such as a slight anemia from hookworm. Some remains showed evidence of arthritis. A pathologist would discern much more.

A volunteer passed around a long bone, a femur, pointing out the syphilitic lesions on it. "The Indians' revenge," he remarked, meaning that syphilis was a New World disease that the Indians had transmitted to the Europeans.

One of the amateur helpers wandered the area. Far from the mound she discovered another interesting feature. Just beneath a small elevation in the earth, she found a pile of rocks with a turtle shell on top. With delicacy she brushed the soil away from the edges. Around the stones was a circle of snake vertebrae.

Anxious to see what rested beneath such a marker, in her excitement forgetting archaeological techniques, she removed the stones and scratched away the earth, exposing yet another grave. The brown skull rested intact. A strikingly beautiful columella pendant had been interred with the person. She had often seen columellae worked into tools. The centers of the conch shells were strong and very durable. She had seen other pendants made from them, but she had never seen one quite like this. As she lifted it, admiring its beauty and peculiar sheen, a sudden cold wind came up. It was July, and it wasn't unusual for a thunderstorm to form quickly from the heating of the day. The large branches of the trees cracked and splintered, and the smaller ones shattered into twigs. The wind whirled the young trees in circles, and the roots of the tall old cypress vibrated in the ground, reminding her how far she was from the group. She huddled by the grave, waiting for the rain to start. The earth beneath her rumbled, making her lose her balance and drop the pendant. Then, suddenly, silence.

The woman looked at the circle of light that poured down on the grave. The wind had clipped the branches just above her so that the light streamed down in a shaft.

"Damn Florida weather," she said aloud, reaching for the pendant. Clutching it tightly, she excitedly trotted back to the group to tell them of her find and of the freak twister that had sprung up out of nowhere.

Chapter One

PERHAPS IT WAS AN OMEN, a warning from her guide spirit.

Teeka watched as Tamuk, the clan's shaman, put a noose around the alligator's snout and began to drag it closer. He readied himself, raising an ashen-skinned arm above the horizon of the marsh, casting it steadily against the blue sky. When the animal was within reach, he would ram the long pointed stick down its gullet. As the thrashing beast tore at the shore, the leather thong noose snapped, setting free the powerful jaws. Twisting, the reptile swung his tail and caught Tamuk behind the knees, slamming him to the ground. The gator slashed to the side and took the man into his mouth, drilling its conical teeth through the oracle's thin scalp, crushing his skull.

Suddenly it released the shaman, only to align itself with a softer part of the spirit man's body. Like the shark of the Big Water, it shook its head, tearing the flesh from Tamuk's girth, speckling the surface of the water with bits of torn tissue. Slowly it backed into deeper water, devouring the great medicine man as it sank. The terrible beast rose to the top and spoke, as in the legends of talking animals.

"You have been warned. Listen well, Little Doe."

The alligator sank all but its eyes beneath the surface,

the yellow spheres glaring over the black water before blinking and then submerging.

Teeka waded into the water, calling to the spirit to explain.

The water had begun to thicken. Each step became more and more difficult, the suction of the mud reluctant to give her up. She looked at the shore to judge its distance and saw Auro standing near the edge.

"Auro, help me!"

Why did he not come to save her, to rescue her?

The sludge covered her, leaving only a few strands of her hair suspended on the top of the viscous slime. How could Auro let this happen to her? She did not understand. As her mouth opened to gasp for air, she felt herself fill with the putrid slime. She let out an unheard scream.

The dream had been so hideous As the eastern sky had shown the first hints of pink, she had gathered her things and quietly walked to the pond. Even now, as she lifted the grooming brush to her long black hair and watched her reflection in the still pool, the nightmare kept recurring. But the water was clear and still, and her jet-black eyes shone back at her.

Even for a Tegesta she was petite. Her nose was delicate and her eyes heavily lashed. Her lips were just full enough to be a sensual contrast to her other delicate features. After a few strokes with the brush her hair hung free from the tangles of sleep, gently flowing across her chest, covering her small round bosom.

The cracking of a dead twig penetrated the quiet. She stood slowly, almost imperceptibly backing away from the pool. Pausing, she listened for any noise, then agilely and deliberately turned. Still nothing. Cautiously she made her way through the brush. She could hear her heart beating in her ears and pounding in her head, and her breath, though she tried to control it, came in short audible gasps and exhalations. Every muscle was straining to do what instinct was petitioning her to do. Run!

The saw grass ripped at her ankles, and the tall sedge slapped her in the face. Then suddenly a shadow darkened the path ahead, and Teeka fell to her knees.

She raised her eyes to see an angular jaw, a straight nose, and onyx eyes. The heavily muscled body was young, strong, and firm. He was masculine in structure and protective in nature. Indeed, he was the most perfect man she had ever known.

"Auro, it is you," she spoke softly, rising to her feet.

"What has frightened you so that you run and tremble?" he asked, searching her face and then looking behind her for some clue.

She bowed her head in embarrassment. "It was nothing. A dream from the night has made me act foolishly. I am glad that it is you who saw me and not someone else."

"Was it a dream from your guide spirit?"

She hesitated before answering. "No. Just a bad dream that made no sense."

"Let the dream leave your head," he said, lifting her face in his hands. "Think of other things. Think of the marriage and how I will soon make you a woman."

Teeka bent her head forward, showing her disapproval. Her slender fingers nervously twirled a strand of hair.

"We want the blessings of the People," she said. "Let us not offend them by breaking the custom."

Auro leaned close and pressed his lips to her hair. Her

ears could hear his breathing, and she, too, wondered if the marriage day would ever come.

"Walk close to me, Auro. Walk with me and speak of pleasant things."

As they returned to the village, he talked of the journey to the Big Water. It was the one thing that could occupy his mind fully enough to distract him from his thoughts of Teeka. This would not be his first journey. He had gone to the Big Water many times since he had become a man.

"We are the strongest of our people, and we are protected by the medicine of Tamuk. When our hunt is done, we will come home, and it will be a time of celebration for many reasons. I will return to you and say the marriage promises."

"But I remember Izo," she said, stopping to argue. "He was brave and young. Pyra was waiting for him for marriage, and yet he was called to walk the Other Side."

"You think too much of the work of men. When we return, we will pay our tribute to Kaho, and then we will celebrate our peace and good fortune. Our marriage will be part of that good fortune. Soon I will show you," he said, taking both of her hands in his. "I will not need to speak of it. Our bodies and spirits will join, and the Joining Spirit will reward us."

"You do not even know when you speak forbidden words," she said, smiling.

"I speak easily of my love. How can that be wrong?"

Teeka lowered her head and blushed with embarrassment. "It does not seem wrong to me, but what if the spirits do not approve?"

Auro turned his head away and pointed to the sky. "Is it not the Great One that gives the gift of love? Do not all the spirits answer to the Great One? No spirit can be angry with the gift of the Great One. We tempt no spirit's anger."

She returned alone to her platform and shook the woven mat of grasses that was her bed. She could see her mother and other women near the fire, beginning to prepare the morning meal. Teeka watched for a moment and then joined them, sitting beside her older sister, Illa.

The fish was beginning to steam in the pot that was suspended above the fire as she stared at her sister, wanting to ask her so many things. Had it been like this for Illa before her marriage to Ata? Had he spoken of such things? What was the gift of the Joining Spirit really like? Why did no one speak of these things? Was it really a silly way of the old ones, as Auro had said? And how did he know of these unspoken mysteries? Were men born with the knowledge? Was it told to them by other men during the secret part of the ceremony of becoming a man? She had so many questions.

To ask was forbidden. The Tegesta placed great value on the purity of their young women. Tegesta maidens were innocent, their virginity well protected by religious custom. The spirits had directed it to be so.

Only once had anyone ever spoken to her of these mysteries. As a child, Teeka had been frightened by the noises in the night, and her mother had tried to comfort her.

"It is not pain or fear you hear, Little Doe. It is the noise of love."

"Do you love me, Mother?" she asked, trying to make some sense of what her mother had just said.

"Yes, I love you. But it is the love of a man and a woman that causes those sounds."

Teeka's face still expressed confusion.

"Do you weep when you are very sad, Little Doe? And

do you weep when you are very happy sometimes? Is the sound of the happy weeping any different from the sound of the sad weeping?"

"No, Mother. They are the same," she answered, beginning to understand.

"The sound of weeping is always the same, but it can mean different things. These sounds should not worry you. They are like the sounds of happy weeping. They are good sounds."

Now, staring at Illa, Teeka wondered what joining was really like. All she knew was that sometimes, when she was close to Auro, she wanted to pull him next to her. When he spoke the forbidden words, she wanted to touch him and feel his flesh on hers. Was that what joining was, being close, flesh to flesh?

The thoughts caused a tingling across her breasts and a drawing deep in her belly, as if something was missing. Teeka adjusted her moss skirt to keep it clear of the embers. When she looked down, she saw that her nipples were erect, as if she felt cold. But the day was warm, especially so close to the fire. She pulled her hair across her chest so that no one would see. She supposed that she would have to wait until the marriage, and then she would ask Auro and the mysteries would end. So many mysteries.

———

The night was filled with dancing until the moon was high in the sky. All of the men gathered in a circle around Tamuk as he chanted and tossed his medicines in a black clay bowl. As he stood, he planted a staff, the crest carved like a snake. The women stood back in the shadows, viewing the ceremony from a proper distance.

The shaman spread the leaves from the bowl on the

ground and spat on them, rolling his eyes while chanting words understood by no one except his son, Auro. Opening his eyes, Tamuk called each hunter by his guide spirit's name. Each took his leaf from the shaman, held it to the mouth of the snake, and then put it into a drawstring pouch fastened about his neck. The medicine man's token would protect them from the dangers of the journey. It would also remind a man's spirit not to be too boastful, else he might take foolish chances.

The men walked in ceremonial procession to a special place draped with hammocks, soft hide slings, in which to sleep. They would sleep away from the women on this night, for a woman could affect the potency of the medicine. Even the men who were too old to make the journey slept in the hammocks. Their experience was well respected. Only the boys, not yet men, returned with the women.

Early, as the mist began to steam from the pool, the clan gathered near the river. The women placed baskets of roots and berries inside the canoes. Each craft was large enough to carry fifteen men. The neighboring villages of Tegesta sent their hunters, and the canoes were full.

Tamuk uttered a string of sounds and motioned with his hands as the hunters began to pole the large open-water canoes down the stream. The water would flow softly at first, and they would have to be careful not to run aground. The work would begin in the current that rushed toward the ocean. When the canoes reached a point where the mouth the river could be seen, a hardwood mast would be fixed in the socket in the bottom of the boat. Sails made from sewn-together animal skins would be unfurled to catch the wind. Only the most experienced men would be allowed to direct the sails and the oars. The others would begin to watch for signs of manatee, fish, sea turtle, and shark.

They would explore oyster beds for food and for the white bead inside. They would harvest the shallows with their nets. They would camp on the beach and smoke their catch at night. When the canoes could hold no more, they would return to their villages and divide the spoils evenly among them. The sharks' teeth would be drilled and modified to become ornaments or parts of saws or other tools. The wheel-shaped vertebrae would be drilled and used as adornments, ear buttons, and counters.

The hunters would return as heroes. The spoils of the journey would be sorted and a portion put with other treasures to be offered to Kaho. For this payment they would be given peace.

Teeka watched the boats slowly make their way down the stream. How many days would they be gone? She would watch the moon.

Chapter Two

AS THE RIVER BEGAN TO CHURN, the clear water turned to a swirling opaque brown. Auro inspected the knife that he had fashioned from a macrocallista shell. He slid the beveled edge across his thumb, leaving a line of separated skin. This was the one tool that always belonged to the man who made it. All the other tools and weapons used on the journey were communal, and each man knew that his life and the lives of the others depended on the excellence of his craftsmanship. If someone was injured because of a weapon of poor quality, the maker would be publicly shamed and never again allowed to make weapons or tools for hunting. He would lose his status as a man.

Only once had Auro seen a man so shamed. It was after Izo had been injured. When Izo crossed to the Other Side, the shamed man could not bear his dishonor and left the clan to wander alone. In this hostile environment, being alone and unable to make weapons was the same as death.

Auro lowered his hand into the water, washing away the blood from his thumb. The village had long been out of sight. The next time he saw it, his patience would be rewarded. It had been a long time since he had gone to Teges, the chief, the cacique, and asked permission to take Teeka as his woman. Six full cycles of the moon had passed, but he remembered the time well.

"Auro, son of the great shaman of our people, why have you come to Teges?"

Auro kept his head low in respect. "I have come to ask permission to take a maiden as my wife."

"And which maiden would this be? The son of a shaman must keep his line pure."

Auro raised only his eyes to the cacique, and Teges gestured for him to lift his head. "She is from the Tegesta clan to the south. She is the daughter of Selo, who is the daughter of Ramut. The maiden's father walks the Other Side. Her line is pure and suitable for the shaman's son. She and her family have been brought here for the courtship. I wish the courtship to end. She pleases me."

"Tell Teges the name of this suitable maiden."

"Teeka is her given name. Little Doe is her spirit guide."

The cacique lifted one hand, palm out. "Does Teeka also choose Auro?"

Auro remained expressionless, though he wanted to smile with the answer because it pleased him so. "She does choose Auro."

The chieftain dropped his hand and closed his eyes. Auro waited, trying not to stir. At last Teges spoke. "Go then and ask the shaman if your spirits are compatible. We have no discontented spirits in the clan of Teges."

In a moment Teges lowered and then raised his head, a gesture that permitted Auro to leave his presence.

He passed Teeka as she pounded coontie into flour. She watched him pass and thought he seemed much taller than before.

He continued to the place of his father, the shaman, which was apart from the main part of the village. Unlike the other open platforms of the village, the shaman's had thatched sides and roofing. The weather was cool, a welcome change from the humid heat that usually plagued them. Auro's mother poked the fire and fed it fresh kindling, hoping to bring it ablaze again. The spirit man was old, and the cool air would make him stiff and sick. She was not the wife of the shaman, as he was not permitted to live with a woman. Instead, the shaman could choose any maid to serve him. He could choose many if he wanted to, and they would hold an honored place in the clan. But Tamuk had chosen only one woman throughout his long life: Shala, Auro's mother.

As a young man, Tamuk had brought Shala to his village to court her. Because he was the shaman, the woman he chose stayed at his village. Tamuk had often gone to Shala's hearth in the night. With age he had stopped, but Shala had continued to go to him. She would rise several times during the night to attend the old man. She would kneel beside him, gently touching his face with her hand. If the air was cold, she would adjust the blankets of deerskin around his shoulders and then return to her platform.

Auro had begun to learn his father's craft as a small child. Most of the other clans of the Tegesta did not have a shaman. When they were in need of a man of the spirits, they came to Tamuk. Even Teeka had been brought to Tamuk as an infant for the naming of her guide spirit. Being the shaman was a very important responsibility.

All members of the clan were related matrilineally. The son of a married couple was only casually related to the father. It was different for a shaman and his son. They had a special bond. As the son of the shaman, Auro was obligated to spend all the days with him, and Tamuk taught him well. They would spend days and nights alone, wandering the land from the wet marsh to the sandier soil to the east, which was covered with tall pines, live oak, cabbage palms, and palmettos. The time was spent in study, identifying herbs, mosses, flowers, plants, berries, and fungi. Away from the rest, the shaman taught him chants, incantations, signs, and gestures for all events. He was taught the methods of contacting the spirits and the way to talk with them. But he would not be allowed to perform any of the sorcery alone while Tamuk lived. Only after the death of his father would Auro become the revered man of the spirits. If he decided to marry before he became the shaman, the woman would have to leave his platform when he rose to that position. No one else's spirit would be allowed to linger at the hearth of the shaman. Such a presence could interfere with his communication with the spirits.

As Auro got closer, he realized how old his father looked. The thought of his own rise to the status of shaman made him wince. It was a great responsibility to which he had once looked forward. But now there was Teeka.

"Forgive my interruption, Shaman," he had begun. "I have come to you to consult with the spirits on an important matter."

"My son has come to me as his shaman. I have watched Auro since he became a man. He wishes to take a maiden as his woman. Is your father not correct, my son?"

"Yes, Father. This man before you wishes to take Teeka, daughter of Selo."

The old man stood very slowly, supporting himself with a walking stick. "Little Doe is the guide spirit of Teeka, and unto my son I gave the spirit of the Alligator. It is a strong and fierce spirit, one that would be needed by the son of a shaman. Come to me in the morning when the sun meets the moon in the sky. I will give you an answer then."

The shaman walked to his platform and began sorting through baskets and pouches for the things he would need to consult with the spirits. He told Shala the things that he did not have stored and asked her to gather them for him.

That night Shala gave the shaman a basket filled with the roots and herbs he had requested. Waving her away, Tamuk carefully measured them into a bowl of hot water. He stirred it and chanted. When the broth became dark and cloudy, he removed the bowl from the fire. As it cooled, the magician shook his rattles rhythmically, uttering melodic sounds. He lifted the pot to his lips and swallowed the hot, syrupy liquid. Then he left the immediate area of his hearth, walking a short distance into the brush. A few moments later he retched until all the contents of his stomach had spilled onto the earth. His hands began to shake, and then his legs jerked in spasms as he fell backward on the ground. With his spine stiff and his eyes rolled back, the shaman began his flight to the spirit world.

Just before dawn he returned to his hearth and slept.

Auro had seen the smoke from his father's fire through the early morning haze. As he got closer, he saw Tamuk standing with a bundle in his hands.

"Have you spoken with the spirits, Father?" he asked anxiously.

"I have." As he answered, Tamuk rolled out the bundle. Inside was a small piece of deerskin that had been scraped and tanned into a soft beige strip. Beside it was an alligator scute, one of the bones that make up the ridges down the back of an alligator.

"What have the spirits answered?" Auro asked, almost too impatiently.

"There was much struggle between them, but they have consented. The spirit of the Little Doe and the Alligator may live as one in harmony. Auro and Teeka may celebrate their marriage after the next journey to the Big Water."

Auro offered his father some pelts and meat as payment for his skill.

"The offering is accepted. After the morning meal, go and tell Teeka."

Auro began to leave when Tamuk called out to him. "Auro, return. I must speak to you as a father."

Auro moved to Tamuk's side. "Is there something that troubles you, Father? Are you in much pain? I can prepare a poultice."

The shaman shook his head. "It is not for me that I am concerned. It is concern for my son and the woman he chooses."

"What is it, Father? Have I offended you or a spirit?"

"Too much love is a dangerous thing."

The young man touched his father's hand. "I have thought about what troubles you. When you are called to the Other Side, I will not let the People be without a shaman."

The old man looked no less concerned. He started to speak, but then patted his son's hand instead. "It is a happy day for you."

As Auro walked away, Shala came and stood next to Tamuk. "You worry too much because he is your son and you are the shaman. Have you seen the way he looks at her? It is the way you looked at me when we were young."

The shaman squeezed Shala's hand. "Do I not still

look at you that way?"

"And that look is in my eyes also."

"We have been fortunate. Love that is out of a man's control goes astray. The love wanders, searching for its boundaries. Sometimes evil sees that the love is lost, and it stalks the love, like a predator tracking its prey. It is sly and traps the love, and the love does not even know that evil has become its keeper."

"Shaman, you are wise, but when you think about Auro, I still say you worry too much."

"My Shala," he began, "it is a burden to be a shaman. It is the price of the gift. I am glad that it is I who must carry the weight and not you."

Auro's recollection of that important day did not include the worry known to his father. He felt himself fill with excitement as he watched the small wake form in the water behind his trailing thumb. The journey would soon end, and he would return to take Teeka as his woman.

———

In these last few days before the hunters' return, Tamuk had been very restless. He slept less and less. He spoke with no one. He had even curtly dismissed Shala. He had seen in his vision the thing that frightened him. He would need to be prepared.

As Shala cooked the morning meal, Tamuk wandered off, casting his weight on his walking stick, until the sounds of the village had long passed. Beneath the trunk of a long fallen cypress, fungi thrived on the dark dampness. The shaman bent forward and jabbed his stick underneath the log. The prying was making him short of breath, and his shoulder and back balked with the pain of the labor. His brows dripped beads of sweat that burned his eyes.

At last, the log lifted and rolled just enough to expose the compost. A scorpion, startled by the light, skittered under nearby leaves. Earthworms protested and wriggled back under the protection of the loosely packed earth.

He had remembered well. The black spongy fungi was plentiful. The shaman opened his waterproof pouch, which he had made many years ago from the entrails of an otter.

The black fungus was exactly what he needed. It lived as a parasite, feeding on dead matter. Its dull, lifeless color separated it from the plants of the living that glowed green in the sunlight. So it hid, feeding on the dead, a heinous thing, and a dangerous one whose potency was known only to the chosen.

The medicine man speared small pieces of it and slipped them inside the pouch before continuing west, collecting a few hard red berries and seed pods. A large, leathery cycad caught his attention, and he stopped and inspected it carefully. From beneath the earth he dug its swollen tuber, which was richly stored with starch and, more important, poison. With his knife he cut it free.

Near the village he detoured slightly and walked up onto the scarred surface of a limestone platform that heroically lifted itself out of the wetlands. In the center, he hunkered low to the ground and lifted his face and arms to the sky.

"Spirits of the People, hear your servant, Tamuk."

The worried, fragile man waited for a sign. A cloud moved across the sun, and the wind came up, blowing the long gray hair away from his rawboned face. A bolt of lightning fractured the air, and the clouds unrolled, covering the sky. In the darkness of the storm, the earth vibrated with thunder, and the temperature of the air dropped, sending a chill down his brittle spine. The animals and insects suddenly fell silent.

The shaman recognized the sign and spoke in an old, old language, used only to speak with the spirits. The flashes of lightning increased in frequency, and the cracking of thunder shattered the air. The wind tried to drown him out, but the old man persisted until he was screaming the words. The wind-driven rain forced his eyes closed and stung his skin. Tamuk stood, lifting his face to the pelting rain and stretching his arms out, repeating and repeating his call. The earth shook beneath his feet. He fought for his balance and won, never stopping his summons.

Near dark the storm passed, and he let himself drop to the earth. His withered body and mind had been spent in the confrontation, but Shala would be worried about him if he didn't return before the sky was dark. Guarding each movement, the weathered old man stood slowly, hoisting himself with the walking stick, and headed toward the village.

The sun was fire red on the western horizon, and the clouds were tinted pink and orange. From a distance, Shala saw him coming, but she pretended not to, not wanting to insult him with her concern. He was still a man, even if he was old and failing.

When close enough, she approached him with a bowl of warm turtle meat.

"You have been gone most of the day. You must be hungry and tired."

He nodded his head. "It was not easy work that I did on this day."

"What has been so important that you would wander without food or drink?"

Tamuk handed her the pouch. "Bring me the bowl," he almost ordered.

"Of which bowl do you speak, Shaman?" she asked.

"The bowl of my father that was his father's, and his father's before him."

Shala stiffened. "What need is there of that bowl, Tamuk?"

The old man's eyebrows dipped, and his forehead furrowed with despair. "It will have a use soon."

She loosened the drawstring of the pouch just enough to see inside, and shuddered when she saw its contents.

"Tamuk, no!" she said, reeling backward. "You have no use for these things."

"Bring the bowl, and prepare the hatchi," he said to stop her protest.

Shala knelt before him. "But I have never prepared hatchi. I do not know how to do this thing you ask me."

"Pound it and grind it to a liquid, but be careful not to let it touch your skin. If it should splatter on you, stop and wash it off. Go now, Shala. Bring me the bowl, and begin your work. There is not much time. The hatchi must have time to cure."

Shala reluctantly obeyed. She was allowed to make the initial preparations, but only the shaman could combine the ingredients of his potions.

She ground the fungi in a rock mortar, and the stench of it made her gag, forcing her to breathe through her mouth. Finally a small pool of foul black liquid rested in the bottom of the mortar. She could still see Tamuk in the moonlight, shaking his rattles and chanting over the ancient wooden bowl. She suctioned the liquid through a reed, carefully drawing it only halfway up, and then releasing it into a clay bowl. Once all the liquid had been transferred, she took it to Tamuk.

The old man inspected it. Deftly, he poured the hatchi into the ancient bowl that he had prepared.

"Go and bury your bowl and the mortar. It can never be used again. When you have finished, bathe yourself. Wash your hair and scrub your skin. Rinse your mouth and nose with clean water. Forget what we have done tonight and speak of it to no one."

"What about the other contents of the pouch?"

"Leave them. Maybe it will not come to this."

Shala stood before him. Her eyes pleaded for an explanation, but he offered none. He had aged since he left that morning. The lines in his face were deeper and his eyes not as clear. His face seemed to sag, and his brows were set with great worry. His lips looked dry and thin, and the hollows of his cheeks looked deeper and darker.

It had been generations since any shaman had used that bowl. It was passed down from father to son, but it was known that only the gravest situation called for its use. It was the only vessel in which the shaman was permitted to prepare the recipe for poison intended for one of the People.

"I can tell you no more, Shala. Go and do as I say. Cause yourself no more concern."

This was too serious a matter to tell her. Today the spirits had confirmed it. For hours he had begged them to deny what he had envisioned. But the spirits had remained firm in their message. He had interpreted it correctly, and they would not intervene. They entrusted it all to him. It was to be his responsibility.

His body was weak from age. A shaman should never weaken, and so his will was strong. But Tamuk had the gifts of a shaman and the heart of a man, and that man's heart ached with love for his son. But he remembered that before anything else he was the shaman of the People.

Just before sleep came, Tamuk felt his skin grow cold. His fingertips grew numb, and a buzzing began in his ears. The buzzing grew louder, drowning out all other sounds. He could see his body below him as he hovered over it. There was no wind, only the stillness of the other dimension. A suction pulled him through a tunnel at an incredible speed and then spat him out into another time.

Tamuk was filled with sadness. Before him sat an ancient shaman, chanting over a potion in the ritual bowl. Tamuk's spirit eye reached out and floated into the shaman. Now he was one with the medicine man. He understood why he had prepared the potion. A man of his tribe was filled with an evil spirit. This evil man had bargained with the spirits for power over the People. The spirits from the Darkside had heard his plea and rewarded him. All men now bowed to him.

The evil man had called the spirits for personal gain and greed, a practice that violated tribal customs and values. Only the shamans were to deal with the spirits, and if another called to them, only the Darkside spirits would listen. Always there was a price to pay. No Darkside spirit granted anything without taking something away in return. And even though the greedy man knew that he would trade the suffering of the People for his own benefit, he was not dissuaded.

Tamuk watched with horror, and he now understood the legends. The forests were disappearing, and the great animals that roamed the earth were dying. Water rushed across the land where there had been no water before. The People suffered for lack of food and high ground. The coast disappeared under the water of salt. The People cried out in pain and anger as they paid the price for the man's greed.

The good spirits visited the ancient shaman and spoke

to him. They told him how to make a special wooden bowl and then how to prepare a poison in it, according to their direction. He was not to alter it in any way. He would have to stop the man. He had the power, and now he had the means. It would also be his responsibility that the People never forget the consequences of such a greedy and evil act.

While the evil man was away from his hearth, the old shaman slipped through the shadows and filled the evil man's shell ladle with the potion. When the man returned, he drank from the ladle and immediately fell to the ground. Tamuk saw the man's face for the first time. He reminded him of Auro.

Tamuk bolted at the shock, setting himself free from the ancient holy man. He trembled with the horror of what he had seen.

A good spirit spoke to Tamuk. "You have seen enough, Spirit Man. Take this vision with you. Know well what you must do. Be strong, Spirit Man. You are Shaman."

The vision faded and blackened, and Tamuk was suddenly transported back through the tunnel and into his body. The experience had taken all of the night. The bowl of hatchi sat just as it had been left. The vision had not been a dream. None of it had been a dream.

Chapter Three

THE MOON HAD TURNED through half its cycle since Auro and the others had gone. They would be home soon. At sunrise Teeka was by the water. A pair of blue jays began their daily argument, attracting her attention. The sky was gray, and the jays fluttered in and out of sight among the mist and the branches. In the distance she thought she saw canoes, but she couldn't be sure. She stood to get a better look, but the fog and hanging willow branches kept obstructing her view. She waded into the water to get a better look. Auro, she thought. They've come home. Teeka started in a trot along the edge of the stream.

As soon as she saw them clearly, she flinched. The canoes that were advancing were not the large Big Water ships. They were the smaller canoes that traveled the inland waters.

She withdrew from the water's edge and hid behind a clump of reeds. Cautiously pulling some of the blades and stalks back, she looked downstream. The fog was rapidly lifting, the boats looming close. Straining her eyes, she searched for some sign that would identify the canoes and the people who manned them. As they got closer, the lead boat became clearer and the identity distinct. In the bow stood a man who had earned her fear. On his head he wore the spiked white plumes of the great egret. His body was decorated with colors that had been etched into his skin with thorns and dyes.

The saw grass cut ragged slits in Teeka's skin, and the undergrowth of grasses entangled her ankles as she scrambled through the brush. A spiderweb caught in her hair, and the huge black arachnid crawled across her face. Whimpers of panic escaped her mouth with each breath. She had gone too far downstream trying to get a look at the canoes. Now there was no clear path to the village. She was weaving through branches and vines, tearing her skirt and abrading her skin. Blood trickled from her shin where a blade of saw grass had slashed the thin skin atop the bone.

Unexpectedly, the thick brush suddenly cleared. She needed to give her people a warning. He was coming. Why? Why? The bravest and the strongest were gone to the Big Water. How would those who remained defend themselves? Why was he coming now? It wasn't the right time.

She ran to the edge of the village but was afraid to scream the warning for fear the raiders might hear her. Panting, she ran through the middle of the village, stopping to tell everyone she passed.

"Kaho! Kaho comes!"

After the first few had been told, the word traveled quickly and quietly. The very name of the man released fear in the village. He was the powerful warring chief of the Kahoosa. The Kahoosa had many warriors, and they dominated by terrorizing other tribes.

The women gathered the children and hid behind the mound, the hammock that supported the village. Teeka held Illa's youngest, while Illa quickly pulled her other two children close to her. The baby was hungry and stirred fitfully in Teeka's arms. She rocked him gently, but he was becoming inconsolable.

The Kahoosa warriors grounded their canoes. Kaho led fifteen men whose oiled skins shone in the sunlight. They were taller, with sharper features than the Tegesta. Their shell necklaces and anklets clanked as they moved, announcing their arrival even before they could be seen.

Teges, Tamuk, and the old men stood in a solid line, side by side, confronting the intruders. They stood tall and straight, trying to bluff the enemy.

The Kahoosa had painted their faces with red, black, and yellow stripes—the colors of the deadly coral snake. Stomping loudly, making no effort to conceal their arrival, Kaho and his men made their way from the water's edge up the slope of the mound. They formed an intimidating line of vivid colors with Kaho at the center, a single step in front of the rest.

Teges, the chieftain, spoke first. "What has brought Kaho to visit the clan of Teges?"

Kaho raised his spear toward the sky. "Does Kaho need a reason to visit Teges?"

Teges did not move any muscle that could be seen by Kaho and judged as fear. His eyes never left Kaho's. Looking away would have displayed weakness.

"Teges acknowledges the power of Kaho but questions his choice of time. Our hunters have not returned from the Big Water. We have not yet prepared your share of the People's wealth."

Kaho looked at his band of warriors. "This cacique questions Kaho's time. Does he not know that Kaho can count the moons?"

Kaho's band laughed at the ridiculousness, but not a smile crossed the taut lips of the clan of Teges. Kaho looked around the village and then turned back to Teges.

"Is this a clan of old men? Are your women your hunters?"

Teeka held the baby closer and offered him a knuckle on which to suck, as Illa tried to reassure and comfort her two other children. The baby twisted in Teeka's arms and let out a cry. She peered through the brush to see if anyone had heard and was coming. Illa grabbed the baby and offered him her breast.

"Where are your women, Cacique? Have they made the journey and left you to do the work of the women?"

Teges understood the meaning. Kaho was trying to provoke him with insults, hoping that he would produce the women in defense.

"Is this the thought of the great Kaho? Has his mind become old and confused?" This time Teges did the provoking, and Kaho responded with anger.

"Bring forth your women. I have come to choose a bride. Even Teges cannot refuse me."

Teges paused a moment in thought, and Kaho allowed it. Both wished the confrontation to end.

Shala stood first. She knew Teges would never compromise the women. He would stand firm, forcing Kaho's hand. In the end, Kaho would have himself a bride anyway. The old men could never hold back the young Kahoosa warriors.

As soon as Shala stood, all the other women followed, bringing their clinging children. Illa shoved the infant at Teeka. "Take him. Let him nurse from your breast. Kaho will only choose a maiden," she whispered.

Teeka looked puzzled. "But I have no milk!"

"It will not matter. He has been nursing. He will be content for a while. Quickly, do as I say."

Teeka felt awkward, but the fear of Kaho overrode those emotions. When she emerged from the brush, the infant was sucking at Teeka's breast.

"I want to see only the maidens," Kaho demanded. "Have them separate themselves."

Now that the women had exposed themselves, the situation altered. Teges nodded at the women. Compliance would be better than inviting a massacre of his people. Still, it turned his stomach. It was more difficult to allow this than to feel the sharp point of Kaho's spear.

The unmarried women moved to one side, eyes focused on the ground, and Kaho strutted before them, looking up and down the body of each. Intermittently he would stop before one, put his hand beneath her chin, and raise her head. At less compassionate moments he would grab one by the hair and yank her head back.

He paused before Erza, a young girl who had just entered puberty. He motioned for her to step forward. As she did, he walked in circles around her, inspecting her. When directly behind her, he suddenly reached his arms around her and cupped both of her breasts in his hands. Erza jumped and closed her eyes tightly. Kaho let go and slid his hands down her sides to her ankles. He felt the rigidness of her muscles and slapped her thighs. A small tear worked its way through Erza's tightly closed eyelids.

Teges took a step in protest, the veins of his neck tight with anger and disgust. As a man he did not want to think of the greater consequences. He wanted to lunge at the invader, drive his spear deep into Kaho's chest, and see Kaho's wicked blood spurt from him. But as the cacique, he had to keep his anger in check. The rest of the clan would follow his lead. Kaho would have to be tolerated or he would take out his wrath on all the clan, all the old men, the women, and even the children.

Kaho stood again and walked in front of Erza, who

was trying to suppress her sobs. He turned and looked at Teges, smiled, and wheeled back around, grabbing Erza and pressing his pelvis to hers. He relaxed his grip, and then suddenly jerked her to him again. Immediately he let her go, laughing. Erza collapsed on the ground as Kaho turned to Teges.

"This one will never keep a man in pleasures. She will resist and fight like the female panther."

Teges again stepped forward. "In our clan, we speak not of such things. The People request that you honor our customs when you visit us."

Teges spoke with respect. That he must give Kaho in order to live semi-peacefully. "She is a child who has just entered a woman's body. During the last full moon we celebrated her first time of the cleansing blood."

Kaho, for a moment, looked as if he understood, as if he felt sorry for her, but then turned his head and spat on Erza, who was still huddled on the ground.

"This is all you have to offer the great Kaho for his bride?"

"These are the maidens of our clan. If nothing pleases you, go out and continue your search in other villages. The village of Teges is sorry it cannot please you."

Illa's baby stirred, becoming frustrated with the lack of milk. The infant sucked desperately, drawing his cheeks into hollows. Unsatisfied, he thrust out his legs and began to cry. Teeka bounced the baby and put him to her other breast. Illa's child tried again, but with no reward he kicked and cried. She tried to keep from looking up, but her fear made her glance up to see if Kaho was watching what was happening. Her eyes fell straight on his. Nervously she lifted the baby to her shoulder.

Without looking again, she sensed that Kaho was watching. She talked and cooed to the screaming baby, again offering him her empty breast. As Kaho came closer, she began to feel more and more awkward with the baby. Her eyes began to burn as they wanted to tear. Her throat tightened, and the cooing became rattled and broken. He had noticed.

"Why is it that you put this infant to your breast and he cries?"

Teeka swallowed, trying to release the constriction in her throat before she spoke. "He is sick."

Illa stood next to Teeka, her face chiseled with lines of fear. She knew her sister well and recognized the fear in Teeka's voice. Had Kaho also noticed?

"The baby has been sick and did not eat for many days," Illa interjected. "The mother has also been ill, and her milk is not so plentiful."

The baby's crying continued to intrigue Kaho. "He looks very strong and healthy. How has he been sick?"

Teeka and Illa began to speak at the same time, but Kaho interrupted.

"Why do you speak for this woman?" he addressed Illa.

"She is my sister, and I have been caring for her and the child."

Kaho's suspicions had been aroused, and his observations were keen. He looked hard at Illa, seeing the clue that confirmed his supposition.

"Are these your only children?" he asked Illa, indicating the children at her knees.

Illa was quick to answer that they were.

"They are too old to suckle, are they not?" he continued to probe.

Illa drew in a deep breath. Why was he asking these questions? There was no way he could know that the child in Teeka's arms was hers.

"Yes," she answered.

"Then why does your breast drip milk from that side?" he said, pointing.

Illa looked down to see the translucent white liquid dribbling from her left breast. She had nursed the baby while they were hiding, but only from the right side. The baby's cry of hunger had triggered the flow of milk from her other breast. Now it dripped, giving away the lie.

"Give the child to its mother," he ordered Teeka.

Teeka resisted, not letting go of the lie. "This is my child. We have been sick, and my milk has dried up. That is why this baby cries. He is mine."

Kaho motioned to one of his band, who came and stood next to him.

"Put your knife to the child's throat and cut it," he demanded.

The man raised his knife to the child and hesitated. Teeka and Illa remained motionless. Kaho gestured for the man to go ahead with the act. The knife touched the baby's throat and drew a small amount of blood as it scratched the skin.

"No!" Illa screamed, grabbing the man's wrist.

Kaho nodded, and the man withdrew his knife. The baby's skin had been only slightly nicked.

"Give the child to its mother," he ordered smugly. "I choose this maiden," he announced, putting his hand on Teeka's shoulder. "I will return for her in a few days. I will take my share and my bride at the same time. The clan of Teges should be proud to offer Kaho this fine maiden. Protect her while I am gone. If this maiden should fall ill, walk the Other Side, or leave this village, the clan of Teges will know the vengeance of Kaho. Not one spirit of the Teges clan will remain."

Kaho signaled his men, and with arrogance they

turned their backs on the people of the village and returned to their canoes.

When the last of the Kahoosa were out of sight, Teges gathered what there was of his clan.

"This is a sad day for the Tegesta. We are a people of peace. It is how the spirits tell us we must be. For that we pay a price, and sometimes the spirits test us. But even if it were not so, we do not have the strength in number to battle the Kahoosa. The People must survive."

Teges walked to the stunned Teeka. "The spirits of the People will go with you. You honor the Tegesta with your sacrifice."

Teges surveyed the clan. "Go now," he said. "We must not let Kaho take more from us than he demands. Our lives must continue."

Within moments the villagers were back to the business of the day. In whispers they spoke of Teeka's fate. She did not have to hear them to know that she was the topic of their muffled conversations. Illa nursed her child and then left the infant to Selo, walking with Teeka away from the village. For much of the way they were silent, and Illa allowed it, realizing her sister was sorting out what had just happened.

Teeka finally spoke. "Illa, I cannot go with Kaho. I am Auro's. Cannot Teges tell him that?"

"You have no choice. Teges has no choice. We are a poor people. Kaho is very strong, and his people are a warring people."

Teeka stopped to pick a wildflower. "I am Auro's. I have been promised to him."

She spoke calmly and tearlessly. "Kaho will have to find another bride. I cannot go with him."

Illa said nothing.

"Did Ata speak to you of forbidden things before the

marriage?"

"What forbidden things do you mean, Teeka?"

"The forbidden things, about love and joining. Did he tell you how he wanted to touch you and give you pleasure? Did he tell you of the Joining Spirit's rewards?"

"Has Auro spoken to you about these things?"

"It does not offend me, Illa. I have mysterious feelings. I think that these feelings have to do with joining. I think they are the same things that Auro feels. Are these feelings bad? Is that why we are forbidden to talk about them?"

"No, Little Doe. They are not bad. It is something special between a man and a woman. If everyone talked of these pleasures and feelings they would not be so special. It would be no more than the pleasure of filling an empty belly with food. It is a gift from the Joining Spirit and is sacred."

"Do you think we have angered a spirit and that is why this has happened?"

Illa could not answer at first. Maybe Teeka was right, but in her heart she did not think so. "I am not a spirit and cannot talk with the spirits."

Teeka had picked all the petals from the flower and watched them blow in the wind. "I had a strange and frightening dream. I still do not know its meaning. I cannot interpret the dream, but it was terrible. There is more to it than having to go with Kaho."

"Sometimes we dream without meaning. Every dream is not a message."

"This dream was sent to me. It was meant to tell me something, something of great importance. It frightens me."

Teeka's conversation had changed, showing her acceptance of what was going to happen. The denial was no longer there.

"I will not endanger the People. I will do what I have to do, but there will be no pleasure from the Joining Spirit for me without Auro—like Pyra without Izo."

Illa was puzzled. "How do you know this of Pyra?"

"I have heard the noises that are made in the night. I have never heard the good sounds coming from Pyra, because her husband is not Izo."

Teeka had not cried, but Illa's eyes filled with tears.

While everyone slept, Teeka tossed on her mat. "Spirit of the Little Doe, help me find my way," she pleaded in a whisper.

Suddenly she sat up. There was something that she had to do. She had to do it now, before it was too late.

In the blackness of night, with only the light of the stars and the moon, Teeka crept to the platform of her sister.

"Illa," she whispered. "Wake up. I need your help."

Illa opened her eyes. "Teeka! What are you doing?"

"Shhh," she whispered. "Come with me. I need your help."

Illa focused her blurry eyes. "What is it that you need? Can it not wait until the morning?"

Teeka pulled on her sister's arm. "Do not ask questions now. I will explain later."

Chapter Four

"WHERE ARE WE GOING?" Illa asked, trying to keep up with her sister.

"Just follow me. I need you to help me launch a canoe. Hurry, Illa."

Illa followed Teeka, slipping through the shadows, to the beached canoes.

"Help me get it into the water."

"Wait. Give me an explanation. Where are you going?"

"I want to find Auro's camp and tell him. Time is short, and when he returns, Kaho will come. We will have no time to talk. Help me now, Illa," she said, pulling on the stern. "Push the bow."

"Teeka, you cannot travel the water alone. You know nothing of canoes."

Teeka let go of the stern, realizing she could not get Illa to help without further convincing.

"I have watched the men. I have traveled in a canoe."

"Yes, but you have not navigated one. It is too dangerous."

"After I leave with Kaho, I will never see Auro again. Please help me, Illa."

"And what if you do not find him?"

"I will be back for Kaho. I love Auro, but I also love the People. What if it were you? Would you not search for Ata?"

Illa put her hands on the bow. "Pull, and I will push, Sister."

The canoe rubbed against the ground. Its movement was minute, and the two were tiring from the struggle.

"Stop," Teeka said. "I have a better idea. Help me gather some fallen limbs. Snap the twigs from them so they are smooth."

When all the limbs had been stripped, they placed them in a row behind the canoe, all the way to the water. They shoved a few under the canoe to form a rolling track.

"Now," said Teeka, "I will stay by the stern and direct it. Go to the bow and see if it will move more easily."

Illa shoved the canoe. The boat made its way down the track, causing the limbs to creak beneath it. When it reached the water, Teeka stepped into the bow.

"Tell the People that I have gone off to be alone and think. They would not accept the idea of any woman taking a canoe. No one will be using the canoes until the hunters return, so I am safe from their discovery."

"They will be afraid, afraid that you have run away and will not return. They have great fear of Kaho."

"Tell them I have accepted my fate, and I have made a promise to you and to the spirits."

"But, Teeka, what if something happens to you, and you do not return?"

"Have faith, Illa. I will be back." She poled her way out into the water.

"Be careful, Little Doe," Illa called to her sister.

Teeka raised her hand and then moved into the darkness. The night had turned black. Clouds had gathered, covering the moon and the stars. She hugged the bank, sometimes banging into rocks and fingers of land that reached into the black waters. The canoe moved steadily and slowly in the direction in which she had seen Auro leave.

She felt the shore with the pole and pushed against it. The canoe moved out and away. Alternately, she would reach to the stream bottom on the opposite side and push the canoe forward and toward the shore. By dawn her shoulders ached, and her eyes felt gritty from the lack of sleep. Her skin had erupted in welts from the mosquitoes that had assaulted her during the night. She had not brought with her the ointment that would repel the insects.

Teeka sat in the canoe and let it drift, reaching into the cool water, splashing it on her face. Her stomach rumbled with the hunger of morning.

She watched the shore for a good place to land the canoe. Just ahead there was a small clearing near the stream. When the canoe touched the bank, she jumped onto the land, never letting go of the canoe with her left hand. She tugged at the boat until it seemed well anchored on the shore. Quickly she gathered some vine and attached it to a notch in the front of the canoe, and then a willow nearby.

Knowing exactly what she would have to do to satisfy her hunger, Teeka searched the ground for a stick that was old enough to char and fresh enough not to splinter. At last she spotted one that looked good. Near the water's edge she found a freshwater mussel shell. It would do the job. With it, she scraped the end of the stick at an angle, bringing the tip to a point.

Leaving the water's edge, she searched for two dry sticks. When she had found what she was looking for, she squatted, laying one piece of wood on the ground, gripping the other between her palms. She placed some small, fine, dry grasses near the wood on the ground. They would make good tinder. She began to twirl the stick between her hands, pressing it into the wood that lay on the ground. After a few minutes she could smell the smoke. Soon a few sparks ignited the kindling, and Teeka carefully blew on the grass, causing it to flame. Gradually she added a little more, until it began to blaze. She held the pointed end of the stick in the fire, tempering it to a hardness that would make it useful as a spear.

Happy with the result, she tied one end of a long strand of vine to the stick and wrapped the other end around her wrist. She then attached another piece of vine to her waist and tied a small sturdy twig to the other end. She wrapped the vine around her waist a few times so that she would not trip on it, and then she walked upstream. Watching her step, she followed a trail of stones into the water.

A long-nosed, slender fish approached her. Slowly she raised the spear, flexing her elbow. Teeka aimed the spear and sent it speeding into the water. When the ripples stilled, she saw that her spear floated by itself on the surface of the water. She pulled on the vine attached to her wrist, retrieving the spear.

Again she waited, the spear raised for striking. Another fish headed in her direction. She waited until it was almost in front of her. The timing was good, and the spear struck the fish just behind the head. It thrashed for a moment and then was still. Now she had some understanding of the thrill that the men felt when they fished and hunted. Fishing was the work of the men, but she had watched it many times. She knew that it took much practice and skill to be a good fisherman. She was both surprised and pleased with her good fortune.

She pulled the spear from the fish and unwound the

vine from her waist, except for the last loop that was tied around her. She took the attached twig and threaded the vine through the fish's mouth and gills and dropped it back in the water, leaving her hands free to hunt again. Another hard-scaled fish passed her. But she needed only one of these to make the salve that would protect her from the insects.

Now she needed a fish to eat, a different kind of fish. Teeka stood perched on the rocks, keeping very still and waiting. A silver flash in the water caught her attention. The water churned as shiners skipped across the surface, trying to escape the larger, feeding bass.

Patience. A strike too soon would miss and frighten them away. As the sun climbed higher, the bass would stop feeding. The timing had to be right.

Teeka balanced herself on the rocks, scanning the water. Suddenly the bass reappeared, flashing in the water. They were moving fast and right toward her. She flexed her wrist, ready to throw. Closer. Closer. Now!

The spear pierced the water cleanly, barely causing a ripple, impaling its target. It happened so quickly that the fish had no warning. Death was swift.

She had always been intrigued by spearfishing, and she had watched the men carefully whenever she could. The years of close observation had certainly helped her now, she thought. And the spirits were on her side.

Having taken all she needed from the stream, she retreated to the land. At the water's edge she stooped and inspected some of the tumbled stones and lifted one from the water. It had a shallow depression in its center. It would serve as a cooking pot.

She laid both fish by her side and took the stone back to the stream, where she filled the depression with water. As she returned to the fire, she picked up a sturdy twig that she could use as a skewer.

She removed the fish from the line and attended to the long-nosed fish first. With the mussel shell she split open the belly and reached inside. Her hands and eyes sought the dark red liver. Locating it, she ripped it loose and put it in the rock bowl. Teeka crowded the coals together, turning them with a stick before setting the bowl on top.

She then turned her attention to the bass. She skewered the fish on the stick, and at either side of the fire she drove a forked branch into the ground, with the fork at the top. She rested the ends of the skewer in the forks. The water in the bowl had started to steam, and already she could see small beads of oil. When the bass was done, she feasted and then pushed the stone bowl from the coals with a stick. Now she would let it cool, rendering the fat of the liver. While it cooled, she wandered and found some succulent berries, which were sweet in her mouth. When she returned, the oil from the fish liver had barely begun to congeal on top. In a little while it would be cool enough to remove.

Feeling full, she stretched out on the soft grass nearby. Her eyes grew heavy, and for the first time she realized how tired and sore her body was.

———

Teeka awoke startled. She had not intended to sleep, just rest while she waited for the oil. The fat of the liver was a yellow-white jelly on top of the water in the bowl. She gathered it with her hands, sparingly rubbing her body with it. It would be an effective insect repellent. She placed the remains in a leaf and rolled it up, tying it closed on the ends with blades of grass. She opened the pouch that hung from her waist and placed the leaf packet inside. She would need more ointment when the sun went down.

Teeka reached the edge of the water, carrying her spear. When she stood near the canoe, she saw her reflection in the water. Her hair was not hanging straight and shining. It was tangled and hung in strings. No matter now, she would do something with it when she found Auro.

She loosened the vine from the willow, tossed it into the boat, and cast off. Now that she was traveling in the daytime, the work was not as hard or as tedious. The midstream current helped carry her. Turtles and alligators basked on the rocks, soaking up the warmth that would hold them through the night. Anhingas—birds that lack the waterproof oil of other water birds—perched atop brush and along the bank, their wings outstretched to dry in the sun.

The sun was beginning to set as she rounded a small bend in the stream. There was some movement near the bank. She reached for the pole and moved the canoe closer to the shore until she made her way onto the bank. On foot, she crept a little closer. The Big Water canoes.

She would have to wait until after dark when all of them were sleeping. She remembered the reflection she had seen in the stream and stripped herself bare, then waded into the water.

After washing, she returned to the shore and let herself dry in the breeze. It was almost dark as she searched nearby for some aromatic flowers. Finding them, she returned to where she had left her clothes. From the pouch she removed the leaf filled with salve. Then she built herself a small fire. Not wanting to call attention to her presence, she was careful that it did not issue too much smoke. She found another small stone with a depression and placed the salve in it. She tore the flowers into small pieces and added them to the ointment. When it melted over the fire, it would take on the fragrance of the wildflowers. While it heated, she gathered some stiff grasses and bound them together to make a hairbrush.

To pass time while the salve cooled, Teeka took her medicine bag and spread its contents on the ground. She had carefully saved all her baby teeth. When she died, it would be necessary for her to be whole if she was to pass on to the Other Side. The spirits would not recognize her if she was without all her parts, even her baby teeth. As a newborn infant, her mother had taken her to Tamuk to be given her guide spirit. Little Doe, he had chosen. In his vision he had seen her as a small female fawn, delicate and wide-eyed. The shaman had placed a piece of tanned doeskin in her medicine bag when he announced her guide spirit. As she had grown, Tamuk had placed other totems in the bag.

Teeka tested the emulsion by lightly touching it with her finger. It was cool enough. The mosquitoes had already begun their attack. She was glad that the repellent was ready. This time when she spread it on her body, the fragrance of wildflowers masked the original odor. Auro had often told her that he liked it when she wore the perfumed oil. Tonight she wished to please him.

She dressed and returned to her canoe, released the binding, and poled the vessel along the edge of the stream. The hunters would be tired and eager to sleep, that they might start the last part of their return early in the morning. One more night away from the village, and then their return would bring celebration for all but two.

Close to the camp, Teeka went ashore. Quietly she moved through the grasses and reeds until she stood at the margin of the camp. She gingerly stepped upon the soft parts of the earth, avoiding dead grasses and sticks. She tried to decide which of the men was Auro so that she would not have to wander through the camp, but there were too many, and she was not close enough.

Quietly she walked among them, looking for the face of Auro. Luckily, he was sleeping near the outside border, not too close to anyone else. With a faint touch, she brushed her fingertips across his cheek and whispered his name near his ear.

Auro stirred and repositioned himself.

"Auro," she whispered again, a little louder this time. "Awaken. It is Teeka."

He opened his eyes groggily, and she put her hand over his lips. Teeka motioned for him to follow her.

"Shhh," she whispered, leading him through the brush to her canoe.

Only when they'd moved farther downstream did she dare to speak aloud. "I need to be with you this night."

He reached for her shoulders and pulled her toward him, letting the pole fall into the bottom of the canoe.

"Why have you come to meet me? What has happened?"

"I love you, and I need to be with you."

Gently, his arms went around her. "And I love you. But something is wrong, very wrong. What is it?"

"Take us to the other side of the stream," she said. "I want to be with you, as you have told me, when a man is with a woman."

Auro lifted the paddle and guided the canoe across the stream.

"The marriage time is almost here, Teeka. Why are you saying this?"

The canoe had made its way to the bank, and she stepped out, holding Auro's hand.

"Come and be with me, Auro. This night, be with me."

"Tell me what has made you come to me this way. This is not the way of our people. Tegesta women stay pure until after the marriage. It is demanded by the spirits."

Teeka's eyes teared. "Why must there be an explanation? Do you not love me and want to be with me, as you have told me so many times?"

"I have told you many times because it is so, but not this way."

She covered her face with her hands so that he would not see the strain in her face. She hadn't wanted to spoil this night by telling him the horrible truth.

"Kaho came to our village," she said, barely loud enough to be heard. "He has chosen me to be his woman. I must go with him when he comes to collect tribute. There will be no marriage for us, Auro. I will be the woman of Kaho."

Auro felt as if the breath had been knocked out of him. He could find no words.

"I want to be with you," she said. "I want to be the woman of Auro, even if it is only for this one night."

Auro's mind was whirling. How could this have happened? Kaho had gone to the village when they were vulnerable and robbed him of Teeka.

"I cannot be with you without the marriage. The spirits would not forgive us."

"Please, Auro. I can forget all the customs and the spirits. They have not protected me from this fate. I do not even believe there are such spirits anymore."

He was shocked at her denunciation of the spirits. "Do not say these things that you do not really mean. We do not always understand the ways of the spirits."

"The only spirit is that of Kaho. He has whatever he wishes."

Auro stood silent for a moment before he spoke. "We do not have a shaman here, but I know the spirits will hear us. We will say our promises of marriage, and they will know us as one. Kaho will not rob you of your spirits and beliefs. You will never be the woman of Kaho. You will be mine in the eyes of the spirits."

If she let go of the spirits now, there would never be anything for her to hang on to, once Kaho came. There would be nothing to live for, nothing to believe in—no hope.

He pulled her close to him and embraced her tenderly. "Raise your hands to the sky, Teeka. Let us call the spirits together so that they may know our intentions. Raise them high and call to them with me."

Chapter Five

"YOU ARE THE WOMAN OF AURO. No matter what happens, the spirits will remember."

"Teach me all of it, Auro. Show me those things of which you have spoken. Make all the mysteries disappear."

Auro took both of Teeka's hands and led her deeper into the cover of the brush. He walked backward and she forward, their eyes never leaving the other's. She could feel the flood of emotion inside her as Auro turned her, resting her back against a tree. Overhead the starlight twinkled between the leaves. Gnarled vines climbed steadily up the trunk, winding their way to the mantle of branches at the top. There they unfolded into delicate white flowers that burst with fragrance during the night.

Auro leaned toward her and pressed his lips to hers with the gentleness that initiates passion. With his body he urged her to sink down on the soft earth as rain began to fall. The world melted into a swirl of watercolors, and nothing had definition anymore, only sounds and sensations. He was an opiate to her, a drug of the medicine man. She bent to his will like a green willow branch. He was the oarsman, and he took her through the river of passion and pleasure. Through pastel waters, they flowed into each other.

Teeka's body yielded to his touch, and she was lost in oblivion. Like an artist, he painted her body with the soft brush of his lips and fingertips. He was taking her above the earth, riding the wind with the eagle.

She soared with him, offering no resistance. All she could do was respond to his miracles, as in some wonderful dream. Her senses were congested with the liqueur of desire as he transported her into a world without reason. She was paralyzed by his expert touch, unable to do anything but react and revel in the intoxicating effect of his closeness. She surrendered all control, all inhibitions, all of herself.

Auro's warm breath fell welcomed upon her body as she reached for him, drawing him closer as he rocked her, filling her with his passion and love. The urgency of her need for him to consume her shook her body until the rapture of quake after quake finally ended.

Her fingers traced satisfied lines up and down his back as he lay collapsed above her. The mysteries were gone.

Breathing through the silkiness of her hair, Auro whispered to her. "I love you. I will find a way. I will never let you go."

"There is no other way. But this night will always give me strength. I will never be Kaho's woman now. He can never take from me what I have given to you."

"He cannot have you. Our people will fight him."

"No, Auro. I must go with him. We cannot be that selfish. We cannot ask that of the People."

Auro's frustration turned to anger. "Then I will find him and slash his throat."

Teeka pressed her lips to his and then pulled his head down to her neck. "No," she whispered. "He has too many warriors. I want to know that somewhere you are well and dreaming of me. I want to close my eyes at night and see you, strong and alive. That is when I will be able to leave Kaho. In my mind, when I am with you. Leave me with that escape."

Throughout the night she gave herself to him, and he to her. Every time there was a new discovery, a new pleasure. Their bodies joined, each knowing the other with some primal sense. Every time they lay spent but with the anticipation of exploring each other yet again, sometimes gently, other times almost violently in their passion. They would have an eternity of loving, a lifetime of tenderness and of ecstasy, in this one night.

At dawn the sky lightened, the gray clouds giving way to the blue.

"I must go now," she told him. "They will wake soon and find you gone."

Auro held her close for a long moment and then helped her to her feet. They walked silently to the canoe, watching the sunrise until they reached the other side. Both of them stepped out of the boat under a pavilion of trees that shrouded the earth. Droplets of light rain rested on the leaves and grasses, glistening where needles of sunlight pierced the branches. The night's rain had caused the stream to swell over its banks, trickles of water running through the grass like strands of a spider's web.

Though they were certain that the spirits recognized their marriage, they also knew that the People could never accept it. If it was found out, Teeka would be shamed and would have to leave in disgrace. As future shaman, Auro could not break the People's law, and he did not want Teeka to suffer any more than she had to.

"Go swiftly and safely," he told her as he held her in his arms for the last time. Fighting tears, she climbed back into the dugout. He pushed the canoe out into the water and watched as she took the paddle.

Going against the current was more difficult than she had thought it would be. The water worked against her, and her arms tired easily. The need to find Auro had provided some energy, but what she would be facing upon her return drained her.

Farther upstream, Teeka banked the canoe and secured it. She gathered some roots and a handful of berries, and put them in the canoe with her. There was no time to stop and camp as the men would. She needed to get back to her people before they did.

Auro returned to his camp. One by one, the men woke full of vigor and excitement. They would make it to the village the next morning, and there would be much to celebrate. They busied themselves preparing for the rest of the journey. They hurried with their preparations, knowing that this was the last full day of travel.

———

Tamuk watched the last of the orange rays spray across the western horizon. Darkness would come soon, and with it would come the beginning. The hatchi's odor had changed with its curing. It permeated the air with its sickening sweetness. He lifted the slab on top of the bowl to see that brown foam had collected on the surface, indicating that the fermentation was complete. The elixir sat waiting, ominously, as if it had a spirit of its own. Tamuk was not fooled by it, as any other man might have been. He recognized the sweet smell and knew it for what it was. His nostrils flared as he breathed deeply.

He lifted the bowl and carefully carried it closer to the hearth. Choosing a fallen twig, he stirred the brown liquid, watching as the foam was absorbed into the thick syrup. The last shadows of the day shaded the fluid, as if light dared not touch it.

The last sliver of the sun disappeared, and night fell swiftly. The hammock filled with the noises of the villagers completing their tasks so they might sleep, banking the fires and shaking the mats to guarantee that no scorpions or roaches would pay unwanted visits. Within moments, noise ceased, and the people slept.

Tamuk did not sleep. Instead, he sat by his fire. He had many things to discuss with the spirits—questions to ask, promises to make, bargains to plead. In the dark of the night, he saw Teeka's slender silhouette slip through the village. The old man drew in a deep breath.

Illa heard Teeka enter her platform and lie upon her mat. Quietly she crept to her sister's side.

"Have you told Auro?" she asked.

"He knows," she answered. "Were the People concerned that I would not return?"

"Yes, but I told them what you said and reassured them. Even Tamuk told them that you would be back."

"Illa—" she began, but couldn't finish.

"What is it? What did you want to tell me?"

Teeka hesitated and then spoke. "Auro and I called upon the spirits, just as the shaman calls them, using the same words. We had no medicine man, but we said our marriage words. I know that the spirits see us as one."

"You cannot belong to Auro. You must go with Kaho."

"I am already Auro's woman. We said our promises in front of the spirits. I have been with Auro. I have joined with him. The spirits will never recognize me as Kaho's."

Illa could not believe that the marriage was a true one. No one but a shaman could call the spirits together for a marriage. But Teeka believed it, and that was what was important.

"You are a brave young woman. Your journey has

been a strenuous one for your body and your spirit."

Teeka closed her eyes, but still the shaman did not. Silently Illa went back to her platform. In the distance she could see the shadowy figure of Tamuk sitting by his fire. His chants were barely audible. His body swayed, coming in and out of the light of the fire. Does he see all? she wondered.

There was electricity in the air as the clan's people began their daily chores. The air was crisp and sharp as it entered the nostrils. The sky was a clear blue with only a few patches of puffy white. No one questioned Teeka about her return, nor did they ask where she had been. There was curiosity, but no one wanted to intrude. They were just grateful that she had returned, and they felt a great relief to find her in the village this morning, but to show it would have been unkind.

An old man sat flaking a projectile point from a nodule of chert. His concentration was deep as he carefully eyed the nodule. He did not want to err. Chert was a valued item they traded for. It came from the north. There were no veins of this fine-grained rock this far south. Just as he raised the hammer-stone, Pyra came running by him, screeching the news.

"They return. The hunters have returned from the Big Water!"

As soon as they heard the news the clan's people stopped what they were doing. The nodule was left untouched, the cooking was abandoned, and the weaving and pottery were deserted. All of the villagers rushed to the shore to welcome the returning hunters. As they crowded the shoreline, they left a path open for Tamuk.

The shaman slowly made his way through the crowd. Shala dropped back, noticing Tamuk's demeanor. His posture made him appear shrunken and old. His face lacked the enthusiasm that he usually expressed when hunters returned to the clan.

The hunters were throwing the cargo ashore when Tamuk arrived. The villagers exclaimed at the sight of the catch. It had been a very profitable journey. Teges inspected everything that the men threw ashore. With each new load, he complimented the hunters. Pride echoed in his voice. He was certain that Kaho could not have done better. His villages were not many in number, but they could be compared to none when it came to Big Water journeys. Teges was not greedy. Every village would get an equal amount. He was a fair man, showing no favoritism toward his home village. The Tegesta were united. They were all the People.

There was silence when Tamuk plunged his walking stick into the ground. He was going to speak. Tamuk had come from a pure and powerful line of shamans and understanding was a blood gift with him. He had knowledge of very old things that he had never been taught. There were very few true shamans left on the earth. Auro was also part of the pure lineage.

Auro had immediately searched the crowd for Teeka's face and found her standing back from the rest, near Shala. He turned to watch his father, reveling in the pride of the moment. He was a hunter, a hero, and he was the son of the man who spoke, the son of the man who received so much reverence. Tamuk had the inborn knowledge. For most of the other shamans, it was only a skill that had been learned through hard training. Tamuk was superior even to his son, for the gift diminished with each generation. As Tamuk spoke, Auro felt the power of his father. That was when the thought came to him. His father was the answer. His father was the key.

Chapter Six

THE CELEBRATION WAS OFFICIALLY to begin. The aroma from the brewing of a strong tea filled the air. It was not drunk for the flavor, which was bitter, but rather for the effect. Its mood-altering effects enhanced the tribesmen's appreciation of the environment, and it increased the energy flow. Hearts pounded faster, and the blood vessels constricted. The men decorated their bodies elaborately with bright-colored paints and wrapped bands of feathers around their ankles and up their calves. Shells hung from their bodies like dripping wind chimes. Medicine bundles, filled with sacred relics, bones, teeth, and small carved images, thought to represent spirits, dangled around their necks.

Teges entered the circle of men, clad in a cloak of animal skin, feathers, and beads. His head was covered by a hide turban with white plumes spiking from it, and his face was streaked with colored lines. His age, coupled with his appearance, demanded awe. He raised a harpoon and a spear to the sky, and the clansmen fell to their knees.

Tamuk painted a bloody stripe down the middle of each man's forehead. It was the official beginning. Each hunter had his turn to act out his part of the journey. They chose the most exciting parts: hurling harpoons, casting and retrieving full nets, tracking the sharks. Exaggerated body movements emphasized each man's personal struggle, courage, and victory. The rest of the clan watched in rapt silence and then cheered each man's victory.

The storytelling, dancing, and feasting continued into the night. The women served the men, demonstrating subordination, crouching before them. It was a time to stress the importance of the man, the hunter, the provider. Women had their rank in the clan, but on this day they honored the men.

Teeka stood by the brewing tea, ladling it into smaller bowls. The women would have their share later. The steam brought perspiration to her face, and she wiped it away, using the opportunity to turn and watch.

Auro stepped forward, and silence fell over the clan as he began to tell his story. From a distance, Teeka watched him almost dance his part in the journey. When he moved, his arms were fully extended, defining every muscle and expressing the tension that had wired his body during the hunt. His jaw was set firmly with determination, and each movement was calculated clearly describing the tale. The clansmen were enthralled with his performance. Every eye watched as he charismatically related his story.

Teeka watched him and relived their clandestine experience. Each ripple of muscle had been hers. His strong hands had been gentle on her body, and his voice had whispered intimacies. She watched him breathing deeply, his chest rising and falling, and remembered how his breath had caught as she touched him and how he breathed so deeply when he fell spent upon her. It was with those thoughts that she would feed her spirit when she was taken away. Kaho could take everything from her but that.

"Teeka, bring more of the tea," Selo told her, interrupting her daydream.

Teeka returned to her work and did not notice that Auro had completed his story. As she ladled more of the tea, Auro captured his father's attention and called him away from the crowd.

Near Tamuk's hearth, he began. "Shaman, you have great magic. Is this not the truth?"

"Yes," Tamuk answered softly, "I have great magic."

"This man, your son, requests that the shaman talk with the spirits. Ask them to keep Teeka unto me. This would be a good thing, and the spirits should be happy to answer this request."

Tamuk found it difficult to look his son in the eyes. "There is no magic that will keep Kaho from taking Teeka."

Auro swallowed, trying to contain his temper. "Are you not from the perfect line of shamans? Do you not have special gifts? Kaho is not a shaman. Do you weaken to him from fear?"

Instantly he regretted the anger he had directed at Tamuk. As soon as he had spoken, he realized how disrespectful he had been. When Tamuk did not immediately reply, Auro seized the opportunity to humble himself. This time he spoke as a son to his father.

"Forgive your son for speaking the way he did. I have said words to provoke you because I am angry and confused. I know that our line is pure and that Kaho's people do not have such a shaman. You are powerful, and you have the knowledge. Kaho's own shaman is from the new lineage. He knows only what has been taught to him. Your power is stronger. I beg you, my father, to use it. There must be a way that you can help me."

"Yes, I have knowledge that was born in me, just as you have. But, as I have taught you, some of that knowledge has been a lesson. The People never summon the spirits for personal satisfaction or greed, especially not a shaman. I have again seen in my visions why we must not. The good spirits serve all the People, not the selfish desires of a single man. The only spirits that answer such a cry are from the Darkside. When you deal with them, they always take something in return, something you may not be willing to give up. Auro, Teeka must go with Kaho."

Auro's muscles tightened in frustration. "Then find a way to keep her heart always with me, forever. She is mine already in the eyes of the spirits."

"What do you mean? She is not yours just through the promises of marriage. The spirits have not recognized you as one, nor has the Joining Spirit given you the Gift."

"But they have. We have said our marriage promises. We called the spirits in the words that you taught me. We have been as one. Father, I am your son. I ask you to call upon all your knowledge and power. If you will not help, I will use all you have taught me, even though it breaks the law. I am not yet the shaman, but I will call on the spirits to work their magic!"

Tamuk heard his son's voice crack. It was a sound that he had not heard from him since Auro was a child.

"Father, help me."

Tamuk's voice was soft in empathy. "There is no magic to keep her here."

"Then have the spirits take her heart and leave it with me. Let her never love anyone else."

"It is too selfish. As I told you, only the spirits from the Darkside answer such pleas. They may promise you Teeka's love forever, but they will also collect the debt.

And what of the woman you say you love? Are you willing to sacrifice some part of her to pay that debt? Even though it seems so now, you cannot dare to take away even the smallest part of her will just to lessen the ache in your heart."

"I am prepared to do anything. If I cannot keep her with me, then at least I will know that no one else will ever have her love, especially Kaho. He will pay for what he has done. He will take a bride who will never give him her heart."

"You are in pain now, but you will heal. It is all right to grieve, but you must not ask the spirits to intervene for you. You cannot see the consequences now. You suffer too deeply."

Tamuk turned his back and faded into the shadows. He would have to stop his son. He was prepared. The father inside him screamed in torment, but he was more than a father. He was the shaman.

Hidden in the blackness, he called out to his son. "Go and think. Reach deep inside, and then come back to my hearth. Together we will work through this."

With all the dancing and excitement, Auro had not been missed. Only Teeka kept watch for him. Everyone had finally tired and had gone to sleep.

Tamuk retrieved the pouch that contained the ingredients to be added to the hatchi. It smelled so sweet, a sensual facade, disguising its deadliness.

Carefully he stirred the brew, remembering how his father had told him of the old knowledge. His father had probed his son, questioning, prying, evaluating. There was some lack of knowledge where the years and the diluting of blood had caused the memory to become imperfect.

Tamuk had retained much of the knowledge. He was a direct descendant of the ancient and pure shamans, and his line had been careful in the selection of mates. But still, Tamuk did not retain as much as his father. The days as his father's apprentice had been happy ones, like the days he had spent with Auro. Kaho had not come in those days, and the clan was strong. They were the People, the only people. There were other tribes to the north and to the west, but each respected the others' territories. They had lived side by side in peace. It wasn't until Tamuk was an older man that a young warrior from the southwest began raiding tribes. His name was Kaho. He had betrayed all the customs of his tribe, and by strength and fear eliminated all who protested.

Tamuk gathered some herbs from his different pouches. Some of them were potentially dangerous, but the shaman's job was to know quantities, and which he could mix without causing ill effects. He chose an herb he had collected the same day he had gathered the hatchi. He combined it with another. Each alone had great benefits. Together, they were deadly. To that he added the hard red berries and the cycad poison. Carefully he poured the potion into a pottery bowl. He wiped the ancient bowl clean and wrapped it in a cover of soft deer hide before returning it to its special storage place inside his platform. When he had finished, he walked back to his fire.

Slowly, as he waited for his son, he brewed the tea, bringing it to a boil and then steeping it. He poured it off into a drinking bowl and skimmed the top, removing the residue of the herbs. The time had come. If he could not stop Auro with his words, he would have to obey the spirits.

He hunkered near the bowl of hatchi and slid off the wooden slab that covered it. Into it he poured his most recent concoction. It hissed and steamed for an instant, sending the sweet aromatic steam through the air. His son should have returned by now. He began to worry.

———

Auro had not been able to clear his head. He was too filled with anger. Neither Kaho nor anyone else would ever have Teeka's heart. She would always be his. He did not care about the consequences. They could not be worse than what he suffered now.

Auro gathered herbs and mixed them. He prepared two potions. He also laid two beautifully polished columellae by his fire. Once he had everything ready and spread before him, he sat, legs crossed and eyes closed. In a moment he would set his plan into motion.

He breathed in deeply, expelling the air through his mouth. With eyelids only slightly open, he grasped the first bowl in his hands and raised it to his lips. He took one small sip, as if hesitating, but then he swallowed the entire potion.

The effect was immediate and dramatic. He stood, swayed slightly, and then grimaced as pressure grew inside his head. He could hear his blood pulse and feel his skin stretch to accommodate his new robustness. Every blood vessel stood out against his skin, and his neck swelled with muscle. Auro felt a power he had never felt before. He was omnipotent. No one could challenge him, not Kaho, not anyone.

His body burst with muscle and strained to be tested. There was a surge building inside him that started in the pit of his belly. The air was his, as was the earth. The young man exploded with the force, shouting to the sky, not calling upon the spirits, but demanding them. An unexpected wind blew through the trees, bending the branches almost to the ground. Auro stood tall, singled out against the buckling landscape.

———

Tamuk went to look for his son. In his hand he carried a small bowl. Loose debris swirled in the wind, making him blink and guard his eyes. When he was close enough, his eyes fixed on the transformation of his son. The man before him was a stranger who had hatred in eyes that pierced the darkness.

Auro's voice rose above the wind. It was not the volume, but the pitch, the depth, and the haunting tone that frightened his father. The voice came from somewhere deep inside him, and it resonated with an unfamiliar sound.

"Stop!" Tamuk shouted. "It must end. Do not do this."

Auro glanced in his father's direction but seemed to look right through him. He took one of the columellae and immersed it in the potion that sat on the coals. The other he wrapped in water-soaked leaves and then tossed it on the coals to steam.

"Auro!" Tamuk shouted again. "Do not finish this. It is the spirits of the Darkside who help you."

Tamuk felt impotent. It was too late to stop. Auro could not listen. His mind was in that other dimension, taken there by the spirits. He looked down at the poison he had prepared. He had thought Auro would come back to his hearth, as he had requested. He did not think his son would make a final decision before speaking with him again. He had even held out hope that he would be able to convince him that spirit intervention was not the way. In the past, Auro had always listened to and heeded the advice of his father. But not tonight, and now it was too late. Even if he could get Auro to drink his deadly brew, the deed was already done.

Tamuk could watch no more, and he left without Auro ever realizing he had been there.

From the fire Auro flicked the columella that sizzled inside the leaf wrapping. The steam burned his fingers, and he recoiled with the jolt of pain. He continued to brush the shell from the coals with short, quick strokes. He unwrapped it, strung a leather thong through the drilled end, and then tied the ends.

The pendant still glowed with heat as Auro lowered it over his head. When it fell to his chest, the skin beneath went quickly from red to blisters that opened and oozed their fluid down his torso. He bit down on his lip, slicing it with his teeth. He leaned forward so that the pendant fell away from his skin, and his mouth filled with blood from his lip.

Auro spat on the ground and then took his knife and cut a lock of his hair, turning his attention to the other pendant. He watched the liquid bubble and fizz when he threw his hair into the potion with the pendant that was to be Teeka's.

"Forever, Teeka," he whispered. "As long as you wear this, you will always be mine."

Auro reached into the liquid and brought out the pendant dripping with syrup. The liquid was tenacious, and he wiped the shell on the ground and then dried it with some leaves. The columella shone with an exquisite patina. He threaded the sinew through it and held it up before him. He was pleased. It was beautiful.

———

Tamuk lowered himself to the ground. Somewhere in a cavern deep inside himself, Tamuk, the man, was relieved that he did not have to take the life of his son. But the part of him that was shaman was ashamed. He had not stopped Auro, and that had been his responsibility. He had failed in his obligation. A shaman should not fail. He questioned and chastised himself. Why had he waited until too late? Had he procrastinated because it was his son? He should have been ready when Auro first came to him. After all, had not the visions predicted this development? Hadn't he anticipated it? He had known what was coming. If he had succeeded, then at least he and his son would one day walk the Other Side together. Now the spirits would probably deny them both.

The pain inside the old man screamed in his ears and ripped at his heart. He did not feel he even had the right to call the spirits and beg for their forgiveness and guidance.

It suddenly became clear to the agonizing Tamuk what he must do. The potion was ready, and it met all the criteria. Perhaps his sacrifice would appease the spirits and they would look at the good things he had done in his life.

As he slid the bowl toward himself, there was a sudden flash of light, and he felt fire on his fingertips. He had been right. This was what the good spirits expected of him, and the Darkside spirits were trying to interfere, to prohibit his redemption.

His grip gave way as his fingers became numb. Tamuk took a deep breath and gathered all his strength. In the last moments of his life, he would prove himself a worthy opponent of the Darkside. He was thankful that he had been given this opportunity. Perhaps after all he would be allowed to walk the Other Side with the many good men who had come before him.

The old man clawed at the vessel, dragging himself on his belly. He shifted his weight to his elbows and pulled himself even closer.

Tamuk drew his knees beneath him and lunged forward. With his wrists he lifted the bowl, rolled to his back, and poured the contents into his mouth. It tasted sweet and felt thick as it slid down his throat. He swallowed and then let his body slump.

The old holy man was filled with emotion. His eyes welled with tears as he watched the stars above him. There were many hearths burning in the sky. He hoped there would be room for his. There, Shala could live at his fire when she joined him. His only regret was his son.

Tamuk's eyes rolled back in his head, and his body shook violently. It was over. The lines in his face became relaxed, and he was cloaked in an aura of peace.

Chapter Seven

THE WIND HAD SUDDENLY DIED. The blowing leaves had settled in new places, and the branches of the trees tried righting themselves.

Auro slipped through the village until he came to Teeka's platform.

"Teeka," he whispered, hoping to wake her and no one else.

She eased herself off the platform.

"This way," he whispered, guiding her through the darkness with his voice. "I have made something for you. Take it with you and wear it always to remember me."

She looked at the amulet in Auro's hand. Even in the darkness there was iridescence to it.

"It is beautiful, Auro. You have made this for me?"

"Yes," he answered. "It is my marriage gift to you. It is a seal, and as long as you wear it, we will belong to each other."

Her mouth turned downward into a frown. "But I have nothing to give to you."

Auro touched her lips with his fingertips. "You have given me the gift of yourself. That is all I want. Take my gift and be glad."

Teeka's eyes wandered over the man she loved and stopped on his chest.

"You wear a match," she said, smiling, seeing the pendant around his neck.

She lifted the pendant from his burned skin, immediately letting it drop back. "Auro, how have you done this? It looks very bad."

"A spark from the fire," he answered.

She gingerly moved his pendant to one side. "This is more than a burn from a spark."

She noticed the warmth that still emanated from the shell's center, but before she could question him any further, he took her hand and pressed the pendant to his chest.

"It is nothing but a small burn. You cannot see clearly in the dark. Here," he said, holding her amulet by the ends of the leather thong, "let me put this around your neck."

He raised it up, and moonlight bounced across it, accentuating the sheen.

"How have you made this? I have never seen one quite so lovely."

"Lift your hair so that I may tie it."

Teeka put her hands under her hair and lifted it away as Auro tied the knot.

"It was made by the hands of the man who loves you. Perhaps it has taken some of his love and shines with it."

"But yours does not have the same sheen."

"This man loves you more than himself. It is only yours that deserves such beauty. There," he said, finishing the knot. "Never take it off or you will betray the love we have for each other."

"Never," she whispered back to him, letting down her hair.

Teeka looked at the amulet around her neck. There was an irritating tingling in her skin where it touched her.

She shifted it, but the tingling came back. She felt an urge to rip it off, a reaction that she could not understand. Why did the pendant make her feel so strange and uncomfortable?

"Wear this forever, Teeka. Do not take it off. It is a symbol of our love. Tell me that you will love me always, that you will never love another."

"Always," she answered.

As they talked, the tingling had subsided, and Teeka was grateful. Auro brushed his lips across hers. "I love you more than life, and I always will. That is a promise that I make. Now, go before we are found out."

She started to move away, wrapping her hand around the pendant, clutching it to her chest. After walking part of the way back, she turned to have a last glimpse of him. She paused a moment, but he motioned her on.

Quietly she climbed the platform and lay down on her mat. The tingling had stopped completely, but she still fought the intuition that she should remove the pendant. Something about it made her afraid. Afraid of what? she wondered. There was no answer.

Her eyes finally closed, but she tossed as dream images filled her head. Again she stood near the water, watching Tamuk. The same drama played in her dream—the alligator dragging the shaman beneath the water, her struggle in the putrid mud, Auro watching, all of it. As her mouth filled with the sludge, she awakened. Her heart was pounding, and she gasped for air. Her body was soaked with sweat, and she trembled. Teeka sat up. What was the message? Why could she not see it? It must be very important for the dream to come twice. There was an annoying sensitivity in the middle of her chest. She rubbed it and felt the pendant.

She lay back down and thought she would see Tamuk

as soon as it was light. If anyone could help her understand the meaning of the dream, it would be Tamuk.

She tried to sleep but was afraid that the dream would come back. And the pendant was so irritating. The medicine bag around her neck had never caused a problem. Did Auro's bother him? Had the pendant caused the burn on his chest? Why did it evoke such fear in her?

Teeka tore away some moss from her skirt and placed it between her skin and the pendant. She instantly felt more comfortable and fell asleep.

Later on she awakened in surprise. She had not thought that she could sleep, but time had passed since she put the barrier between the pendant and her chest. The sun was rising above the horizon as she left her sleeping place and went to the stream. There she washed her face with the cool water. She used a green twig, stripped of leaves, to clean her teeth. When she had finished, she walked across the village to Tamuk's hearth. She saw Shala, already awake and crouching over something. As she got closer, she saw that Shala was weeping. Something, half hidden by her body, was the object of her sorrow. Teeka slowed her pace and approached quietly.

Tamuk lay on the ground, not moving.

"Shala," Teeka called as she picked up speed again. "What is it?"

Shala turned and looked at Teeka as she came to her side. "It is Tamuk. He is dead."

Tears streamed down Shala's face. Teeka reached for her and pulled her close.

"Oh, Shala," she uttered, recognizing the woman's grief.

Shala pulled away and looked back down at the old man. "I came to fix his morning meal and found him here. Look at his hand, Teeka. The flesh has been burned from it. What could have happened? He did not even call for help."

Teeka looked at the medicine man's hand. Blackened, dead flesh clung in small clumps to the tips of his fingers. She gathered some leaves and covered it.

Shala stroked the old man's face. "Why did he not call for me? Did I sleep too soundly and not hear his cries?"

"Do not think that, Shala. Tamuk was old, and he has been ill for a long time. It was his time. The spirits called him to the Other Side. There was nothing you could have done. Perhaps his hand fell into the fire as he left us. He would not have felt any pain."

"Look at the hearth, Teeka. His hand is nowhere near it. He must have suffered this burn before he died. Why did I not waken? I have never slept through the whole night without checking on him."

"You worked hard for the celebration. You were exhausted. You did nothing wrong. It was his time."

"He has been troubled for many days. He has had me prepare strange things. He knew that something terrible was going to happen."

Shala saw the bowl that had held the hatchi. It was uncovered and empty. Another small bowl rested on its side near Tamuk. She lifted it and smelled it.

Teeka took the shaman's wife by the arm and helped her to her feet. "Come and sit away from him. I will go and get Auro and Teges."

After Teeka left, Shala picked up the bowls. Then, with a hoe made from a horse conch, she dug a hole in the earth and placed the two bowls inside. With a rock she smashed them, shattering the bowls into pieces. She covered the hole with soil and then spread leaves across the top so that no one would notice and question the disturbed earth.

"No one will know," she whispered.

She went back to Tamuk and held his uninjured hand. The warmth of life had already gone from him. His skin was cold and lifeless. Shala looked to the sky. "Do you hear me, spirit of this medicine man?" She gazed back at the body of the man she had loved for so long. He had been a good man, respected by all. He was a powerful shaman and had used his magic wisely. She would never allow that image to be destroyed. Softly she touched her lips to his and then rested the side of her face against his. Her tears stopped as she realized that the body in front of her was not Tamuk. It was only the shell that had served as a home for Tamuk's spirit while in this world. She raised her eyes again to the sky. "You have found the peace you wanted. There is no more burden to carry. Whatever the torment, it is ended."

Auro rushed to his mother's side. "What happened?" he asked.

She told the story again of how she had found him. This time she left out the part about his hand. *Let him rest peacefully,* she thought.

The burn on Auro's chest had all but disappeared. A small flushed patch of skin was all that remained, and that was hidden by the pendant. He bent over the body of his father, his shaman. The man's face looked more relaxed than he had seen it in a long time. He looked in death as he had been in life: kind, wise, and gentle.

He placed his open hand across the breadth of his father's face. "Take this man who has served you well," he said to the clear sky. A gentle breeze rustled the leaves as if Tamuk's spirit approved. But Auro's heart was heavy with guilt. Was his father's death part of the bargain he had struck with the spirits?

He lifted Tamuk in his arms and carried him to the shaman's sleeping platform. Before the sun set, Auro would be declared the new shaman, and his first act would be to perform the ceremony at his father's grave.

Teges stood back with grief on his face. Tamuk had been his boyhood friend. His generation was coming to an end. One by one they were dying, and his time would not be so far away. He worried that there was no young man of the clan ready for the responsibility of being the cacique. The young people paid less attention to custom and tradition. The Tegesta would change. They would lose their identity, which was so closely tied to ritual, custom, and tradition. Those very things had kept them strong and allowed them to survive through all the many generations. Sadness filled him as he watched the son carry his father.

Tamuk's hand dropped to his side as Auro lifted him. Teges noticed that there was something wrong and followed Auro.

Auro laid his father down gently, as if Tamuk could feel his son's tenderness. Teges stepped forward, reaching for the injured hand. Shala quickly stepped between and blocked him.

"He was a good man," she said, looking at Teges.

"Yes, a good man and a magnificent shaman."

She stood between Tamuk's hand and Teges, trying to think of something to distract the cacique. Teges nudged her backward.

"Let me have a better look at my old friend," he said to her.

She could do nothing but move aside as Teges lifted the burned hand.

"Did he fall into the fire?"

Teeka looked at Shala, who hesitated before she spoke.

"His hand must have fallen on the hot embers. I hope he did not feel it."

Teeka started to speak but stopped herself. That was not what Shala had said before. Why was she now denying all those things that had bothered her just moments before?

Teeka walked away, confused, and sat by the hearth. There was something missing. The bowl that Shala had lifted and smelled was gone. So was the other one. Surely Shala had not been concerned with housekeeping for the few minutes she had been gone.

She called to Shala to come and sit with her as Auro and Teges prepared Tamuk's body.

"The bowls that were here, what happened to them?" she asked.

"Be still," Shala snapped. "Leave him in peace! Tamuk is gone from us. Let it be."

From the shaman's hearth, Teeka saw a sudden throng of people in the center of the mound. They looked confused, scattering in all directions, like ants dispersing after their nest had been stepped on. Yet there was urgency with a purpose in their motions.

Ascending the mound were the painted men of Kaho's tribe. They were the reconnaissance party, alerting the clan to Kaho's impending arrival. They surveyed the village and then stood as sentinels.

Teeka ran to Teges and Auro. She first met Auro's eyes, and his mouth dropped open.

"He is here?" Auro asked, though he already knew from Teeka's face.

The blank stare in her eyes answered his question.

Teges climbed down from the platform and walked slowly toward the rest of the villagers.

Kaho's craft had arrived. He stood at the edge of the mound watching Teges approach.

Teges walked with the dignity of a king. He hurried for no one. His head was erect, his spine straight with shoulders back. Each deliberate step was calculated. His gait was rhythmic, his eyes steady and focused. His manner was arrogant enough to irritate, but not enough to enrage. He sacrificed his pride for no one, not even Kaho.

Auro had followed closely behind Teges; Teeka and Shala lagged slightly behind him. As Teges got closer, Kaho walked to the center of the village. Teeka dropped back, gathering the last hope that Kaho would not look for her.

The two kings faced each other squarely as some of the people of the clan began to lay portions of their fortune before Kaho.

"The journey was fruitful." Kaho spoke.

"We are great hunters and fishermen. All our undertakings are prosperous."

"That is fortunate for the clan of Teges. You provide well for Kaho. It pleases me," Kaho said, scrutinizing the bounty.

Kaho gestured to his men, who began hauling the tribute to the boats. Auro held his breath. Perhaps the intruder would not ask for Teeka and would leave. Maybe it had just been a ploy to antagonize the People. Kaho enjoyed such things.

Ata walked closer to Auro, anticipating that he might become difficult when Kaho asked for Teeka.

"The clan of Teges deserves peace for offering Kaho all these treasures. You have a wise cacique," Kaho said, looking at the gathered clan.

"Then take your tribute and leave these good people in peace. We are grateful for your continued kindness to the Tegesta."

Both leaders observed these formalities at each visit. None of it was sincere, but it was expected.

"Has Teges grown old since I last spoke with him? Is there not something that you have forgotten?"

Auro straightened, and Ata stepped even closer.

Teges did not speak but continued to stare at Kaho with an expressionless face.

"The maiden, old man. Have you forgotten my bride? Surely you must have forgotten. This cacique would not try to keep her from me."

Teges did not acknowledge the comment. Kaho walked around him and into the crowd of people.

"Where is the maiden I chose?"

Teeka stood in the background with her heart hammering. Her throat tightened as she stepped through the crowd.

Auro started to move toward her, and Ata reached for his shoulder, holding him back. "No, Auro," he whispered. "It must be."

Kaho turned to Teges as he saw Teeka coming forth. "Another wise decision. It would have been unfortunate had something happened to this maiden."

Kaho looked her over as she stood before him. His eyes raped her before her people, and the women looked away. He lifted a handful of her hair and held it to his nose.

Teeka stood motionless, showing no emotion. The tingling of the pendant had been replaced by a comfortable warmth. Kaho moved it aside and slid his hand down her center and back up her arm.

Ata held on to Auro. "Look away. Do not punish yourself."

Auro backed through the crowd, knowing that he could stand no more. To see Kaho touch her and look at her was more than he could tolerate. He had lost his father and now Teeka. But the pendant caught his eye, easing his rage. She would never truly be Kaho's.

Kaho led Teeka away from everything she knew and to his canoe. Her mind whirled, retreating into a dark, hazy corner where she did not have to deal with the horrible reality. If she had to face it, she knew she would collapse. She could not do that to her people. It would steal the masculinity from the men. No, it was better that she wrap herself in a thick mist in her mind. It was better that she not let herself feel. It was better that she leave with dignity.

"Always!" Auro screamed from a distance. Like a wisp of smoke, something from her nightmare floated in her head and then was gone.

She lifted her legs, one at a time, as she boarded the boat. She faced the other side of the river, trying to catch the elusive puff of the dream.

A man, somewhere behind her, pushed the canoe off of the soft earth and into the water. After it had cleared the shallows, the oarsmen took over with silent paddles.

Teeka reached for the warm pendant. In the daylight, the sheen looked different. It was strange but not such a curiosity. It was the moonlight that had added the shimmer, she thought. The pendant was still quite beautiful but closer to ordinary than it had seemed in the moonlight.

The familiar surroundings were disappearing as the canoes made their way down the river. The smell of the company was peculiar, and the places she recognized along the shore became fewer and fewer.

Kaho lowered himself so that he sat next to her. "Tell me your name."

Teeka looked at the man who had caused so much pain in her life, but she did not speak.

"This beautiful maiden must have a beautiful name. Will you tell me what it is, or shall I name you? Why do I not call you Amisa? Yes, I like that—Amisa of the Tegesta."

Teeka did not care if he knew her name, but she would not give it to him. She would give him nothing she did not have to.

She felt him staring, watching her breathe. She hoped he wanted her. It was going to please her to refuse him.

Teeka fondled the pendant, feeling the warm glow in her hand travel through her body. She sleepily lowered and raised her eyelids as she provocatively tossed her hair to one side.

Chapter Eight

KAHO WAS AROUSED by Teeka's coquettishness. Her eyes seemed larger and darker than he remembered, black pools too deep to see the bottom.

"Is this the same maiden who trembled with fear when I chose her?"

Teeka rocked her head to one side and let her lips slightly part. "Is there something I should fear?"

"There is nothing to fear, but when I chose you, you quaked like the leaves of a tree during a storm."

She again teased with her posture and subtle gestures, while she moistened her lips with her tongue.

"Are you not pleased with your choice?"

He was confused by her boldness. He had taken her against her will, and yet she offered no resistance. There was something about her that made him uneasy, yet she struck a primal, animalistic chord that he could not ignore.

"I am pleased," he answered, still studying her. "We will be at the village of Kahoosa in another day. You will find it different."

His thoughts had become scattered. Why was he so intrigued with her? She had not been so remarkable the day he had chosen her. Her hair had been disheveled, and she had had scratches on her cheek and legs. Her body, as he remembered it, was slight, and her breasts were not very large. The face was pretty and naive, and her eyes were clear and innocent. That was what he found most alluring.

He always read personalities by looking at people's eyes. He liked innocent women and enjoyed taking their virginity. He was proud of his sexual prowess and found special pleasure in spending hours guiding a young woman through her first sexual experience. He considered himself a master. He would slowly arouse her, gently, tenderly, and then as her passion rose, he would explore her more fervently, more aggressively. She would clutch and beg as he teased her with the promise of fulfillment, and then he would slow his pace, withdraw, and let her hang at the edge. Finally, when she screamed for him and raked at his back, he would resist no longer.

But this woman would be different. How, he wasn't certain. For some reason his power seemed diminished, and yet he was drawn to her. He wanted to know more about her, and he wanted more than anything to dominate her.

Teeka watched his face as the thoughts poured through his mind like water over a waterfall. She smiled slightly and turned away from him.

Kaho stood and appeared to be checking their location. He scanned the bank, seeming to know each Sabal palm, each blade and reed, every cypress. Darkness would come soon, even though the moon was waxing; it was better to camp at night than to travel. Just ahead was a bend in the river, and just beyond that was a campsite he and his men frequented.

"We will stop for the night," he ordered them sternly, reasserting himself, as if to make up for the impotence he had just felt while thinking about Teeka.

He would wait to take her, he thought, as he looked at her back. She sat tall and erect, her long black hair cascading down her back to her waist, and then spilling over onto the femininity of curved hips.

The canoes rounded the bend and moved toward the eastern shore. A clearing would be their overnight camp, and some of the food given by Teeka's people would be the evening meal. The Kahoosa quickly started a fire and then gathered around it. Kaho sat across the circle so that he faced her. Every now and then she would look up at him and curve her lips into a smile.

As the curtain of darkness draped over them, the moonlight and the firelight danced their ballet over the faces of the men. Teeka was far enough away from the fire so that only shadows and moonlight played on her face. The pendant she wore seemed to collect the light. What special skill did her people have to make a columella so iridescent? He would have to ask her, he thought, as he watched her settle beneath a tree and close her eyes.

The men selected their spots for sleep, and Kaho posted two sentries near Teeka. But as he gave them instructions, he saw that she was breathing the deep breaths of sleep. Even so, he posted two more lookouts near the water.

Kaho closed his eyes and waited for sleep. But in those moments that preceded sleep, when disjointed thoughts tumbled in and out, Kaho saw images of her and flooded with desire. There was a dull ache in his loins, and if it had been any other woman, he would have gone to her bed. What was this trepidation? He rose and walked to his sleeping prize.

"Do you wish to be alone with the maiden?" the sentries asked.

Kaho looked down at her. "No," he answered.

He returned to his sleeping place, but when sleep did come, it was interrupted. Several times during the night he woke startled, as from a nightmare, but he remembered no dream. Each time he would glance across the clearing to see if the sentries and Teeka were still there.

When the sun rose, he was relieved. He was the first awake, but Teeka was the first to get up. She busied herself with her morning grooming, even though the sentries stayed with her. Kaho watched from a distance, trying to seem detached. Every move she made was suggestive, though the action was suited to her tasks.

On the last leg of the journey back to his village, Kaho placed Teeka in a separate canoe from him and instructed his men to watch her. Her canoe was to stay in the middle of the fleet, which would aid in guarding against any rescue attempt. He did not think the Tegesta would come for her. They were not strong enough. But he would be prepared just in case. He had learned long ago never to make assumptions.

Teeka watched the shore, observing the landmarks. She noted a tree that had grown crooked, guided by its search for some small sprinkle of sunlight in the thick cover of the older trees. A fallen tree had dammed leaves and debris as it stuck a dead finger into the water. Another area had been burned off by a fire from lightning. The new shoots of saw grass were just beginning to come through. All of these scenes she would need to remember. They would help her track her way back home. Home to Auro.

The river had birthed several tributaries, and the small flotilla had left the main water flow and begun to travel one of the branches. The farther they traveled, the more choices they made in direction. Teeka continued to memorize the landmarks that would help her identify the route. Today she felt more frightened. Again the pendant began to aggravate her flesh, and she wished she could remove it or at least find a way to wear it that was more comfortable.

She looked up to see Kaho in the boat ahead. Her stomach churned. He repulsed her, and yet she was trying to entice him. She wanted him to find her attractive, desirable. How could she possibly act that way? Suddenly she felt embarrassed and ashamed. Her people would have been appalled. What was wrong with her?

In a day or two the moon would be at its fullest, and there would be enough light for her to steal away when all were sleeping. If she continued not to struggle, perhaps he would dismiss the guards. She resigned herself to the need to tolerate whatever was asked of or done to her.

Before late afternoon, they arrived in the village of the Kahoosa. Kaho had been right—she did find it different. Compared to her home, this place was immense but still well organized. The earth had cast up an enormous outcropping of limestone that rose high above the marsh. It was a splendid vantage point as well as a rampart against the fluctuating water table. It was speckled with gumbo-limbo, live oak, cabbage palm, red maple, and other trees. Palmettos clumped together in patches. In the lower, wetter areas, cypress took over, and beneath them grew the beautiful, delicate ferns.

The site was three times larger than her village, which was the largest of the Tegesta. The wealth of the tribe was reflected everywhere. Thatch covered the roofs of all the living platforms, and a large spoked hearth lay in the center of the habitation mound. Women were cooking small portions at their own fires, and hot stones steamed in pouches of liquid-filled animal hide. The central hearth was attended by a small group of women who were preparing the meat for the entire village. It appeared that all of the Kahoosa shared the evening meal.

Teeka watched as Kaho proudly displayed the latest collection of food, hide, and shell that he had taken from the other tribes, including hers. Two men suddenly seized her arms and led her forward. Kaho spoke in a language of which she knew little, even though there were many common root words. Without understanding all he said, she knew that he was including her in his boastfulness. Teeka again looked as she had the day he had chosen her, innocent, naive, and virginal. She was a prize, a piece of meat brought back from a hunting trip.

Two women came and stood next to her, touched and examined her, and chatted between themselves. She gathered that these were Kaho's wives. They wore carved bone pins and combs in their hair. Necklaces of shell beads hung around their necks.

The women gestured for her to follow them, but she stood still, not sure what she was supposed to do. To Teeka's surprise, they directed her again but in her language. They sounded strange, the inflections and pronunciations not always exact, but she easily understood them.

"How do you know my language?" she asked.

"You are not the first woman of your tribe to come here. Kaho has brought others," one of them answered.

"Where are they?" Teeka asked excitedly.

"They did not please him. They were sent away."

Teeka looked hopeful. Maybe all she had to do was displease Kaho. "Back to their clan?" she asked.

The two women stopped, looking at Teeka in disbelief. "Kaho would never do that. No, they were sent to smaller Kahoosa villages."

The sudden spark of hope that Teeka had felt was quickly extinguished.

She passed the central hearth, and the aroma of venison roasting on the spits made her mouth water. She followed the women to a newly built platform, the thatch still green. One of Kaho's wives indicated that this would be Teeka's home and that Kaho would be nearby. When he desired her, he would have her go with him, or he would be with her here. Teeka cringed at the thought, but nodded her head to express understanding.

The mat for sleeping was plusher than what she was used to. It was two woven pieces sewn together and stuffed with soft grasses. There was even a smaller mat on which she could rest her head.

"When will the marriage be celebrated?" Teeka asked the one who spoke to her.

"Kaho will find out if he likes you first. This will be a trial. If you please him, he will keep you."

"And what if I do not please him?"

"Then you must find someone else who will take you. A woman must have a man who will hunt for her. You must try hard to please him. No man wants another man's discard. Please him, and you will not have to worry about such things."

Teeka sighed. *I will escape. I cannot please him. I do not want to please him,* she thought. Every time she thought about him, her stomach drew up into a hard ball.

The sun began to sink in the western sky, and Teeka sat alone in her new home. She did not know the Kahoosa's ways and did not venture out into the group. The venison had been consumed by the time darkness fell, and her stomach grumbled with hunger. She had not seen Kaho since the women had led her away, and she had not seen the wives since they had shown her to her platform.

Teeka looked through the maze of deer hides that were strung and stretched between posts and trees. She wondered which nearby place was his. She watched in the light of the moon as the Kahoosa prepared for bed. One of the wives came to her with a bowl of broth.

"I have brought you food."

Teeka motioned for her to bring it up. She could smell the wonderful hot broth. She was so hungry. The woman climbed the short ladder and placed the intricately decorated bowl on the floor of the platform.

"What are you called?" she asked.

"Teeka. What are you called?"

"Cala," she answered.

"And the other woman?" Teeka asked.

"Rebet," she replied.

"Thank you, Cala," Teeka said, picking up the bowl.

The woman nodded at her and left.

She sipped the broth and looked at the moon, wishing there had been more in the bowl. She wanted something solid, but this would do. When she had finished, she stretched out on the soft mat. She wanted to see the stars, but the thatch obscured her view. She turned on her side to look at the sky. Every star in the heavens was lit, and the moon was bright. *Auro,* she thought, *this should be our night.* Her eyes closed. She could feel his touch and hear his breath in her ears. If she had to, she would live each night this way with him in her mind. She clutched the pendant. "Always," she whispered, remembering her promise.

Another day and the moon would shine its brightest. Tomorrow she would wander the village and find the best way out. She would ask Cala and the other woman questions. She would study the Kahoosa routines and store some food away. She hoped she could do it without alerting anyone to her plan.

She snuggled into the mat and looked across the village. Resting in the shadows was all the evidence of the Kahoosa wealth. It seemed they wanted for nothing. She had already seen so much and knew that she could never have imagined it. She had heard stories about the way the Kahoosa lived, but she had found them hard to believe. Even the number of baskets about the village that abounded with wild berries, fruits, edible stalks, leaves, and roots had taken her by surprise. There was so much of everything. She wondered how much of the bounty had been stolen from other tribes.

Suddenly she realized that two men stood beneath her platform. Kaho had not dismissed the guards. Teeka turned the other way. She could wait them out, she thought. Tonight she would rest so that she would be strong for the next night. She would watch them and wait until their eyes closed. Then she would quietly cross the village and take a canoe. By the light of the big moon she would trace her way back. She would not be missed until the morning. By then, she would have enough of a lead to escape safely.

Then the truth crashed to the front of her brain. Even if she did escape, they would know where to find her, and they would punish the People. Tomorrow would not be the day. She would need a plan—a better plan.

Teeka reached for the pendant. It was all she had of Auro, except her memories, and she clutched it tightly as she drifted off to sleep. In her dream she felt Auro's gentle hand stroke her hair. His strong hand was tender as it brushed her cheek. She sighed at the comfort of his presence. Snagging her from the depth of her dream, something nagged at her, deep in her belly, and she shifted with the discomfort. Another drawing pain coursed through her side and crept to the center of her lower abdomen.

Auro's hand touched her face and throat, and she shifted at his touch, stirring from her wonderful dream. Her heavy eyes opened.

Kaho was kneeling over her. It was his touch she felt, not Auro's. Her first reaction was to balk, but she quickly remembered the importance of cooperation. Again she felt a slight pain, an emptying of her fruitless womb. It was the onset of her moon cycle. Now that she was awake, she recognized it for what it was.

Kaho looked down on her and let his fingers trace the outline of her lips. She held very still, awaiting his next move. His hands wandered over her body, brushing all the hollows and crests that defined her as a woman. Slowly he lowered himself upon her and tasted her throat. His hands moved over the length of her torso, sensing the profile of her breasts and the indentation of her waist. He continued, letting his hands cup the arch of her hips, and then he reached as far as he could, finding her thighs. Leisurely, he slid his hands up her thighs until he reached the junction, where Teeka's hands halted him. Kaho respected her wishes and placed his hands behind her head, lifting it so that her lips met his. He would not press her but would take her slowly until the animal that existed in all women yielded to its instinctive need. His lips and tongue darted into her ear and down her neck until he found the soft tissue of her breasts. Again he lowered his hands, and again she stopped him. Gently he stroked her cheek and looked at her, as if to reassure her that he would be tender.

Teeka remembered how he had treated Erza and

wondered about his inconsistent behavior. Was he afraid to let anyone see another side of him, the gentle and patient one that she witnessed now? Might it undermine his image?

"No," she said softly. "It is my time."

Kaho rolled to one side and sighed. She lay still next to him. In a moment he rose and left. Soon two figures approached. As they got closer, she realized that it was Cala and Rebet. Both of them climbed the platform.

"Stand up," they ordered.

Both were tired and aggravated that their sleep had been interrupted. Teeka stood, and Cala leaned over to examine her. As she did, a trickle of blood streaked the inside of Teeka's leg.

"She tells the truth," said Cala.

They gathered Teeka's things. All of her personal things that had been given to Kaho and sent with her, rested in the two women's arms.

"Follow," said Cala.

They left the village and crossed a small slough that separated the habitation mound from another mound. She quickly realized that they were walking along the edge of the burial ground. A tall marker stood at one end, a totem honoring the deceased members of the Kahoosa. On the edge of the burial mound, but away from the graves, was another platform suitable for a handful of people. The women climbed up and laid Teeka's things on the floor of the platform. She looked puzzled, and they saw that she did not understand.

"Stay here until you are clean."

She still did not understand.

"When your time is finished, bathe and ask the spirits to cleanse you. Then you may return to the rest of us."

Teeka saw four other women sleeping on the small

platform, their personal things piled near them. Each of them rested on a flat mat.

"There," said Cala, pointing to an empty space on the far edge.

Cala and Rebet climbed down and left Teeka standing, still a little puzzled. Being careful to move quietly and not disturb the sleeping women, she gathered her things and crossed the platform to the empty space. With no mat as a buffer, she found the bare floor of the platform hard and uncomfortable. The mats the other women slept on were different from the one she had been given in her quarters. These were lighter and more portable, like the one at home. She would be here for the next five days, if they had meant that she wasn't to leave until her time was finished. Strange, she thought, that the women having their moon cycle would be separated from the rest. At least it had held off Kaho. For that she was thankful.

She looked through the things that Illa and Selo had prepared and had given to Kaho. The leather straps were there, but there was nothing to line them with. It would have to do for the night. She would ask the other women where she could gather the fiber that she used to line the leather straps. Even if they did not comprehend her language, she could make them understand. It was one element that all women had to deal with. It bound them.

She found it hard to get comfortable. Splinters of wood pricked her each time she moved. She settled for a position on her side, though it made her shoulder ache.

Again the pendant irritated her, and she felt a strong dislike for it. It upset her that she could feel this way about something that Auro had made especially for her. It was already difficult enough to sleep. The floor was hard, the strap had no lining, her belly cramped, and the pendant annoyed her. It would be a long night.

Chapter Nine

FINALLY, SOMETIME IN THE WEE HOURS of the new day, before light, she had managed to fall asleep. The women had awakened and looked at the stranger in their midst but tried not to stare. Living in the open as they did, they had developed the convention of not watching others. There was little privacy in the way they lived and housed themselves. To protect some privacy, they respected one another by not intruding with their eyes.

The women whispered to one another, inquiring if anyone knew who she might be. Because of their temporary exile, they had not seen Teeka's arrival in the village. She certainly was plain-looking, they thought. She wore no adornments in her hair or any other ornaments, except that pendant. Such necklaces were common, but this one imparted a particular luster that attracted their attention. Her other personals were rather ordinary. She must have come from a very poor tribe. Kaho had probably brought her back, they decided. Their suspicions were confirmed when they saw two men standing guard across the mound. Could this be the woman for whom the new platform had been built? Yes, they whispered, she was pretty, delicate, and nicely shaped. Her face was lovely, but she had no markings of high rank. Kaho would probably treat her as he treated the many others he brought from the lesser tribes. He would have his mock trials with her for a short time and then tire of her. She would be an outcast, a woman with no man.

Kaho's marriages to Cala and Rebet had been family arrangements made during their childhoods. Cala and Rebet had come from different clans. Sometimes such marriage arrangements were made to keep the ties strong between the villages, thereby strengthening the tribe. Ultimately, after he came of age, the man would decide whether or not to honor the arrangement. Kaho had obliged and taken both women as his wives. They served him well, produced many children, and kept him respectably within the limits of the customs and traditions he had so often blatantly defied. For every act of rebellion, he submitted to some act of tradition. It had kept the old ones quiet and had given his advocates support for their arguments.

He was a manipulator and a genius at managing people. He had the ability to whip up the ardor of the young men whenever he found a cause. He had surrounded himself with zealots and proved himself a leader at a very young age, so that when he was older and led a small rebellion against the peaceful policies of the tribe, he had been overwhelmingly victorious. Whenever there had been an objection to his methods and actions, the wealth he had accumulated for the tribe always squelched the complaint.

His people admired him as a leader, aggressor, and arbitrator, but they also feared him.

Teeka gradually awakened, still feeling the cramping. It was the smell of the strange surroundings that finally made her open her eyes. The other women turned away, as if they had not been watching her. The atmosphere was strained, and the Kahoosa women tried to ignore the stranger. Finally Teeka spoke.

"I am Teeka," she said, getting the attention of the round-faced woman who stood closest. She was small, with long trailing hair that needed some attention. She bore stretch marks across her belly and breasts, attesting to the fact that she had borne children. Her facial features were broad, including a wide nose and fat cheeks. In her eyes there was a glint of friendliness that Teeka relied on.

"Teeka," she said, pointing to herself. "My name is Teeka."

She waited for a moment, hoping that the others would respond with their names. At least it would be a start if she could address them by name.

"Teeka," she said again, poking her chest with her finger. She rotated her hand and pointed to the woman on her left, who had looked friendly.

"Teeka," the woman said, pointing back. She turned her finger to herself. "Tosa."

Teeka grinned, tapped herself, and repeated her name, then pointed to the woman and said "Tosa."

Tosa appeared as though she had just discovered a secret, then pointed to the woman next to her, who was small and delicate, not unlike Teeka.

"Basee," she said, and then took the hand of the next woman to be introduced.

"Lamita," the woman said, almost shyly.

Lamita was tall, thin, bony, and angular. Her collarbones jutted from a flat chest, and her shoulders were square-cornered. Teeka guessed that she was the youngest of the four. It was unusual for people of either the Tegesta or the Kahoosa to be so tall and thin. Lamita's posture was stooped, as if she tried to shorten herself. Teeka supposed that Lamita was self-conscious, and that accounted for her apparent timidity.

She smiled at Lamita and repeated her name. Teeka's accent made the woman giggle.

The last of the four had still not seemed to approve and had not offered her name. She gave the impression that she was a little disagreeable and had walked to the far end of the platform when the introductions began. She was short, pudgy, and older than the other three. Tosa walked over to the woman, who grumbled at her approach.

"Pansar," Tosa said, touching the woman on the shoulder.

Teeka repeated the name and stepped closer, hoping to cure the woman's unpleasantness.

Pansar said something to Tosa, which Teeka could not understand. Tosa replied in a soft, easy voice.

Pansar looked at Teeka, as if giving in.

"Teeka," she said, feebly lifting a finger toward Teeka, and then "Pansar," she said, finally introducing herself.

Tosa pointed to herself again. "Tosa, Kahoosa." When she stopped speaking, she directed her hand toward Teeka, gesturing for her to answer.

"Teeka, Tegesta."

Both women grinned at their simple communication. In unison, all the women repeated "Tegesta" and raised their eyebrows with interest.

Now Tosa and the others understood the plainness of Teeka's apparel. The Tegesta were poor compared to the Kahoosa, but even so she was strikingly nice to look at. A pang of jealousy struck Pansar. All her youth had gone except for the last physical attribute, her moon cycle. Her breasts were pendulous from the weight of them through the years. She had never been particularly attractive, and her aging was flattering neither her face nor her body. Her waist and hips had spread with age without benefit of bearing children. No man had ever looked at her with interest, much less chosen her. If it had not been for her brother assuming the role of her provider, her fate would have been disastrous.

Some of the clan women brought small portions of food to the isolated women. They placed dull, undecorated bowls on the ground before the platform. The food had been prepared for them in these simple containers that were used only by women in their moon cycle.

"Why do you stay here?" Teeka asked, turning and sweeping her hand to indicate the platform.

Pansar was the first to understand the meaning of Teeka's question, rubbing her belly and then signing the moon. Teeka rubbed her abdomen and copied the sign. The women nodded in confirmation.

Teeka knew the physical reason but wondered about the social or moral reason for such a peculiar custom. How could she relay that question? She turned her face into quizzical lines.

"Tegesta, no," was all she could think of that the women might comprehend.

They looked surprised. Pansar seemed a bit wiser and not as surprised as the others. Through her years, she had heard about some of the strange customs of the Tegesta and others. She knew that the women of the Tegesta were not separated from the rest of the tribe when it was their moon cycle time, though such a custom made no sense to her at all. Being separated was the right thing to do. Women were unclean and harbored undesirable spirits during that time.

Pansar climbed down from the platform and called Teeka's name. With her leathery hands she lifted some soil from the ground and smeared it up and down her arms, then rubbed her stomach and made the sign for the moon.

The meaning was clear—menstruating women were unclean. The onset of the bleeding for women of the Tegesta was a time of celebration. It marked the passage from childhood into adulthood. The whole tribe knew when it was a young girl's first time. She became a maiden, with all of the attendant responsibilities and freedoms. She was allowed courtships and was given a voice in informal discussions. It was a time that young girls anxiously awaited. Yet here it was looked upon as something unfavorable. She felt a little sorry for these women who had never been able to enjoy the phenomenal miracle that the spirits awarded the body of a woman.

Teeka walked to her part of the platform and picked up one of her other straps and took it back to Tosa. She needed to know where she could collect some of the soft fiber for the lining material.

Tosa led her down the platform, off the mound, and away from the village, at times having to wade in the thin layer of marsh water. They made extra noise, sloshing the water with their feet to frighten away any snake that might be hiding in their path. Within a few minutes they reached a low plain that was dotted with tall, thin plants that bore pink fuzz as their flower. Teeka stripped off some of the feathery material and compacted it in her hands. Tosa helped her collect more and put it into a pouch she had brought along. When they had collected enough, Tosa showed her the way to the bathing place.

The five women went to a secluded portion of the stream that bordered the village of Kahoosa. The sky was azure with great puffs of white that with a little imagination could be seen as larger-than-life animals. The day would be clear and warm, Teeka thought. A banded water snake lay on a rock across the stream, collecting the warmth of the sun, and turtles poked their heads out to breathe the fresh, clean air. Teeka held the pendant away from her as she cleaned the sensitive skin beneath it. She took a mouthful of the sparkling liquid and rinsed her mouth. From the bottom she took some of the rough sediment and rubbed it on her elbows and heels to keep them soft. The women bathed and washed their leather protectors, then left them to dry on the rocks and lined soft, clean ones with the plant down. Teeka felt much better.

When they returned, they each took a portion of the gruel that had been left for them. The warmth of it relieved some of the cramping in Teeka's lower abdomen and back.

Tosa began to gather all her things together to get ready to leave. She offered Teeka a leaf to chew on that had pain-relieving properties. She gladly took it, tore off a small piece, and chewed it with her back teeth. Slowly the drug was released and absorbed, and she could feel her muscles relax. She was sorry that Tosa's time was over. She had been the most amicable of the four.

Tosa began to walk away, carrying her basket of belongings. Teeka watched her as she stopped within a circle of rocks, lowered her basket to the ground, and knelt. She stretched out her arms and bent her head until her face touched the ground. Three times she raised herself, arched her back, and lifted her hands to the sky. She was saying something, but Teeka could not hear. She made some signs with her hands, touched different places on her body, and then lowered herself to her initial position. After a few moments, she stood and picked up her basket.

That must have been the request to the spirits for cleansing, Teeka thought. She expected Tosa to walk out of the circle and on to the village, but she turned and walked back to the platform. She put the large reed basket on the ground, removed her folded mat, and handed it to Teeka. It was such a kind gesture. Teeka reached out and touched Tosa's hand.

Though Pansar had been a little helpful to Teeka, she was still not very pleasant. Smiles were few. The next day, both Lamita and Pansar left.

———

The days were long and filled with nothing. There were no tasks, no weaving, no cooking, and yet she found relief in them. She had time to think. The time was there to work out a plan, but she did not know the people and their daily routines. She was isolated and did not even know the entire layout of the village. She would have to postpone her escape even longer, until after she had had a chance to study the situation. She was torn between having the safety of the exile and needing the freedom to return to the village so that she might devise a way of escape.

The fifth day did come, and her time had passed. That morning she cleansed herself particularly well. She was not sure where she should go or how to call on the spirits, but was certain that Cala or Rebet would show up and watch for a moment, just as they had done every day. When Teeka returned from the stream, Rebet was standing with the sentries.

She picked up all her things and left. Rebet walked to meet her, carrying a basket that Teeka could use. They paused at the circle, and Teeka stepped inside, waiting for some clue from Rebet. Without confidence she knelt, as she had seen the others do. The ground was hard and free of any plants, standing out from the surroundings with its barrenness. She leaned forward, looking at Rebet for approval. What would she do now? She did not know the words or the spirits that she was to call. Rebet watched and waited, but Teeka remained on her knees with her face to the ground and her arms outstretched. Rebet stepped closer to the edge of the circle and called Teeka's name.

"You may not return until all the bad spirits are cast out."

"But I do not know your ways."

Rebet's patience was growing thin, and it showed on her face and in her voice. "Call the spirits. Make yourself humble."

"But I know not which spirits to call. This is not the way of the Tegesta."

"What is the custom of the Tegesta?" she asked.

"Women do not need cleansing after their cycle. We do not leave the clan."

Rebet looked repulsed by the idea and thought that the Tegesta were not only poor but also very primitive. She would have to show Teeka what to do if she was to return to the tribe. Rebet knelt down outside the circle.

"Do as I do," she told Teeka.

Teeka watched and copied every movement and sound. The words were nonsense, and some were difficult for her to pronounce. She hesitated, appeared stiff in her movements, and stumbled over the words. It would have to do, Rebet thought.

After the completion of the ritual, Rebet led Teeka back to her housing. Teeka looked back, seeing the totem marker at one end of the mound and the platform on which Basee stood at the other. The two sentries followed behind.

Teeka clutched the pendant, wondering what would come next. As her fingers curled around the smooth shell, she seemed to derive some strength from it. Auro had known this would be difficult for her. He must have known how important it would be for her to have something she could touch and feel that represented their love. Somehow her fears and reservations had diminished. But why did the pendant bother her sometimes? The inconsistent properties of the amulet puzzled her.

One of the sentries was particularly attractive, and to her surprise she found herself speculating about what it would be like to join with him. She pictured herself persuading him to come to her in the cover of darkness. He would be unable to resist her. She would take him places where he had never been, making him writhe with the need to have her completely. She could almost smell and taste him. Teeka's pulse increased as she continued her fantasy. A drop of perspiration crossed her brow, and her breathing became shallower and more rapid.

Teeka returned to reality, shocked at how such a scene had played itself out in her mind. Where had such a horrid thought come from? It was unacceptable. Joining was only something beautiful, like what she and Auro had had. And if the People knew that she had these thoughts, they would feel shame. Was just being among the Kahoosa enough to make her betray her values, the morals of her people? She frightened herself and wanted to be alone. Tegesta women did not think of such things. She was not an animal.

Chapter Ten

THE MOON CONTINUED TO TURN in the sky, changing its face to those that watched, altering the silver light that fell over the earth during the night. Teeka watched it, and so did the People.

Teges sat at his hearth, the flames flickering low. The Tegesta had been emotionally wounded, and it seemed so needless. A wound of the flesh was quicker to heal, he thought. He had had these thoughts often since Kaho had come and taken Teeka. For him to ponder the same thing over and over must be a sign from the spirits, he decided. The next evening the Council would meet at his request. It was time to end the suffering.

Teges unfolded his stiff legs and stretched them out. His knees were sore from sitting so long in the same place without moving. He reached for the walking stick that would help him lift his heavy body from the ground and, grimacing with each step, he climbed the ladder to his platform. He would do no more thinking this night. Tomorrow, beneath the moon, he would share his worry.

———

The Council of men sat cross-legged, solemnly watching Teges through the orange glow of the central hearth. His quiet but resolute voice fell unfaltering on their ears.

Those across the fire leaned closer.

"We must be the first. The People must be the ones. The spirits have charged us with that. The spirits have put peace in our hearts, not the Kahoosa's.

Teges searched the men's faces, reading their reactions. Auro's face was strained. He had hardened since losing Teeka to Kaho. He was filled with anger and hate, emotions that a shaman should not harbor and nurture. This worried Teges. These feelings that Auro could not let go of would influence his visions and perceptions, and that would harm not only Auro but also the People.

Yagua, a strong young leader who had captured the eye of Teges and many others as the most likely to become the next cacique, cleared his throat and then began to speak.

"Teges has the wisdom that comes with age. He has observed and evaluated the events throughout his life. It would be prudent of us to listen to his advice."

Olagale, Auro's apprentice, fidgeted with nervousness. He also agreed with Teges, but he knew it would not be appropriate for him to speak out, knowing that Auro did not agree. He would hold his tongue, unless of course he was asked to state his opinion.

There was silence in the circle of men. There was silence across the whole village. The women whispered to their children, quieting them so that nothing would distract the men.

Ata finally spoke, dismantling the silent tension. "We must think of the children of the Tegesta and the children of the children. It is our obligation to do all that we can to leave them a peaceful world. We must take the steps."

Auro heard the muffled agreement. Some were still unsure, but too many seemed to be concurring with

Teges. He had promised himself to hear them out, but this was too much. The Council was actually considering groveling at the very door of the Kahoosa. Where were the warriors? Did they exist only in Tegesta legends? Where was their pride?

"You listen to this?" Auro nearly shouted, throwing his hands in the air with exasperation. He lowered his hands and balled his fists into tight knots, trying to regain his composure. "Kaho has ravaged, plundered, and marauded the Tegesta, and you are dwelling on peace. Where are the warriors of the Tegesta? Have they all died? We stood by like women and watched Kaho take Teeka. No wonder the Kahoosa find us such easy prey. We do not stand and fight like men. We cower and crawl on the ground at his filthy feet. The Tegesta are a nation of cowards."

"Auro!" Ata interrupted. "We have all felt the pain caused by the Kahoosa. You are not alone. But we must let that go and think of the future. Do you want this terror to continue forever? Surely you want it to end. And if you do, then you understand that we must concentrate our energies on finding ways to bring about a full and truthful peace, not just safety from war but freedom from fear."

"You are blind," Auro retorted. "The only way is to seek vengeance, be strong, fight instead of cringe, stand tall, as our ancestors would have."

Auro stopped and looked around the circle. There were one or two men he seemed to have incited. On the faces of the others he saw expressions of discord and dissent.

Teges took his walking stick and pushed himself into a standing position. He was outraged at the insults. "You shame your heritage."

Auro stepped inside the circle, asserting his rank among the men. His handsome face was disguised, hidden by the sour lines of bitterness. "The Tegesta shame themselves. You quiver with fear and call it the peaceful way. You disgust—"

Ata again interrupted, suspending the affront. "You are still riddled with anguish and misery. See through that, Auro. No one should ever need to feel such grief again. We must prevent it. We can. And it will take much more bravery than killing. It does not take a brave man to run a spear through an enemy. The Tegesta will confront the Kahoosa without weapons."

"You talk in circles. What is it that you want, the annihilation of our clan, of our tribe? What kind of man are you? Do you not hear your wife, Illa, cry in the night? She grieves for her sister. Do you turn your head from her? Do you offer her no comfort? Now you say we will confront the Kahoosa with no weapons. Your words are stupid."

Teges pounded the earth with his stick. "Enough! The Tegesta will not hurt one another with barbed words. It will not be the Kahoosa who destroy the Tegesta. We will do it to ourselves if we betray one another. You forget the procedures of the Council, our code. We come together to arrive at solutions. Auro, you have disgraced the Council. You turned this gathering into a squabble. You spread your anger like a poison."

Ata interrupted yet again. "I think I have a plan that would satisfy all of us. It is filled with risks, but as you will see, Auro, we have not become a nation of cowards. What I propose will take all the courage we can find."

Auro sat down, relinquishing his spot to Ata. "Speak, then," Auro snapped. "Tell us of your bold scheme. I fear that it will make me laugh."

Ata ignored the remark. "We always allow Kaho to come to our village, stomping, demanding, threatening. I suggest that we extinguish that fire inside him. Throw water on his flames."

"And how do you propose to do that, Ata? Should we beg at his feet? We almost do that already."

"Kaho intimidates the Tegesta because we wait for his next move. What if we are not intimidated? What if we let him know we are not afraid? What if we make the first move?"

Teges squinted. "What do you mean, 'make the first move'?"

"Attack?" questioned Yagua.

"No. Go in peace," Ata answered. "Take some of our goods to the Kahoosa village, to Kaho. Do not wait for him to come. That is what gives him the advantage. Let him see the true courage of the Tegesta."

Teges raised his brows. "I think you have a good plan, Ata. Not only do we display our bravery, but we also start the move toward peace."

"That is right," Ata agreed. "Kaho cannot demand of us what we give freely. It will be the first step."

Auro grumbled. "Is there not a man here? A warrior?"

"Hear it all, Auro," Ata continued. "We will also see Teeka and bring her news of the Tegesta, and she can send news of herself. Do you not wonder about her condition? Forgive me—how could you not?"

Ata's references to Teeka only further incensed him. "Warriors would bring her home."

"And the Kahoosa would come for her again," Teges said. "And then they would come for someone else. Those brave warriors on both sides would die for something that would never be resolved. This would be a beginning."

Ata nodded in agreement. "Perhaps we should all give the idea some thought. We do not need to make decisions this very night. Teges," he said, turning his face from Auro to the cacique, "maybe we should not ask the Council tonight. Send us home. Let everyone think about it, and then the Council can meet again. It is an enormous step we contemplate."

"You are right," Teges agreed. "The Council is dismissed."

"Yes," Auro called to the dispersing Council. "Reflect upon what has been said. Consider what Ata has proposed and then think about your ancestors. Would they have continued to bow to Kaho? Would they have taken him the treasures of the People or would they have believed that if Kaho wanted something, make him come and get it? Would they have humbled themselves to make peace or would they have stood tall and brave and died in protest against his evil? Yes, go and think. Dream tonight and let your ancestors speak to you as the spirits speak to me. Let them tell you what a proud people the Tegesta used to be."

Auro stepped out of the light and into the darkness. His teeth were clenched in anger, and his stomach turned in his belly.

Teges also felt the nausea. Auro had still not recovered from the loss of Teeka. He remained caught up in it that he had forgotten about the well-being of the People. His eyes did not yet look outward on the rest of the world; they still looked inward. It was not a sign of a well mind, and it was no good for a shaman. He hoped that as time passed, Auro would heal.

Ata was worried and concerned. Auro was not the same. He had alienated many, and he had isolated himself from the rest of the villagers. No one grieved any more deeply than Teeka's mother and sister. He often found Illa weeping quietly when she thought she was alone— but she had not turned on her people.

Now that the men had returned to their platforms, they would lie next to their wives. Those who were troubled would tell their women, needing someone to listen patiently to their concerns. Though the men did not seem to realize it, subtle facial expressions, sighs, and head movements would indicate how the woman felt about what the man was saying. Without verbal responses, the woman would sway her husband's thinking. When the man was finished, she would soothe him and wash away his apprehension, focusing his attention on the matters of pleasure. Morning would come soon enough. The privacy of the darkness was not for disquieting thoughts.

———

Ata leaned over the baby next to Illa. Both mother and child were sleeping. Gently he lifted the child and moved him to a small mat between the older children. Tonight he ached to feel his wife's warmth. He needed her to quell his anxiety. He wanted the solace, the oblivion that he found in their lovemaking.

"Illa," he whispered, settling next to her slender body.

Illa shifted, turning toward her husband. Her eyes were heavy with the sleep that she did not want to leave.

"Illa," he murmured softly. "I may have the chance to see Teeka again."

Illa's eyes opened quickly. "Ata, what did you say?"

"I may get to see your sister."

Illa sat up. "What do you mean?"

"I have proposed that we initiate a peace between the Kahoosa and the Tegesta. The Kahoosa will never do it.

109

They will never take the first step."

"How? We cannot ask for peace. Kaho will laugh."

"First, we would deliver some of our goods to the village of the Kahoosa. Kaho will respect our bravery. Perhaps our actions would eventually lead to some small trading and finally a mutual peace. No more terror. No more grief."

"What about Teeka? You said something about Teeka."

"If we go, I want to be included in that party. I will look for her and hope that we will have the chance to speak."

"Oh, Ata. Do you think that you really could?"

"If the Council agrees with the proposal. Auro was strongly against such an idea."

Illa sank back into the mat. "Does he not see that it is this animosity between the Kahoosa and the People that has brought on his grief? He should want to end it. And just the thought of news of Teeka should have made him agree."

"Auro has never left that place where a grieving person hides to soak himself in his misery. It is a short part of the healing process. Remember how alone you felt, how full of sorrow?"

"I remember. It was a time to immerse myself in my pain. It was a way to release that pain, to put it outside me and finally leave it there. It was a time when I wondered how the rest of the clan, and even all the People, went on about their daily chores. Did they not realize what had happened? I was angry with everyone who did not suffer as I did. But those feelings passed. That short time was a cleansing process. There is still pain, but it does not choke me."

"But Auro has not left that feeling of anger. It makes

him turn on his own. He is choking on his torment and lets himself be swallowed by it. He feels only his pain. Nothing else matters. He does not care if the suffering continues. He cannot see into the future. He has no visions. He is trapped in the day that Teeka left. He will never seek peace. He would rather feed on his grief, and he is frustrated that he cannot pass his agony on to the rest of us. He calls us cowards."

"How could he not see the courage it would take to go to Kaho's village? Can he not understand the danger that ..." Illa's voice trailed off as she realized the scope of what Ata proposed and the possible consequences.

"Ata, not you. You cannot go. We cannot predict how Kaho will react. What if he receives you with weapons? I think that he has no conscience."

"It is my proposition. Auro and his supporters, if he has any, will claim that I am not confident in my own recommendation. It could undermine my argument. I would have to go. I want to go."

"Please, Ata. I could not bear to lose you also."

Ata stroked his wife's hair, brushing it from her forehead. "Shh," he whispered. "No decision has been made. Think no more of it tonight."

"No, not tonight," she whispered back, placing her head next to his chest and snuggling closer. She reached one arm over him so that she could run her hand up and down his muscular back.

"Turn onto your stomach," she told him.

Ata obeyed, and Illa sat astride his back, her hands smoothing out the kinked muscles that tensed in his shoulders. Softly she hummed a melody as she relaxed his tight body. He finally turned beneath her and looked into her face. Ata let out a heavy breath. He closed his eyes as Illa's touch first tranquilized him and then lit the fire of arousal inside him. She was pleased with his response, knowing that his mind had already left the question that had been put to the Council.

———

Auro had not immediately returned to his platform. Instead he had stood on the bank by the water. He could almost smell Teeka's sweetness on the wind. For a moment he thought that if he concentrated hard enough, he could make her appear. Why had Kaho selected her? It made him so angry. He recalled the last time he had seen her, stepping into Kaho's canoe, and Kaho following so closely. It was Kaho who could now smell the perfume of her skin and hair. It was Kaho who could see into the black sea of her eyes. It was Kaho who was with her now. Was he touching the soft flesh of her breasts and tasting her lips? Were her hands exploring his detestable body? Was she trembling beneath his hands, moaning and thrashing with a need for him?

Auro slammed his fist into the trunk of a tall Sabal palm, splitting his knuckles. He walked away, enveloped in his rage. The village was quiet. The air was heavy, laden with heat and night moisture. Auro stopped beneath Erza's platform. He had been told how Kaho had humiliated her the same day he had chosen Teeka. Kaho should have taken Erza, he thought. If Erza had not shown her weakness, Teeka would never have been taken. But Erza was like the rest of the Tegesta, he thought—a coward.

He was stepping onto the platform before he questioned what he was doing, but the thought never fully developed. Instead, he looked about in the dark. Erza's parents were sleeping soundly. On a mat at the opposite end of the shelter, Erza slept. He walked to her side, reached down, and shook her shoulder.

"Come with me," he ordered.

Erza's eyes flew open with the shock. Her eyelids fluttered as she tried to focus and understand what was going on.

"Auro? What are you doing? What is it?"

Erza's parents awakened and sat up, her father rising to his feet. "What is happening?" he asked.

"I am taking Erza with me," Auro answered. "Come," he told her again.

"Why?" Erza's father asked. "Why are you taking Erza with you in the middle of the night?"

"I am Shaman. It is my prerogative to have any woman. I want Erza."

Erza looked back to her parents. She was frightened and confused. "Father?"

"He can do nothing," Auro said impatiently. He jerked on her arm, pulling her to the top of the ladder. "You go ahead of me," he commanded.

Erza eased herself down the ladder, feeling her throat tighten with the need to cry. Auro forced her across the mound and up the ladder to his platform. In the corner, he reached for a bowl and swallowed its contents, afterward wiping his mouth with the back of his hand.

"When I am finished with you, I want you to get out."

Erza nodded her head.

————

The next day the Council gathered after the morning meal. Yagua wanted to begin, but Teges rejected the idea.

"We will wait for Auro. All the Council must attend," he argued.

"But Auro will only continue his verbal assaults. We need to make decisions and proceed," another contended.

Olagale sided with Teges. "We cannot proceed with any plan unless all agree that we should initiate a peace. If we cannot agree on that, there will be no plan. Auro is our shaman, and we must listen to what he says. His advice should be valued."

"But Auro is not thinking as the shaman," Yagua responded. "He is thinking only as a wounded man. We cannot take his opinions into consideration. Not this time. Not when we have such important matters to weigh."

"We will wait for our shaman," Teges said, ending the debate.

The men sat, waiting in the sun as it climbed in the sky and beat on their backs, drawing sweat that dripped down every small crevice of their bodies. If they had not held Teges in such esteem, they would never have tolerated Auro's recent behavior. They certainly would not have been sitting here, being tortured by the heat.

As many grew impatient, Teges sat staunchly until Auro finally sat with the others. The argument continued under the blazing sun. It went as had been predicted, but late in the afternoon Auro walked out on the Council when the tally was taken. All of the others scratched their marks in the dirt in favor of setting forth a plan for peace.

———

In a matter of days the Tegesta had decided who would be the members of this first eventful journey to the Kahoosa village. It was decided that it would be a small number so as to provoke no dangerous confrontation. A small party could not be mistaken for a group of warriors attacking the Kahoosa. Kaho would have to see that they came in peace. They would go in two of the small canoes, the second carrying only two men and the cargo. The lead canoe would carry four men.

Auro was not asked to go, but he had already said quite clearly that he wanted no part of it. Teges was probably too old, but he insisted that he go. Ata, of course would go, and also Yagua and Olagale. Two others were also chosen by the Council.

On the morning of the departure Illa held Ata close before he left the platform. At the water's edge she watched him leave in the direction of the Kahoosa village. She had seen her sister leave in the same direction. Her arms tingled with the apprehension she felt, making her rub them vigorously as if she felt chilled. She hoped this was not a foolish plan and that the Kahoosa would be receptive. All she knew of the Kahoosa was how they terrorized her and how they had caused so much pain to so many in her village.

Auro also watched, but he stood back from the crowd. He rubbed his cut knuckles, breaking the scabs, making fresh blood ooze to the surface.

Chapter Eleven

AS THE VAPOR ESCAPED from the river into the air, the small Tegesta group left the land where they had camped for the night and got back into the canoes. Today they would reach the Kahoosa village. A new adventure for the People would begin this day. Teges wondered how it would all end. What would future generations know of this day? Would the importance of it be lost somewhere in time? Would their names and their deed slip out of the legends that were to come?

Today the men in the canoes did not talk much. Most of the time they were deep in thought. Teges stood in the canoe and looked into the distance. He knew where the village was, though he had never been this close. Now, far in the distance, a thin swirl of smoke floated above the foliage.

"There," he said, pointing.

The men's eyes searched the river and the bank for signs. They were not far now, and Ata felt his heart beat faster, as did all the other men on the journey. The last curve in the river straightened. Into their sight came their first glimpse of a culture that seemed strange to them. The mound was enormous, sitting high above the wetland. The landing was well protected, and intruders could be easily detected. The platforms were all built in an orderly fashion, opening to the south. There were so many of them that from a distance they appeared as dark splotches half hidden by foliage.

As the men came closer, they saw the Kahoosa gathering, watching the small canoes approach. Both men and women had gathered, but now the women began to back away. Most of the men seemed to have curiosity carved in their faces.

The Tegesta stopped the canoes before they actually reached land, so that the Kahoosa would have more time to survey them and see that they had not come with harmful intent. Teges watched the Kahoosa. Those who had been gripping weapons finally lowered them. Children scampered through the gathering crowd, eager to see Tegesta men. The news had traveled quickly. The women began to walk back toward the river, less frightened when the strangers did not appear to be aggressive. *How extraordinarily courageous,* many of them were thinking when the two small canoes sat openly in the river across from Kaho's village.

Through the center of the glut of people, Kaho made his way to the water. The Kahoosa moved aside as he walked, making a path for their king. Kaho stopped and stared out at the Tegesta.

Teeka heard the clamor from her platform. She stood on the open side looking and listening and was astonished at what she could make out. It could not be, she thought to herself. If only the Kahoosa spoke her language. She kept hearing "Tegesta—Tegesta." Had they come to rescue her? No, she quickly deduced. There did not seem to be any evidence of confrontation. She remained bewildered.

Teges motioned for them to move the dugouts onto the shore of the Kahoosa village. Yagua's knuckles turned white from his tight grip on the paddle as he pulled it through the water. Shortly, the canoes scraped the bottom. Yagua jumped from the first dugout, turned his back on the Kahoosa, and pulled the canoe onto the shore. Olagale did the same with the second canoe.

Teges stepped onto the dry land and planted himself squarely in front of Kaho. "We come in peace," he said.

Kaho did not respond. Teges could tell that he was confused. Of course he would be, Teges thought. He only understands the way of the Kahoosa.

"We wish to share our goods with you. You need not come and demand them from us. We have enough to share."

Kaho turned to a young warrior behind him. "Increase the guards about the platform of the Tegesta woman."

"We do not come to take her back," Teges said. "We have been sickened by the sadness such acts have caused. We want it to end someday. But the woman you took is Tegesta, and we wish to know that she is being treated well." Teges was careful not to give away her name. Names held special powers, and if Teeka had chosen not to tell Kaho, Teges would not let it be given away.

"No harm has come to her," Kaho answered.

"How can we be sure of that?" Ata asked.

"Because I say it is so," Kaho barked back.

"Her sister is my wife. She has asked that I inquire."

"And I have answered your inquiry."

"I want to see her. I want to reassure my wife."

"No," Kaho answered firmly, asserting his authority.

"Are you afraid?" Ata asked.

"Of this small, weak band of Tegesta? Never."

"Then let me speak to her. We bring you bounty to show our good faith. The Tegesta can be trusted," Ata pointed out. "Perhaps the Kahoosa do not trust anyone else because they do not trust one another."

Kaho tightened at the implication. "We are a people of honor. I will allow the old cacique to see her. No one else."

"Alone?" Teges asked.

"Kahoosa guards will wait below. But then I wish you to leave."

"Show me to her," Teges said, stepping forward.

The others began to unload the cargo, throwing it on the bank. It was not nearly the amount that Kaho usually took from them, but it was a token. The Kahoosa began to whisper. How had such a poor clan gathered so much courage? Perhaps the Tegesta had always been underestimated. Why this peaceful offer? Maybe they should be taken more seriously.

Teeka had seen Teges coming. She could not believe it and began to sob with excitement and joy. Teges ached as he climbed the ladder. When he balanced himself on the floor of the platform, Teeka lowered her head in respect.

"Have you come to take me home?" she asked, trying to sound patient.

Teges cautiously lowered himself to the floor. Teeka sat across from him, looking into the eyes that had clouded with age. None of the wisdom had faded, only the clarity of youth.

"No, Teeka. We cannot do that. Kaho would just come for you again. You know that, Little Doe."

Teeka blinked away a tear. "Yes," she said, "I know that. But you are here, Teges. No Tegesta has ever been in the village of Kaho."

"We want this hostility to end. We have come in peace to show our courage and our intent. But our visit would not be complete without seeing you. Illa will be pleased to know that you are well."

"Teges, tell me of Auro."

Teges shook his head. "He is consumed with grief. He cannot seem to recover. I hope that it is not the same for you."

"I love him. I miss him. I miss Illa. I want to go home."

"Auro is not the same. I cannot explain, but you must deal with what the spirits have decided for you."

"I am trying, Teges. It is the most difficult thing I have ever faced. But I will come home. I do not yet know how, but I will find a way."

"Enough time, Cacique. Come down and be gone," Kaho shouted from under the shelter.

Teges touched Teeka's face. "I will tell the People of your courage. I will tell them that you have been treated well."

"And tell Illa and my mother that I love them. And tell Auro," she added, reaching for the pendant, "that I will love him always."

"I will tell them all," he answered.

"Now, Cacique!" Kaho's voice echoed from under them.

"Help me to my feet, Little Doe. My old bones bicker with my desires."

Teeka stood and helped him up. She had much to say, but no words would come.

As soon as the cacique touched his feet to the ground, Kaho had his men escort him back to the water and the canoes.

"Be gone," Kaho ordered.

The Tegesta poled their canoes out into the water. When they were out of sight, the crowd broke up. By the return of the villagers to their daily activities, Teeka knew that Teges had gone, and again she was alone. There was no one to count on but herself.

In small huddles where Kaho could not see or hear, the Kahoosa discussed the strange visit by the Tegesta. They were amazed at the courage shown by the tribe. They had dared to come—without weapons. Indeed, there was much to think about.

———

Clear of the Kahoosa village, Teges and the others congratulated themselves. The visit had gone very well. A tiny seed had been planted. With time and continued care, it would one day flower. The spirits know all, Teges thought. As tragic as Teeka's fate seemed, it was all part of the greater plan. Her presence would certainly help the mission of peace. She was an instrument of the spirits. Auro should be the one to see that, he thought. He was the shaman, the man of the spirits.

They camped at dusk, and when night came they found it easy to sleep. The soft wind blew across their bodies, and the sky sparkled with the hearths of the spirits. It was a sure sign that the spirits approved.

———

Anxious to return to their village, the men brewed themselves a light tea just before the sun rose. As soon as it was light, they were ready. It seemed that they would never reach home. The day lingered on and on. But, just as night fell, they pulled the canoes onto the land.

The clan of Teges gathered to greet them, all anxious to hear their story. By the light of the central hearth, the clan assembled. They hung on each word, each detail of what had been seen, said, and intuited.

Ata searched the crowd for Auro but could not find him.

"He keeps to himself," Illa told him. "Did you really expect him to come?"

"Yes," Ata answered. "He knows that we bring news of Teeka. If for no other reason, I expected him to listen."

As the fire burned low, the villagers slowly walked to their platforms to sleep through what was left of the night.

Illa walked next to Ata. "I was afraid."

Ata put his arm around her. She carried the baby over her shoulder, and the other two children followed closely. Rarely did they stay awake late into the night. Their small bodies drooped with fatigue, but they continued to giggle and play.

"It will be difficult to calm them," Illa remarked. "They are too excited."

Ata touched each of his children's heads before they climbed the ladder. He helped the little one up, being careful that his feet did not slip. It was a shame that Auro and Teeka would never know such simple joys.

The children did finally sleep, and Illa cuddled close to Ata.

"It was a good journey, was it not?"

"Yes," he answered, sounding distracted. His lips touched hers, and Illa returned his kiss, but then broke away.

"What is wrong?" he asked.

Illa stared into the distance. "Nothing. I am sorry. I was thinking of something else."

Ata leaned over her and brushed a strand of hair from her face. "You are so far away," he whispered and then softly nipped at her ear. "Come back to your husband."

Illa turned her head away and then made him look into her face. "Ata, I must ask something of you. I want to go. I want to see my sister."

"Illa," he said and almost chuckled, "where do you get some of your ideas? That is out of the question."

His hand cupped her breast, and his mouth teased at it. Illa sat up. "Why is it out of the question?"

Ata raised himself up on one elbow, nuzzling his face in her softness. "It is too dangerous," he mumbled, his mouth full of the tender flesh of her shoulder and then her breast.

Illa held his head to her, enjoying his attention. But her mind was spinning. "No, it is not so dangerous. I am a woman, and you believe that limits me. Not from this, Ata."

Ata finally gave in, lifting his head. "I see that we will have to settle this first."

"I want to see her," Illa repeated. "There were no threats made to any of you. I listened well tonight. And think of it this way, my visit will only continue what you have started. I am not afraid. Will you take me?"

Her argument was fair, as much as Ata hated to admit it. "Do we have to decide this tonight?" he asked. "Let me think about what you have said."

"Do you promise to take my request seriously?"

"I know how much you love your sister."

"Yes," she whispered, reaching for him and pulling his weight onto her, "I do."

Chapter Twelve

TEEKA VENTURED DOWN the ladder. The day was hot and humid and staying inside the platform was torture. The guards followed as she made her way to the water. When she reached it, she followed along its edge, distancing herself from others, from Kahoosa sounds and smells. Tightly gripping the amulet, she felt her stomach churn as she turned over Teges's words in her mind.

Teges had brushed off her questions about Auro, and she had noticed that his face was taut, as if he was withholding the strength of what he really wanted to tell her. Actually, he had given her very little information about Auro. She could not imagine what Teges had meant. How could Auro be different? Teges's voice seemed to lack the respect that she should have heard when a cacique spoke of a shaman. Something was wrong.

Suddenly she felt someone grab her arm. It was one of the guards. He motioned for her to turn around and go back. She must have wandered too far.

Teeka looked down, away from the face of the man who led her by the arm. Since her strange fantasy she had tried not to look at any of the sentries who alternated the duty of watching her. Again she felt the shame. This was a secret that she could never tell. The Tegesta would have found thoughts like those strongly objectionable.

She would have to return to her platform, she realized. Though she was allowed to wander through the village, the constant closeness of the guards irritated her. The brief walk had broken the monotony. The fresh stirring air and the sweet smell of the vegetation had been splendid; if only the sentries had not spoiled it with their conspicuous presence. They kept so close that at times she felt she could even feel the heat from their bodies. At home she had often wandered the paths that led away from the village. There was always so much to see and learn, always some new discovery. There the air smelled of the fragrant flowers that bloomed at the top of the vines. Her mouth watered, and she could almost taste the sweet grapes that hung in clusters near the village. Perhaps she would request some, she thought.

Ahead she saw Rebet. Kaho's wife accompanied them on their way back. She said nothing, just walked beside them. Teeka knew that Rebet was looking at her, and she could feel her hard stare. She realized that she must still be quite a curiosity.

Rebet walked the distance to Teeka's platform but did not climb up.

"Kaho comes soon," said Rebet.

The woman left, but the sentries remained posted at the base of the shelter. Teeka tried not to look at them, but her eyes kept wandering and focusing on the man she had fantasized about many days ago. He was not so spectacular that women would find him in their dreams, but he was taller than most and had a muscular body. What was it about him that set off such a shocking fantasy? The thought that kept creeping into her mind was not what it was about him, but what it was within her.

When the sun was straight overhead, Tosa appeared and beckoned her down. She led Teeka to her hearth where she was preparing turtle meat and some bread from coontie. The two escorts were replaced, and the new watchmen followed them.

Tosa's children played around the hearth with other children. Some things were certainly the same from tribe to tribe. The sound of children at play and their made-up games were like those of the Tegesta children. They chased one another, complained, and found excuses when they were caught.

Suddenly one of the children let out a cry that crossed all languages. Tosa quickly ran to him and examined his injury.

During a friendly tussle in which the boys often participated, the neighboring boy had scratched the face of his friend, Tosa's middle son. The boy's face had a small nick that bled only slightly. The other child stood shocked and shaking. Teeka heard Tosa speak to her son and heard her call him by name, Boro. Boro stood up and faced his friend.

The mother of the visiting child quickly ran up and scolded her son, Nakosa. The two women backed away as Nakosa and Boro stood looking at each other. Nakosa was still shaking when Boro reached out with a sharp stick and scraped it across his playmate's face, leaving a thin line of blood. Nakosa reached for his cheek.

Tosa and the mother of Nakosa nodded at each other and returned to their own fires and meals. The boys resumed their playing as if nothing had happened. The matter seemed ended, and Teeka thought that what she had just witnessed was a strange custom.

When the meal was finished, the escorts returned her to her place. For the next two days she was invited to join

Tosa for meals. When Teeka visited, Tosa's husband usually took his meal and then went to visit some of the other men sitting at the central hearth. Teeka felt that she might be interfering and, through crude gesturing, asked Tosa about it. Tosa shook her head and laughed. And from what Teeka could glean from Tosa's words and gestures, he probably enjoyed the opportunity to sit and talk with the men.The two women had begun to teach some common words and signs to each other. Often they found themselves laughing at each other, but neither was insulted. Teeka was beginning to feel more comfortable with her strange surroundings and with herself. She had not had any other fantasies and supposed that the one had been caused by the shock and adjustment to her new way of life. She even had a friend. It was not as terrible as she had imagined it would be. Teeka felt the pendant around her neck. The thoughts that she had just had were close to a betrayal. Of course she had to focus on finding a way to go home. But there was one unrelenting problem. Every time she thought about escape, she ran into a dead end.

———

Teeka had not seen Kaho since her return from isolation, except for the brief glimpse she had had of him when Teges came, and quite a few moons had passed since then. During a late visit with Tosa, she decided to ask about him. Just as she began her combination of simple gestures and new words, Rebet came and spoke with one of the guards. The guard listened intently and then spoke to Tosa, who nodded in understanding. The man took Teeka by the arm and began to lead her away. She looked at Tosa for some kind of explanation, but Tosa just motioned for her to go with him.

At the edge of the village was an extravagant platform that had posts decorated with brightly colored designs. It was larger than the others she had seen and distinctly more elaborate. Even the thatched sides were embellished with shells. The people who had gathered at its base talked in whispers and turned in curiosity as Teeka was led to the platform.

Teeka tensed. Obviously this was the dwelling of Kaho. Rebet nudged her to the ladder and indicated that she was to go up. In the twilight she made out a man stretched out on a mat in the center of the floor. A man in a mask sat next to him, and Cala stood at the far corner.

"He asks for you," Cala told Teeka.

She walked closer, seeing Kaho struggling to focus on her. Kuta, the medicine man, wore the mask of a wolf, and he chanted over the cacique. Kaho raised his hand, dismissing the shaman, and Teeka knelt by his side. Bandages of leaves lay over his right thigh, but they did not hide the swelling. The skin was pulled tight, and a red streak ran down his leg. Teeka reached out and touched the poultice. Carefully, she lifted it to see an angry, deep wound that exuded pus. She had seen wounds like this before, caused by a bear.

"How did this happen?" she asked.

Kaho's parched lips quivered as he spoke. "Bear."

Cala explained. "Some of the hunters had gone for game. They came across a panther and tracked him. When the tracks became deeper and fresher, the band spread out in a circle. The men came closer together, narrowing the circle, hoping to trap him. They heard skirmishing and darted in to collect their prey. The panther had gotten himself a small bear cub. The aim was sharp, and the panther fell to Kaho's spear, freeing the young bear. Kaho taunted and played with the cub, making him swat at his spear. The men were watching and laughing when the mother bear came from nowhere. In one swipe, she grabbed him by the leg. Bad spirits have gotten into the open flesh, and he battles with them. The shaman has been with him constantly, but the wound grows worse."

Teeka supposed that he was very close to death. She inspected the leaves and herbs that had been placed over the wound. The Tegesta had never used them on such severe wounds. They were effective only for small abrasions and scratches.

"What else have you applied?" she asked.

Kuta straightened at the question, and Teeka was surprised that he was so familiar with her language.

"Do you question my medicine?" he asked angrily.

"No, I do not question it, but the Tegesta have knowledge of another medicine that may help him."

"The Tegesta are backward. They know nothing."

"There is no intention to insult. I only want to offer you something else."

The shaman was still angry. No one challenged him, especially one of another tribe—and a woman. He knelt next to Kaho, replaced the poultice and leaves, and began chanting again.

Kaho groaned in agony and pushed away the shaman.

Teeka touched his burning head. She tore a piece of moss from her skirt and soaked it in the water that was placed near him for thirst. She wrung the moss out and laid it across Kaho's forehead. The coolness made him open his eyes. She continued to wipe down his body as the medicine man grumbled at the top of the ladder and then descended.

Cala and Rebet sat next to Teeka and watched her

swab Kaho's body with cool water.

"Do you know of other medicine?" Rebet asked.

"Rebet!" Cala scolded in her language. "You have no faith in the great Kuta?"

Rebet looked ashamed but then gathered her self-confidence. "I have faith, but what if the Tegesta know of something else? There is no harm in asking. Kaho is not getting better. He is worse."

"You know that the Tegesta do not like the Kahoosa. Perhaps she wishes to harm Kaho?"

Teeka listened, understanding only a few of the words but knowing what they said.

"He is going to die," she said, looking at Kaho's wives.

"Do you think that if you save him, you might earn your freedom?" Rebet asked.

"Perhaps," she answered.

By the middle of the night, Cala and Rebet had dozed off on the other side of the platform. Teeka stayed at Kaho's side, cooling him down and applying the leaves and medicine provided by the shaman. She ran the moss over Kaho's chest and felt his rapid heartbeat. His body was fighting the invasion, but she was convinced that it was losing. His skin was still dry and hot. She lifted the leaves again to apply a clean dressing and saw that the wound had stopped oozing, and the swelling had moved up and down his whole leg. This was a bad sign. The abscess would need to be lanced so that the poison would drain out of it.

Teeka awakened Cala. "Go and get your shaman. Kaho needs more treatment."

Cala scrambled down the ladder and into the night. While she was gone, Kaho opened his eyes.

"Can you hear me?" she asked him, taking his hand.

Kaho was weak and found it difficult to speak. Teeka

felt a faint squeeze of her hand.

"Good," she said. "The medicine man comes to help you."

Kaho's dry lips and mouth struggled to form into the shape that would enable him to speak. His breath was forced across his vocal chords as he managed to whisper, "Help me."

She looked down on the face of the man she had hated such a short time ago. It was not the Tegesta way to harbor hatred. And she had seen another side to this man. When he had come to her in the night, he had not been brutal or harsh. He had touched her tenderly and gently. He had not been demanding. How different he was from the savage she had seen torment Erza. No, even though she wished to go home, she did not hate him enough to want him to die. Now she could only feel sympathy.

"I will help you," she reassured him. "I will not let you die."

He had heard what he wanted and closed his eyes. Kuta returned with Cala and bent down next to Teeka.

"What has happened?" he forced himself to ask.

"The wound has closed, and the poison cannot escape."

The shaman looked closely. "It is healing," he said.

Teeka was shocked. What kind of medicine man was this?

"The poison is trapped inside. It must come out. You must open it and let it drain, or he will die."

"Are you a medicine woman?" he asked smugly.

"No, but I know what I see, and I have treated wounds before with the knowledge learned from Tamuk."

"Ah, Tamuk. I have heard of this shaman. But he has not done any more magic than I. And what makes you think that you know the magic of Tamuk?"

"When we went to Tamuk for help, he taught us how to treat ourselves. He shared his knowledge."

"A real shaman never shares his magic. That is why the tribes have medicine men. They know of things that the others do not."

Teeka was frustrated. She didn't know how to make Kuta understand. He knew the Tegesta language well, but he did not know the People.

She moved away and watched the shaman's pitiful attempt to cure Kaho. He checked the wound again, and his face showed delight that it had closed. His ignorance made her feel helpless.

———

In the morning, Teeka tried to get Kaho to drink some broth, but he refused. His skin had begun to lose its resiliency as he dehydrated. The leg looked even worse in the daylight, and he began to shake.

"Go and refill the bowl with clean, cool water," Teeka requested of Rebet. "This water has warmed through the night."

Rebet challenged her. "He is cold. Look at the way he shivers. Why would you put cool water on him?"

The shaman and Cala had fallen asleep before sunrise, and Teeka did not want to awaken them.

"Shh. Do as I tell you."

"I must ask Kuta first. What you do may not be good."

"Touch him with your hand," she directed. "Do you feel the heat? We must make his body cooler. Now go and get the water."

Rebet refilled the bowl but was still unsure. Teeka dipped the moss sponge in the cool water and began to wipe him down. His groin was filled with large lumps, and Kaho moaned when she touched them.

"He is very sick. I am afraid that he will die. I can help him if it is not too late. Go and gather some aluit, and bring it back before Kuta wakes."

"I know not aluit. Is there a Kahoosa name for this plant?"

How could she explain? She didn't know the Kahoosa name, and if she hesitated too long, Cala and the medicine man would be awake and Rebet would probably change her mind.

Teeka put the moss in the bowl and whispered for Rebet to follow her beneath the platform. With a stick she drew a picture of the plant in the dirt. It had pinnate leaves on a tall slender stalk. In the spring it had small yellow flowers. Rebet seemed to recognize it.

"Wokee," she said. "There is none of that stored in the village. But I know where to find it. I will go and get some."

"Bring the whole plant, including the roots. Hurry now. We have little time."

Rebet hurried off, and Teeka returned to the platform. She would need to grind and boil the leaves as well as the roots. She hoped that Cala and Kuta would sleep a long time. They had been awake most of the night, so she knew that they were tired. The villagers were beginning to stir, and the noise worried her.

If she could save Kaho's life, it might mean her freedom. She would have to treat him secretly, for if he died, she would be blamed. After watching the scene with Tosa's son and Nakosa, she knew that the code of the Kahoosa was based on immediate retaliation. Rebet would have to keep a secret.

Rebet returned with a basket of the medicinal plant,

and Teeka helped her with the grinding.

"If I save Kaho, he may give me my freedom. I would be a fool if I brought any harm to him."

Rebet continued to grind and listen.

"And if I help you, and you harm him or he dies, I will also be blamed," Rebet said.

"It is too late. You have already helped. Now it is important for both of us that you tell no one."

"Why do you do this secretly if you can really save him?"

"If anyone knows that I—we—are treating him, if it is too late, and Kaho cannot be saved, then we will be blamed for his death. I am not a shaman and neither are you. Do you understand?"

"If no one knows, then how do you think that you will be freed?"

"Kaho will know."

"Why should I trust you?"

"Because you must now. You have already gotten the plants."

They placed the ground leaves and pulverized roots in the boiling water.

Teeka gingerly carried the bowl with leather pads so that it did not burn her hands. Halfway up the ladder she handed it to Rebet.

Carefully she lifted the old dressing. She opened the medicine bag around her neck and removed a shark's tooth. It would serve as the lance.

"This may startle him. Touch my back if Cala and Kuta seem to be awakening."

Biting her bottom lip, Teeka pierced the abscess, making a short but deep incision. Kaho opened his eyes at the sharp pain.

"Trust me," she whispered to him. "I will make you

well."

His eyes closed again as the infection spewed from his leg, and Teeka quickly wiped it up. The yellow pus was blood-streaked, and it continued to flow as quickly as she sponged it off. Finally it subsided. She soaked a clean swatch of moss in the medicine that she and Rebet had prepared; the elixir was still hot, and the heat would help draw the poison out. She then replaced the leaves that had covered the previous dressing and tucked the old dressing under the waistband of her skirt. Kuta would not know that the medicine had been changed.

Teeka reached for the shark's tooth to put it back in her medicine bag, but she couldn't find it. She stood, thinking that perhaps she covered it with her body. It was not there. For an instant, she panicked, but then she saw it wedged between two of the wooden beams of the floor. Her fingers pulled at it, but with each attempt she pushed it deeper.

Rebet touched Teeka. "Kuta, he wakens."

The medicine man sat up and then rose to his feet and walked to Teeka's side. "Leave him," he ordered.

Teeka winced at Rebet, hoping she understood that something was wrong. Rebet caught the expression. As casually as she could, Teeka pointed to her medicine bag and shrugged her shoulders. Rebet had watched Teeka lance the abscess and quickly understood that she was missing the tooth. As she walked away, Teeka looked down at the spot in the planks. Rebet walked closer, spotting the shark's tooth. Kuta had seated himself just next to it. Rebet slid her foot over it so that it was hidden from view.

Kuta suddenly stood. "I will return shortly."

As soon as he had descended the ladder, Teeka and Rebet scrambled to pry the tooth loose. Cala was beginning to stir, and both of them stopped and looked at her. Cala turned onto her side, eyes still closed. Neither of them could dislodge the tooth. It had wedged itself even deeper.

"Quickly, bring me Kaho's small spear," Teeka said.

Rebet ran to the post where the spears were propped. She chose the one with the narrowest point and brought it back to Teeka.

Teeka dug at the tooth, splintering the wood around it. At last it was free. She placed the tooth in her bag and handed the spear to Rebet.

"What do you do with Kaho's weapon?" Cala asked, sitting up, startling the two frantic women.

Rebet did not know what to say. She looked at Teeka, her eyes wide with fear.

"Kaho asked for it, but he went back to sleep as we brought it to him," Teeka answered.

Cala seemed satisfied, stretched, and yawned. "Is he any better?"

"There is no change," replied Rebet.

"I am sorry that I did not awaken early," Cala apologized. "Where is Kuta?" she inquired, stretching again.

"He has gone to take care of his morning needs," Rebet answered.

"I should do the same," commented Teeka. "Rebet, would you come with me? Maybe if you are there, the sentries will give me some privacy."

Rebet nodded in agreement. "Cala, can you stay and watch until I return?" Rebet asked.

"I will wait for you or the shaman. Both of you go."

On the first rung of the ladder, Teeka reached through her skirt and grabbed the old dressing. The guards could not see with her back to them.

When they reached the bottom of the ladder, they walked away together, the guards following.

Rebet turned around. "I will stay with this woman. I will call out if there is any trouble."

"We must stay with her," one of the guards told Rebet.

"You may come with us, but can you allow her some privacy?"

The guards looked at each other and decided that they would follow but respect her privacy.

When the two women reached their destination, Rebet nodded to the guards who stopped and let them proceed into the brush alone.

When just out of sight, Teeka slipped Rebet the wadded mass in her hand.

"Dispose of this. I am afraid that they still watch me."

Teeka emptied her bladder in the cover of the brush and began to walk out toward the guards. The two men were walking toward her. Cala had come, and she walked with them.

"The shaman wishes to see you," Cala said, as both guards seized her arms and led her away. Rebet remained behind, watching in terror.

Chapter Thirteen

TEEKA CLIMBED UP the platform. She tried to maintain her composure, but her hands trembled. She had been found out. Why else would Kuta have sent for her? She almost froze at the last step, realizing the precariousness of the balance between life and death. Was everything predestined by the spirits? It was a powerful thought.

Kuta stood at her entrance, his hair gray and astray. The old eyes, set too close, peered from beneath slouching eyelids. His skin was pallid and plowed with furrows from sun and age. The thin lips were pinched as he spoke.

"Come, see what has happened."

Teeka slowly walked toward him. The shaman lifted the herbal bandage and moss. The abscess looked less angry since it had drained. A canal had formed from deep within, the skin lipping inward, allowing the discharge of pus and body fluids.

"The demon is fleeing. Kuta's medicine is too strong for him," the shaman proudly declared.

She nodded with relief as he seized the moment to promote himself.

"The wound closed in battle, and Kuta has won. Did I not tell you it was the beginning of the healing?" Kuta continued.

Teeka knew better than to argue. Kaho was still gravely ill. The poison had traveled through his body. He was going to need more medicine, and she would have to tell Rebet exactly what to get and how to prepare it.

During the noon meal, Teeka had an opportunity to talk quietly with Rebet. She gave her directions and described the plants in detail. Some she knew would be more difficult to find than others. Some were rare, growing only on dry ground, so often lacking in this place.

Rebet seemed to recognize all the plants that Teeka described.

"Collect shells in the village," Teeka added. "You will need to boil them and save the water to mix with the medicine. Rebet, you will have to do much of the work. I am watched too closely."

"I understand."

"Do you still fear that I will harm Kaho?"

"I have seen what you have done. Your medicine would have saved one of my sons."

"Where are your children?" Teeka asked, noting that she had not seen any children with Rebet or Cala.

"My brother and my mother watch after them while Kaho is ill. I must stay with him all of the time."

"What happened to your son?" Teeka asked with sympathy.

"He was mauled by a panther. He played by the water one morning, and the panther came to drink. It was a season of little rain, and all the animals ventured closer to the village for water. The animals were dying, and their thirst made them bold. My son suffered for days after his wounds turned bad like Kaho's. Kuta stayed with him, but he could not save him. I wish Kuta had had your medicine."

"I am sorry, Rebet."

Both women sat for a few minutes, not speaking, finishing their meal.

"Then you will help me?" inquired Teeka.

"Yes," Rebet answered without hesitation.

———

During the next few weeks Kaho slowly recovered. Teeka and Rebet quietly gave him medicine and applied their dressings out of sight of the others. Kuta bragged about his success, and others applauded him, but as Kaho became more and more lucid, he noticed the conspiracy of Teeka and Rebet.

"You have made me well, is that not so?" he asked Teeka quietly as she made him sip her medicinal tea.

"Yes," she answered simply.

One day, as evening drew near, Cala, Rebet, and Kuta returned to their own shelters and fires. Kaho was going to survive, and they did not need to attend him through the night. But Teeka would stay, and the sentries would stay.

The moon was growing larger in the sky. While Kaho slept, she changed the dressing.

Before covering the wound with the external dressing, she found herself staring at his naked body. He had strong muscles, like Auro. Her eyes wandered across his chest, and her fingers danced around his nipples. Sliding her hands down his rib cage, she paused at the rocklike muscles of his abdomen and then let her fingers trail onward to his groin.

She ached inside to be with Auro. She needed to feel his weight on her and to feel him fill her with his love. She closed her eyes, letting her other senses take over.

She could hear his breathing and smell his scent—the distinct scent of a man. Carefully she touched her cheek to Kaho's chest, and stretched out next to him. The warmth of his body flowed through her. She wished he were Auro and that she could lie by his side the rest of the night. She wished he would reach out and touch her, hold her breast in his hand, and kiss her. With no one to see, she slept by his side. Before dawn, she moved away. It was the most restful sleep she had had since coming to the village of the Kahoosa.

The huge silver ball in the sky made the village shimmer as branches and leaves, blown by the breeze, came between the moonlight and the earth. The full moon was a marker of time, and Kuta notched his stick.

Each day Kaho improved, and Teeka continued to give him the medicine that would make him rest. His body gained strength as he slept, and Teeka enjoyed this time, when she was alone, except for the ever-present guards. More than once, when convinced that Kaho was deep in sleep, she had lain next to him, felt his skin next to her, and dreamed of Auro. She knew that she should feel ashamed. It was not the way of a Tegesta woman, and she was sure that Auro would not approve. It seemed that her yearning for him was inducing her to do things that would shock the Tegesta—things that the Tegesta would find objectionable. But she was so alone.

She sometimes used this time to think, plan, and analyze, but often she just enjoyed the quiet moments. And there was always the amulet to remind her, to heap the guilt, to arrest any passing serenity, so that she would continue to plot. She had given up on escape. First, she would wait and see if Kaho would set her free, let her return to her people and to Auro.

This night she stretched out on the sleeping mat that

had been given to her; but she was restless. She needed to empty her bladder before she could sleep. Finally, giving in to the urge, she descended and greeted the guard who was awake. The other sat, eyes closed, head sagging on his chest.

As she walked ahead, the moonlight reflected off her hair as if it were obsidian. It trailed down her back, past her swaying hips. The escort behind her concentrated on her sensuous movement. She was the epitome of sex, and he found it difficult not to stare at her and think about her, and Teeka sensed it. But then he thought of Kaho. He would not pursue his thoughts about the woman he guarded. She was Kaho's. It was not worth it.

Teeka stepped into the brush, and he stayed behind, giving her some privacy with her personal needs. She relieved herself and checked to see if her moon cycle had come. It was later than usual. Her body must be adjusting to her new life, she thought. It would come soon enough.

When she stepped out of the bushes, she held the warm pendant in her hand. The guard saw her step free of the tall grasses, but then she stopped. Teeka looked past him, to something behind him. He spun around, also sensing a shadow moving, hiding from the light of the moon.

"Who is there?" he called out.

There was no answer. The wind picked up, making it difficult to hear sounds, other than the plants' responses to the breeze.

"Who is it?" he asked, with more tension in his voice.

Teeka stood frozen. She was frightened. She could have wandered at night without fear among the Tegesta. But she did not know the Kahoosa.

Again she thought she saw the dark silhouette ducking behind a clump of grasses. The guard lifted his spear and backed toward her.

By moving his spear back and forth, the sentry motioned for her to come to him. After every few steps, she stopped, looked into the distance, and listened. At last, when she neared the guard's side, he turned to her. They began the walk back to the platform. Teeka did not look back, but the sentry did. He saw no one following.

She felt safe once she was up the ladder. Kaho slept soundly. She was safe just by being with him. What a strange thought.

Stretched out on her side, Teeka faced the ill chief. He was so young to be a chief. She supposed that many of the Kahoosa women thought that he was attractive. He was, in a Kahoosa way.

She studied his face. It had many sharp angles, like Auro's. His nose was straight but not large. His skin was clear and smooth.

She relaxed and closed her eyes. In her dream, she stood in a mist under the canopy of the thick foliage. She wandered through the ferns and trees until she saw him. She could barely make him out as he walked through the fog. It was Auro, and he was walking to her. She held out her arms to hold him, embrace him. As his arms folded around her, she buried herself in him. He touched his lips to hers and lowered her to the ground. She was home.

Her dream was suddenly interrupted. She heard Kuta's voice and then one of the guards'. She did not understand what they were saying, but she could tell that they were very upset. She crawled to the edge of the platform and peered over. Kuta was speaking to the guard who had been sleeping before. He was shaking his fist and ranting.

"Wintu," she heard him say over and over again. That was the name of the guard who had escorted her earlier.

Where was he?

Chapter Fourteen

BEFORE THE REST OF THE VILLAGE awakened, Kuta and the guard climbed up the ladder to Kaho's platform where Teeka slept.

The guard shook her shoulder, making her wake.

"Come with me," Kuta ordered.

Teeka rubbed her eyes. She remembered hearing the disturbance in the night, but when things quieted, she had gone back to sleep.

"What is it?" she asked.

"Follow," Kuta answered sternly but soft enough so as not to awaken Kaho.

She followed the shaman away from Kaho's platform. Kuta motioned for the guard to drop back and leave them. Teeka knew that Kuta felt threatened by her. He did not hide his dislike for her, and she did not like being alone with him.

Finally he stopped and looked around. It was barely light; the birds were not yet singing.

"You have an evil spirit about you. The Tegesta have sent you to try to destroy the Kahoosa. I will not allow it."

"What?" Teeka asked, confused by the shaman's accusation. "My people did not send me here. Your cacique brought me against my will. Have you forgotten?"

"Then you must have lured him, enticed him, directed by the evil spirit that touches you."

"Why are you saying these terrible things? Because I questioned your medicine? I mean you no harm, Shaman. I am not here to hurt anyone."

"The proof is around your neck. Your amulet has been touched by a spirit—I believe an evil spirit."

Teeka reached for the pendant. How could he say such a horrible thing? Auro had given the columella amulet to her as a wedding present. It sealed their love.

"You are here to discredit me." Kuta said. "Without a shaman, the Kahoosa will not have the strength to continue. The Kahoosa must have the spirits on their side. Your people wait for our fall."

"If you feel this way, why not tell Kaho? Surely he will send me back to the People, and that is all that I want. Then we will both be happy."

"You know I cannot do that. I cannot tell Kaho that he has been tricked. But I will take care of you. My justice has already begun. Your scheme will not work."

Teeka felt a shiver as the old man spoke. He was obsessed with her destruction. He could not accept that she had challenged his medicine or that Tamuk might have been a greater shaman. This humiliated Kuta, and now he wanted revenge.

Kuta returned her to the platform. He stayed below.

———

Teeka's lower back ached. Her moon cycle was coming soon, and again she would be sent to the isolation platform. Rebet would have to take over. She hoped that Kaho's recovery was far enough along so that there was no threat of relapse. This was not a good time to leave Kaho. As long as she was with him, she felt safe from

Kuta. What was the deranged medicine man's plan? She needed Kaho on her side. How strangely things had changed.

Teeka checked on the cacique. She lifted the dressing and saw that the wound was healing nicely. The red lines that had spiderwebbed out from it were all gone. She touched his groin, feeling for the lumps. They had grown much smaller; she could barely feel them. Her freedom would come with his complete recovery.

At Teeka's touch, Kaho opened his eyes.

"Have you slept well?" she asked, making him drink her tea.

"Your medicine has been good."

"How do you know that it was my medicine and not that of Kuta?"

"Much of the time that my eyes were too weak to open, my ears still heard. I learned your voice, and I know that of Rebet. I have also learned your touch."

"Kuta would not let me give you the medicine of the Tegesta."

"Then he has learned a lesson."

"No, he does not know that Rebet and I treated you."

"Then he is blind, and you are very clever. What if your medicine had not healed me?"

"But it did," she said.

"Why is it so important to you that I live?"

Teeka did not want to speak of her freedom. It was not yet time. "To the Tegesta it is important that every man live."

"Even your enemies?"

"Are you my enemy?"

"You are a strange people. If I were you, I would have hoped for me to die."

"But you are not me. I am Tegesta, not Kahoosa."

"I will tell Kuta what a fool he is."

"No," she protested. "He is an old man, and he has not many days left. Let him think he has the most powerful medicine."

Teeka did not want Kaho to aggravate Kuta. But when the time came, she would need Kaho to protect her.

Kaho gave her a puzzled look. The Tegesta way of thinking was very strange indeed.

"It is time you called me by name," she whispered, touching the bowl to his lips again.

"You have decided to tell me? Amisa did not please you?"

"I am known to the spirits by my name, Teeka."

"Teeka," he repeated. "I like the way it sounds. Say it again for me. I like the way it floats so nicely on your voice."

Teeka ignored his request, offering the bowl to him once more. "All I surrender is my name. You should know the name of the one who has healed you. When you thank your spirits, you should tell them my name."

Suddenly there was confusion in the village. Two of Kaho's warriors and one of Teeka's guards climbed the platform, seeking an audience with their chieftain. Kaho signaled that they might speak.

"Wintu has been found slain. It was during the night, but we did not wish to interrupt your sleep."

Kaho unsteadily pushed himself into a half-sitting position.

"Who has done this?"

Teeka's face paled. Wintu. They *had* seen something in the darkness. It had not been a shadow of some moving branch or their imaginations. Someone had been out there.

"No one has an answer. He was found alone, away

from the village."

"In what manner was he killed?"

"His throat had been gouged open."

"Find the murderer. Wintu's blood relative will avenge him."

Kuta stepped onto the platform. His face was twisted with anger. "Perhaps you should ask the Tegesta woman what she knows of this."

"Why should she know about this?" Kaho asked, leaning forward.

Kuta almost smiled. "I saw her with him last night. It was late. My body does not sleep easily anymore, and so I walked about the village."

"Is this true?" he asked Teeka.

"A guard walked me to the brush so that I could take care of my personal needs. I think he was called Wintu."

Teeka realized that it must have been Kuta hiding in the darkness.

"We saw a shadow," she continued, "a silhouette, slipping through the grasses and trees. It startled us. Was that you, Kuta? Why did you not reveal yourself?"

Kuta grimaced. "I saw you as you passed. Maybe you have made up this story of someone hiding in the bushes."

Kaho looked to Teeka for her response.

She had a hard time finding her voice. How would she answer him? Her voice would be full of tremors, and her breath was coming in nervous, uneven spurts. Kaho would mistake her fear for guilt.

"I know nothing," she said. "I stayed the night here. How would I know what went on below this platform?"

"But you did leave with Wintu. You said that yourself."

"He was only my escort. I told you what we saw and

heard. I last saw him when he brought me back."

Kaho turned to the other guard. "What did you see?" he asked.

The guard squirmed, and beads of perspiration broke out across his worried brow. "I had fallen asleep. Wintu did not waken me. I saw nothing."

Kaho braced himself, his face glowing red with anger. "You slept while guarding my platform?" Kaho was outraged, and he started to stand.

"No," Teeka said. "Your leg."

"She orders the king." Kuta laughed, forcing Kaho to defend himself.

Kaho proceeded to stand, ignoring Teeka, proving to Kuta that no one, especially the Tegesta woman, gave him orders.

"Tell me," he said, looking squarely at Teeka, "what is the method of murder of the Tegesta?"

"The Tegesta do not murder."

"No tribe murders their own. How do the Tegesta murder an enemy? Is it by driving a stake through the throat?" he asked pointedly.

"Why do you ask these questions?"

"Have you done this in revenge? Or did you lead Wintu away from the village while someone of your tribe hid and waited for the chance to kill him? Did Teges bring an assassin? Did he use what he called a peaceful visit to study this village and then leave a warrior behind to do this? The Tegesta are not a courageous people, a furtive stabbing would be the coward's way. Was this crime planned before I went back to your village for you? The Tegesta are not brave enough to wage war."

"You are wrong, Kaho. I did not kill Wintu. And you do not know the People. The Tegesta are brave. If they were to avenge me, they would strike all the Kahoosa. But we do what is best for all. Leaving with you was my sacrifice for the People. If I had asked, they would have fought you. We do not have as many warriors as you do, but our men are braver than the Kahoosa. Even though their number is small, they would have painted their faces for war, and they would have battled you."

"The Tegesta are afraid of Kaho. They would not have the courage to wage war with me. They know that it would be the end for all of them."

"The murderer was not one of my tribe. That is not the way of the Tegesta. You had better find out who of the Kahoosa would do this. He is a danger to all of you. He is possessed by evil spirits."

Kaho said no more. He weaved and then sat down on his mat. He waved them all away and drifted off into the sleep that had been prompted by Teeka's tea.

Teeka sat, her face in her hands. What had happened to Wintu? Who had been in the brush? It must have been Kuta. Was this part of Kuta's scheme to destroy her? Would a man of the spirits kill one of his own? If the blame ever settled on her, what would happen? Teeka was afraid to answer her own question.

She removed her medicine bag, loosened the tie, and laid its contents before her, looking for something that would give her a clue as to what to do. Her life was spelled out in the contents. Each object defined her character, which was why the shaman had given her each item. They marked the events of her life, the journey of her spirit. She fondled each, turning it in her hands, searching for an answer or even the right question. There was nothing.

She lifted each article and built a circle by laying them evenly spaced around her seated body. The spirits would see and protect her.

Teeka lowered her head, and chanted the prayers to the spirits and to Little Doe. She pleaded for their guidance and their protection. As Kaho continued to sleep, she called to the spirits. This was all part of the dream that she had had. She had been warned, she knew that, but she still did not understand.

As she leaned forward, head bowed, the pendant swung free. She opened her eyes, focusing on the dancing pendant. She stopped her chanting and lifted the amulet so that she could see it better. Kuta's words rang in her head. What did he see in the pendant? Was there any basis for his suspicion of it? Was that why the pendant irritated her skin? What had Auro done? The words of Teges still haunted her. Auro was different—changed. She had been able to tell that this change deeply distressed Teges. Was this the Auro in her dream, the one who had stood by as she sank beneath the water? Teeka let go of the amulet. It swung gently before her. She wanted to take it off, but Auro had told her never to remove it or she would betray their love. But for some reason the pendant seemed to cloud her vision. She lifted the necklace over her head.

Suddenly she felt as if the breath had been sucked out of her. Her chest was being crushed. She clutched her head to stop the stabbing pain, and her eyes found the pendant lying on the floor in front of her. Everything around her faded to black except the small circle of light around the pendant. She almost stopped breathing. In the distance a voice was echoing, but she could not make sense of the words. She reached for the pendant and frantically lowered it again over her head. The pain left her head as the gift from Auro touched her skin. Her vision cleared, and she gasped for air. Perspiration dripped from her and streamed between her breasts. Now she could understand the voice that had been echoing. It was that of Rebet.

"What is wrong?" she was asking.

Rebet had come back and stood at the head of the ladder.

Teeka looked up. "Nothing, I am fine," she said, collecting all the symbols and placing them back in her medicine bag.

"What happened to you?"

"I just had this pain in my head. It is better now. It is close to my time again, and often my head hurts with it."

"Does it always hurt that much?" she asked.

"It has not been so bad as that before, but it is gone now."

"Should I get Kuta for you?"

"No, I told you, it is gone. Really, it was nothing," she insisted, drawing the pouch closed.

"Do you need me to gather more medicine plants? I will be gathering other things this morning, and I can get herbs for you as well. It is a good time. There would be no questions."

Teeka walked to the storage baskets and checked under the common plants that rested on the top, hiding her secret collection. She was low on all of them, though Kaho did not require so much medicine now.

"Bring some of each. We may not need them, but as you say, this is a good time."

Rebet nodded an acknowledgment, and climbed down.

As Teeka went to check on Kaho, she felt a drawing in her lower abdomen. Her time had come. She would wait for Rebet's return and then go to the platform for menstruating women. She was thankful. It had been a long time since she had been able to sleep through the night. She needed to be alone. She was tired of the guards. She felt watched, crowded, and tense. In the isolation platform, she would be safe from Kuta. The guards would have to keep their distance. Maybe if she was alone she could think more clearly. Kuta was wrong about everything, but still he unnerved her. Auro would never have kept anything from her. He loved her. There was only one thing that kept her from denying all of Kuta's horrible insinuations and all of her terrible doubts.

The pendant. The pendant. The pendant, she thought.

Chapter Fifteen

THE EARTH WAS BEGINNING TO SHOW signs of ripeness and fullness. New, thin blades of green rose from the rich soil among the stiff brown grasses. The cypress were dotted with the pale green of rebirth. It was the beginning of a new season. Teeka thought about her life and how drastically it had changed. But the earth went on with its cycles. It did not stop or pause. She was such a small part of life, she thought.

Tosa had been with Teeka only one day at the exile platform. Her time had almost passed when Teeka arrived. Pansar, whose cycle was changing and could no longer be counted by the moon, had not come at all. Lamita and Basee had also preceded Teeka by a few days. There was no one new.

To Tosa, something seemed a little different about her friend this time. She was more withdrawn and preoccupied, and it concerned her. Tosa was not one who enjoyed everyday chores. She preferred to find some small adventure to pursue, but those things were limited for a woman of the Kahoosa. Teeka offered something different. She added some sorely needed spice to Tosa's life.

Again the bland, unappetizing food was brought for the women and laid on the ground. Eating was as much a ritual as everything else. Each time the hunters left, their departure was preceded by meals that would aid them on the hunt. They consumed venison to attain the swiftness of the deer. Panther meat would render unto them stealth and cunning, and the tail of the alligator imparted strength and ferocity. The gruel served to the menstruating women was believed to be most benign, forcing spirits to become passive, letting the woman become clean again, so that she could return to the people of her tribe.

Soon Teeka was left alone in the isolation area. She wanted the time alone, but it also frightened her. With others about she could always find some distraction to keep her from confronting her fears. Many times she remembered taking off the pendant. She would never take it off again. She never should have done so the first time. She had betrayed Auro. It made her sick and dizzy again just to think about it.

What had Kuta seen in the pendant? Had Auro used his father's magic? Was it more than a wedding gift? Had he made her promise without telling her everything? Teges's words still rang deep in the crevices of her mind: "You must deal with what the spirits have decided for you."

By her last day, she had decided that when she returned to the village, she would wait for the right opening and then ask Kaho for her freedom. She was certain he would grant her request. He was much kinder than she had thought while she lived with her people. It was just a matter of time before she would be home. Then she would not have to think about all this anymore. He would give her back to the People, back to Auro, and she could try to forget everything that had happened since leaving her village.

———

Teeka returned to her platform now that Kaho had recovered. The days were full of rain. Sometimes it poured, and thunder echoed across the land. Other times it drizzled. The great lake to the north had swelled and spilled over, discharging its overload into the shallow river that now washed across the land.

Kuta was out alone, slipping through the water in his canoe, making observations. The medicine man was extremely proficient at reading the natural signs of his world. Holding one hand above his brows to prevent the drops of rain from blurring his vision, Kuta scrutinized the shoreline near an uninhabited mound. He finally poled closer and watched the flurry of white feathers as the herons took to the sky, frightened by his approach.

Kuta searched the edge of the hammock where the ground-nesting birds usually built their nests. There were none. This was a bad sign. Farther up the slope, closer to the crest, he began to spot the nests. These birds usually brooded close to the water, but this season they incubated their eggs at higher elevations. He knew what this meant.

Later in the day he surveyed several other hammocks. All of them told the same story. The birds and animals expected a substantial rise in the water level. It was the season of the big storms that sometimes came. The animal spirits had been kind to share their knowledge, and he thanked them. It was important that he inform Kaho. Preparations needed to begin as soon as possible.

Kaho listened intently to Kuta's predictions. "Yes," he agreed, "the signs are all there. The women have even complained that the wild grape vines have fruited higher in the trees where they often cannot reach them."

"The nests are very high. There will be an

exceptionally wet storm. I also think it will come soon. The birds would not nest so far from the water if they did not know that it would rise soon."

"Tomorrow we will begin. Spread the word through the village."

As the rain continued, the deer sought the sparse high ground, congregating on the small cypress heads and hammocks, ultimately stripping those areas of vegetation. Some of the deer began to starve after consuming most of the food.

The deluge went on for days, drenching the earth, which was already saturated from the normal frequent rainfall of the season. Now there was another, more serious threat. A mighty storm was brewing somewhere and would soon blow in, leveling much of the land. Those people who lived near the Big Water moved inland, heeding the warnings of their own shamans. Men and women of all tribes dug trenches alongside their mounds, moving the spoil onto their small islands to keep the water from swallowing their homes. This was one of the activities that Teeka was allowed and expected to join in. She did not eat her meals at the central hearth, and she was still considered an outsider. But now she worked alongside the Kahoosa. The rain soaked them, and the wind made them chill.

Teeka stood next to Tosa as Tosa's husband loaded baskets with spoil from the borrow pit. Her hair hung down across her face. She wiped it away, smearing mud along her cheek. Her feet seemed mired in the soggy muck, making the task even more difficult. Teeka thought of the Teges clan, her home. For an instant she closed her eyes in dread. What if Auro was unable to read the signs? From what Teges had said, she feared that he lacked the skill. Tosa's voice made her return her concentration to the task at hand.

"Teeka?" Tosa handed her an empty basket to hold for filling. Teeka stood quietly, letting Tosa's husband fill it with the heavy load as she blinked away the drops of rain that spilled through her long, full lashes and into her black eyes.

"Here, Tosa," she said, handing the basket up the chain.

The last person would empty the contents atop the crown of the mound. Tosa's husband stood ankle deep in the pit, holding a hoe made from a large whelk shell lashed to a long stick. He looked to the horizon in the west. It would soon be dark, he realized.

"One more basket," he told Tosa.

Tosa handed Teeka another basket from a collection of others at her feet. The children gathered them as they were emptied and hurried with them to the end of the lines, depositing the baskets near the edge of the pit.

Teeka stepped closer to Tosa's husband, holding the basket with both hands and bracing it against her body. With effort, he scooped through the water, coming up with a load of marl. Teeka held the basket as he dumped his load into it. A few more times and the basket was filled. Any more and it would rip and be too heavy to carry.

Teeka turned, handing the basket to Tosa. Just as Tosa went to grasp it, Teeka lost her balance. The mud was so slippery that her feet slid from under her, and she collapsed onto the ground, spilling the marl, covering herself with soupy, gray, lumpy soil and rock.

At first she was startled, but then Tosa started to laugh. As Teeka stood, the dark mud slid down her chest. Again her feet slipped, but this time she stayed upright. Teeka imagined how humorous her fall must have looked—and then to almost tumble again. Tosa's giggle was contagious, and in an instant both women were laughing. Tosa reached out to help steady Teeka. Teeka grabbed her hand and took a step. The mud from the basket seeped beneath her feet. She could feel the slippery gush when she stepped, but there was nothing she could do. She tugged on Tosa's hand, desperately trying to prevent another tumble. But it was useless.

Tosa slid forward, feet in front of her body. Instantly, it seemed, both women lay sprawled in the mud. Sputtering, spitting dirt out of their mouths, they laughed until tears ran from their eyes. The more they looked at each other, the harder they laughed.

Tosa pointed to a small clot of mud near Teeka's nose. She tried to talk, to relay her meaning with hand signs, but she found it too funny and rolled back in unrestrained laughter. Teeka looked at Tosa. She, too, tried to speak, to ask what Tosa found so funny, but watching the woman lie back with riotous laughter just made Teeka laugh even harder.

For those few moments, she forgot about the guards. She forgot that she was unhappy.

Finally spent, the two of them crawled a few feet and then slowly stood. They washed in the river. As they made their way back, the rain slackened, becoming no more than a very wet mist.

Teeka went back to her platform and sat in the shadows looking out, watching the Kahoosa gather at the central hearth. She wished for company, for someone with whom she could enjoy her meal. She supposed that either Rebet or Cala would soon deliver her portion. Maybe she could persuade her visitor to stay.

She finally did see Cala approaching. Teeka stood at the head of the ladder, watching Cala come up.

"Thank you," she said.

Cala nodded, acknowledging the courtesy of the Tegesta woman.

"Will you stay?" Teeka asked. Though Cala was not particularly friendly, she was not sour, and Teeka yearned for company.

Cala set the food on the floor and backed to the ladder. She looked as if Teeka's invitation made her uncomfortable. When she disappeared below, Teeka's face fell. Another solitary meal.

When she had finished picking at the food, she checked her mat for insects and then lay down on it. Her body ached with exhaustion. Her intent was to close her eyes and, as she did every night before sleeping, sort through all those things that might work to get her home again. But tonight she plunged into sleep without contemplating a single option.

The next day brought the same hard work, building up the" mound from the earth around it. The borrow pit even had its own function, becoming a small sump that collected water, but it would fill rapidly when the storm came. Today the wind blew, and clouds moved quickly across the sky. Colors became distorted, and except for the increasing wind, the land was frighteningly still. By dusk it was obvious that Kuta's seasoned observations had been accurate and keen. The big storm was imminent.

The Kahoosa slept on their mats, seeking the rest they would need. There was no necessity for anyone to stay awake and wait for the storm. It would make itself known. Kuta chanted into the night, beckoning the spirits to protect them. His song was a ballad that lulled them to sleep.

Teeka slept with one hand around her pendant. She

feared for her people. Touching the amulet before sleeping let her drift back to Auro and beyond him, to the days of her childhood. As she fell into sleep, she took those memories with her, dreaming of the days when life had been simple. It was a time that was free and uncomplicated. In her reverie, she tumbled in the grass with her playmates. She could smell the scent of childhood sweat and of the freshly crushed grass beneath them.

The groaning of the wind gradually turned to a shrieking that could not be ignored. Teeka's platform shuddered, creaking as it listed to one side. The storm had come.

She sat up, wrapping her arms around her chest. The night was completely black. A large section of thatch was suddenly ripped from one side of her shelter, leaving a gaping hole that the wind gusted through. Her belongings were swept across the floor, a basket slapping the side of her face. She scrambled on her hands and knees, trying to save those things that the wind had not already stolen. With so little light, her effort was like chasing shadows, grasping handfuls of air, lurching for something that already spun out of reach.

The platform began to shake violently, and the guards below ran to safety. Teeka crawled to the edge just as the roof blew away. The whole structure bent before the wind, swaying and then splintering as if it were made of twigs.

Teeka extended one foot to the ladder. Just as she stepped on it, the entire platform collapsed, crashing to the ground. Some parts of it blew away, vanishing in the darkness.

A tree limb flew through the air like a spear thrown by a warrior, slammed into her shoulder as she tried to stand,

and knocked her back to the ground, leaving a slash in her skin. She screamed with the surprise and the pain. Debris from other fallen platforms was hurled through the air.

Teeka lay flat on the ground, looking for refuge from the wreckage that the wind carried. She put her hands over the back of her head, curling her elbows around her ears with her face buried in the dirt. She could hear people screaming, children crying, and the wind howling. It all blended into one horrid sound.

Suddenly a violent gust picked up a plank from the floor of a platform and pitched it across the mound, end over end. The plank struck Teeka's head. Everything went dark and silent.

———

A shaft of sunlight, so bright that it penetrated her closed eyelids, pierced the leaves of the tree overhead and woke Teeka. The sky was a magnificent blue, and the dazzling sun had already begun to dry up the standing puddles. Had the storm ended?

Rebet leaned over her, looking down into her face.

"You are awake. That is good."

Teeka's head pounded, and she reached for a tender spot on the left side. Rebet moved her hand away.

"Something hit you during the storm. Do you remember?"

"I do not know," Teeka answered, her thoughts still cloudy. She looked around the village. There was debris everywhere. All of the platforms had been destroyed. There was much work ahead.

"It does not matter," Rebet said. "When the wind finally died down, Kaho found you and carried you here. He asked me to look after you. You have a big lump on your head and a bad cut on your arm, but you will be fine."

"Mmm," Teeka moaned in agreement. "I will be fine."

"I did not want to ask Kuta to help you."

"No! Do not ask him," Teeka snapped, sitting up. Her face paled with the dizziness that engulfed her, but in a moment it passed. "I will tell you what to get for me."

A strong hand on her shoulder urged her backward, making her lie down.

"You are not badly hurt?" Kaho asked.

Teeka was surprised. She looked into his face, noting that it was etched with sincere concern.

"No. A little bruised and sore, and my head is throbbing, but—"

"Rebet," he said, not letting Teeka finish, "what does she need? Can you gather the medicines? Will you understand her requests?"

"I gathered her medicine for you," she answered.

"Of course you did. I have not forgotten. Go and get them and prepare them in whatever manner she suggests. Keep Kuta out of this."

"I will go as soon as she tells me what to gather."

Teeka smiled at his anxiousness to have her healed. "The spirits have a way of turning things about, do they not?"

"They do indeed," he answered, remembering how she had risked so much to make him well again. Now she was injured, and there was nothing that he could offer her— especially not his medicine man. This Tegesta woman bewildered him and complicated his life. He did not understand why those feelings pleased him.

————

Within days, the Kahoosa had well begun to rebuild.

Replacing the shelters did not take long. The women searched for their scattered belongings, but many of their things had disappeared with the storm.

They began to replenish the roots, leaves, stems, flowers, lichens, and other usable plant parts that they normally stored in the village. A hunting party found the compactly congregated deer easy prey, but they brought back only what they needed. Some of the women tended to the grates over the fires, smoking the meat so that it would not become rancid too quickly. The village was soon functioning as it always had.

All the people of the area had been through similar storms many times before. Their platforms were perfect for the climate; because of the simplicity of design, the Kahoosa could rebuild them in a short time.

Teeka's medicine quickly healed her arm and shrunk the lump on her head. Rebet remained amazed at the effectiveness of Tegesta medicine.

Teeka looked around the village; all the shelters had new green thatch. It would not be long before it turned brown. She hoped the Tegesta had made out as well as the Kahoosa.

She looked all around her. "Ah, the wonder of the spirits," she said aloud, looking out from her new shelter. In a few days the land would dry out and the tender young shoots of saw grass would feed the hungry deer. The deer that were left would be the strong ones, the ones that could endure, and their offspring would be strong like their parents. The rain and the storms were part of the cycle, like the fires that seasonally burned off the land. The fires cleaned the old brush away so that the new growth could begin. Sometimes it seemed that the land was always in distress, but that was the way the spirits had designed it. The miracle never ceased to enthrall Teeka.

————

Rebet was coming, as she did every day. Teeka climbed down to meet her. The guards stood silently, always watching, listening, crowding her.

"Let me see your arm," Rebet told her.

Teeka held out her arm. There was only a small red line where the gash had once been.

"It is amazing," Rebet remarked. "The wound closed so quickly, and no evil spirits got into it."

"It is really not so amazing. Tamuk was from the pure line of shamans. He knew much, and he shared his wisdom with all of the People."

Rebet wanted to ask Teeka to teach her the Tegesta medicine, but she was afraid.

Suddenly there was a stir in the village. Both women turned toward the commotion. A warrior came running and whispered to one of Teeka's guards. The guard reacted immediately, taking Teeka by the shoulder, turning her toward her platform ladder and motioning for her to go up.

"Rebet, what is it? What is happening?"

"I do not know," she answered.

Just then the guards started shouting at Teeka.

"They are telling you to go inside, Teeka," Rebet said.

One of the sentinels poked Rebet with his spear, urging her to leave.

Rebet twisted her neck, looking back for Teeka as she walked away, but she had faded into the darkness inside the platform.

The guard who had hurried her along dropped back. Rebet broke into a trot, moving with the rest of the crowd that had begun to run toward the landing bank.

Rebet was weaving through the crowd, darting from side to side, peeking around the mass of people. What had they all come to see, and why had Teeka's guards been alerted?

Rebet broke clear of the mob. At last she could see through the tall grass and reeds. Just off the bank was a small canoe. Inside was one of the Tegesta men who had come before, and this time he had brought a woman. Something about the woman made Rebet's mouth drop open.

Chapter Sixteen

TEEKA PACED INSIDE HER SHELTER. She could hear the noise of the Kahoosa gathering. Instead of two guards, there were now five below her platform. She wrapped her fingers around the pendant. Had her people come for her? For an instant she hoped they had, but then she remembered that Kaho would never let that be—it would mean bloodshed. What was happening? If only Rebet would come back and tell her.

She stood in the opening again, ignoring the alerted guards. Kuta was passing in the distance. His pace was painfully slow as if he were going reluctantly. She watched him until he was hidden by the brush.

Kuta approached the crowd and made his way through it. It was what he had thought. More Tegesta. What was becoming of the Kahoosa that they would even allow any Tegesta to come close. Under his breath, he mumbled his disgust.

Rebet pushed the tall grass away and then trampled on it, clearing her view. The woman in the canoe looked so much like Teeka. The resemblance was unquestionable, and yet she lacked Teeka's remarkable beauty. From a distance, Rebet was sure that they could easily be mixed up.

What bravery, she thought. What astonishing courage.

It was remarkable that the small party of Tegesta men had come, but it was incredible that a woman would dare. Rebet's opinion of the Tegesta people was changing rapidly, as was that of many other Kahoosa.

Kaho stood at the water's edge. He acknowledged the visitors and finally indicated that they should bring the dugout in.

Ata drew his paddle through the water. Illa turned to her husband, smiling. It was going to be all right. She was going to see her sister.

Two of Kaho's warriors escorted Ata and Illa to the center of the village. Kaho stayed by the water with some of his men after everyone else had left. They scanned the water in the distance for other canoes. Still not satisfied, Kaho ordered a group of lookouts to surround the village. He did not trust the visitors' intentions.

Ata and Illa sat on the ground. Most of the Kahoosa pretended to go on about their daily chores, but they could not hide their curious stares. Kaho passed the visitors without acknowledging them, but he did encourage the Kahoosa stragglers to disperse. He would let the Tegesta sit, but they would not demand an audience with him. He would meet with them on his terms.

Rebet ran back to Teeka's platform. When she reached the base, the guards prevented her from going up.

Teeka heard the argument below and went to the open side.

"What is it, Rebet?"

"I saw—" she started, but a spear was suddenly pressed against her throat.

Rebet fell silent and backed away. The point was clear enough.

"Let her talk!" Teeka said, raising her voice. "Why can

she not tell me?" She knew it was useless. The guards did not speak Tegesta, or at least they pretended not to, and she could not speak to them in their own language. Besides, she knew her request would make them angry if they understood her.

The platform seemed to grow smaller and smaller as the day wore on. It radiated the heat from the sun, and the air almost seemed heavy inside. She felt cramped and uncomfortable. If only they would let her go for a walk. She had asked the guards once when she needed to take care of her personal needs, but they had refused. Much time had passed, and she had become very uncomfortable. She had no choice. As repulsive as it seemed, she urinated into a pottery bowl. She would throw it out once she could go down. She even once thought of throwing it below, letting it smash at the feet of the guards, splattering their legs with her waste. She amused herself with the vengeful thought but knew that she would never do it.

As the hot afternoon sun faded, Ata and Illa still sat in the same spot.

"Why does he not talk with us? Why do we just sit here?" Illa asked her husband. "Is this what you had to do when you came before?"

"I am not certain why he makes us sit here, but I believe it is to show us that we are on his territory and cannot demand anything from him—not even an audience with him. It is a show of authority, that is all. He will come. Kaho has to be curious as to why we have come. We must be patient."

"I am patient, Ata. I do not wish any audience with him. I only want to see my sister."

"Do not forget the Tegesta and Kahoosa relationship. It is not a friendly one."

"If Kaho likes Teeka, then he likes the Tegesta. Whatever he sees in her is Tegesta," Illa commented.

His wife was naive. "It is not the Tegesta way that attracts Kaho to Teeka."

"I know that," she retorted, annoyed with Ata for thinking she did not have a good grasp of the situation. "But that attraction is shallow, and if she pleases him, it is more than just physical. Believe me, he is drawn past her body to the Tegesta inside."

"I hope you do not reveal this insight to him. I do not think that he will want to hear it."

"Oh, Ata, sometimes I think you do not know me or trust my judgment."

Ata looked away from his wife as he caught some movement out of the corner of his eye. "He comes," he whispered.

Kaho walked very slowly, a signal that he had no interest in visitors but would accommodate them because he was a gracious host. He sat across from them, legs folded, the setting sun his backdrop.

"You are one who came before. Is that not so?" Kaho asked Ata.

"It is so. And again I come to you on a mission of peace."

"I am not so certain that your last mission was peaceful. Not many moons after your departure a Kahoosa was slain. If it were not for the persuasion of the Tegesta woman, I would still be certain that you left a warrior behind to slay one of us—a cowardly way to seek vengeance. Sometimes I wonder if it is not so."

"Believe the woman," Ata responded. "As you see, none of the Tegesta are cowards—neither the men nor the women. My wife dares to come to the village of the one who has harassed and terrorized the People."

"For what purpose have you come?" Kaho asked.

"As I told you on my last visit, my wife is the sister of the woman you took from us."

Kaho was eager to let them know that Teeka had given him her name. "Yes," he said, looking at Illa. "I can see the resemblance between you and Teeka. It was your child she held the day I chose her."

"Yes," Illa said. "It was my child you threatened to kill. And you speak of cowardly ways. What brave man orders a knife held to the throat of an infant?"

Ata's eyes widened. "Illa, be still."

"She does not provoke me. She has fire—like her sister. I like that in a woman. You are a lucky man to have a woman like this."

"I have come a long way. Will you permit me to see Teeka?" Illa asked.

"I will permit it," he answered her. "Your request is granted because I respect you. Your bravery and forthrightness impress me. If you had come for any other reason, I would know by now. Neither your tongue nor your face is comfortable with lies."

Illa stood, anticipating his lead. "Will you take me to her?"

"The man stays. He will wait here."

"No. My husband escorts me. He has brought me here and will see it through with me. What harm could there be?"

"There is no harm. You feel very strongly about this, do you not?"

"Yes, I feel strongly. He is my husband. To leave him here is to ask him to endure an insult on my behalf."

"So that you will see that I am not an unreasonable man, I will permit your husband to go with you. I will respect your commitment to him."

Kaho led them to Teeka's platform.

"The Kahoosa have rebuilt from the big storm. The Tegesta have also recovered," Ata remarked on the way as he looked around the large village.

Kaho spoke to the guards, explaining that the two visitors had permission to go up. The warriors moved aside giving them access to the ladder.

"Do not give them too long," he told his guards. "Too long a visit will make her sad," he said as Ata followed his wife up the ladder. That was the other thing that made him uneasy about their visit.

Teeka sat in the back of the platform sorting through some of the plant parts in a basket. Illa's face rose above the floor of the platform, and she called to her sister.

Teeka jumped to her feet. Were her eyes playing tricks?

"Illa! Illa!" she cried, the tears already beginning to stream down her face.

Teeka grabbed her sister's hand and helped her into the shelter. As soon as Illa was standing, the two of them embraced, crying with the joy of seeing each other again.

Ata also made his way onto the platform. He stood silently letting the women continue to hold each other. Teeka looked over Illa's shoulder and saw him.

"Ata! How have you done this?" She looked past him for anyone else who might be coming up the ladder. "Has anyone else come?" she asked, hoping that Auro, too, was here, that he had come for her and secured her release.

"No," Ata answered. "It is just Illa and I. She wanted to see her sister. How can I refuse this woman?" he said, smiling.

Teeka realized that her wish was no more than a fleeting fantasy. Auro was never coming for her. It was like her dream when he stood by the water and did not save her. Though she did not like it, the dream was slowly beginning to unravel.

"Kaho has let you come to see me?" she asked, already knowing the answer but amazed by it. Teeka wiped her eyes and sniffed. "I am so happy to see you."

"How are you being treated?" Illa asked as they all sat.

"Captivity is not so bad. I am not mistreated, but the constant presence of the guards annoys me. I wish that Kaho would release them, but I dare not ask too much too soon. Even Kaho is not as horrible as I thought. He has a different face from the one he shows as king. He also has a considerate and just side."

"Has he been gentle with you, Teeka?" her sister asked, not really certain how to bring up the subject.

"Are you asking about joining?" Teeka asked blatantly.

"Well, yes," Illa answered uneasily. It was such an awkward subject, and it was also forbidden. But Teeka had spoken of it with her before, and what did it matter now?

"I have not been with him."

Illa looked surprised.

"When I first arrived," Teeka began, "I started my moon cycle. And then Kaho was very ill. By the time he had recovered, it was my time again. And of course there was the big storm, and everyone worked so hard to prepare for it and then to rebuild afterward. Were the People prepared?" Teeka asked, though she was really asking if Auro had read the signs and warned them.

"Oh, yes," Ata spoke up. "We were well prepared."

"Then Auro is a good shaman?"

"What do you mean?" Ata asked.

"When Teges and I spoke, he told me that Auro was different, that he had changed. Teges did not seem to have any confidence in him."

"Auro predicted the storm," Ata said.

"You are not telling me everything. Illa, what is it?"

"Teeka, I am your sister and I will tell you the truth. When you were taken, Auro grieved for you as I suppose you grieved for him. But it has become a sickness with him. He does not have the interest of the People in his heart anymore—only his interests. Everyone is concerned, not only for him but also for the clan. Do not let your heart ache too badly."

Teeka swallowed, and because she was fighting tears it pained her. Her fingers touched the pendant. She recalled how she and Auro had called the spirits together and how wonderful that night had been. She could not imagine him being any other way. But it seemed so long ago. So much had happened since then.

Illa took Teeka's hand. She pressed it to her belly.

"Illa! Do you carry a child inside?"

"It will be a girl. I have had dreams. Ata and I have already decided on a name. She will be called Teeka."

Teeka leaned across and hugged her sister and Ata. "I am so happy for you. A new baby. It is wonderful. But," Teeka said as her expression changed, "I will not be there to give her a gift when she is born." She looked around the platform. There was nothing she could give to Illa now for the baby either.

"You give her your name, Teeka," Illa said. "There is no better gift."

"There is so much I want to tell you, Illa. I lie here at night and say it all as if you were listening, and now that you are, I do not know where to begin. The customs are so different. Illa, the Kahoosa think that women are dirty, unclean, during their moon cycle. We are sent to a special platform, near the place of the dead, until the cycle is over. We eat bland food from plain bowls. It is very strange."

Illa looked shocked.

"Do you wish for me to take back any messages?" Ata said, changing the subject.

Teeka thought. There were so many messages she wished to send. "Illa, assure Mother that I am well and that it is not terrible for me here. Tell Shala that I think of her often. Is she well?"

"Her health has not been as good since Tamuk died. And I think she is concerned about her son," Ata answered.

Teeka continued. "Illa, will you give Auro a message?"

"No," Ata protested. "Auro does not hear anything that comes from us. Let him go, Teeka."

"I made a commitment before the spirits and another to Auro before I left. Illa understands. She knows. Auro and I love each other. No one but Illa knows how much. It is not something I can just throw away. I am going to come home."

"Let her send him a message, Ata. It cannot hurt."

Ata nodded his head, though he knew he would be able to persuade Illa not to deliver it. If Auro was to ever recover, he was going to have to put away his grief. Messages from Teeka would only prolong it.

"I will wait for you under the platform," he told Illa. "Teeka, I pray the spirits will continue to protect you," he said before leaving.

Ata climbed down and sat in the shade beneath the platform. The guards were ready to end the visit anyway, and one of them soon went up. A moment later he led Illa down the ladder. Teeka stood at the edge of her platform, watching her sister leave. Tears slid down her face, some of them working their way into the corners of her mouth.

Chapter Seventeen

REBET HAD WORKED UP the courage to ask Teeka to show her the Tegesta medicine. She wanted to learn some of the incredible things that Teeka knew about healing. She stood near Teeka's platform, hesitating. Then confidently she walked close and called up to her.

Teeka was glad to see her. "Rebet, I am glad you have come." Illa's visit had reminded her how lonely she was.

"I have been thinking," Rebet stated when she got to the top and went inside. "I have seen you do magic with the Tegesta medicine. Will you teach me some of the Tegesta magic?"

"I do not know any magic, only some medicines."

"Kaho's recovery was magic to me."

"The Tegesta's shaman does the only magic. He teaches the People how to use the medicines that the spirits have given us. We do not believe that is magic."

"Kuta tells us nothing. We are completely dependent upon him."

"If I teach you about the plants that we use for medicine, it may anger Kuta."

"Kuta does not need to know. I want to be able to help my family if Kuta's magic fails. It will be our secret. Kuta will not find out."

Teeka thought for a moment. Rebet had helped her.

She was obligated. "It will take some time," Teeka finally responded. "The Tegesta learn all their lives."

"I will work hard. The loss of one son is enough."

"Then we will start with some of the plants that you already store. I will show you how to prepare and use them. I am sure that the Kahoosa have much of the same medicine."

"I wish I could stay with you now and that we could begin, but there are other things I need to do this day."

"I understand," said Teeka. "We will begin soon enough. But may I delay you long enough to ask you a question? I am curious about one of your customs. I often wonder about it while I am in isolation."

Rebet nodded.

"When your young women have their first cycle, are they also sent to isolation?"

Rebet laughed. "Our customs are different, but we do not lack feelings. It is a joyous time for a young woman of the Kahoosa, just as it is for the Tegesta. All of the young women who have recently made the transition to womanhood are gathered together for a special celebration. Each is taught by an older woman of the tribe and is told of the duties of womanhood. For four days we sing spirit songs and ritual chants to thank the spirits. There is dancing and feasting. It is a time to give gifts. We celebrate with games. And the young women themselves play special games. At the end of the four days, they return to their own homes for another three days. During those days they do not see anyone other than their own families. At the end of that time, they are accepted as women of the tribe. It is during the next cycle that each must go to the secluded platform. Once she has spent that time alone, she is eligible for marriage."

"It is not much different from our own custom,

except that we are never isolated. We are really not that much different from one another."

Rebet grinned and touched Teeka's shoulder. "No, we are not so different."

"Is it terrible to think that perhaps we all came from the same people, many generations ago? Could the same blood that runs through my veins also run through yours? Could the spirits of the Kahoosa and the Tegesta be the same, only called by different names? Have our tongues learned to speak differently as we have spread apart, just as our customs have changed? Teges and Tamuk would be angry to hear me speak such things."

"Kaho and Kuta would not like it either. There are Kahoosa legends about how all men were one when the animals could talk. One story tells of a man raising his hand against another man. This angered the spirits so much that they made their tongues speak differently. Then the men who could speak the same language grouped together and moved away. Do the Tegesta have a legend that is similar?"

"It is the same legend, but it tells of brother raising his hand against brother. Would such legends be told by both the Kahoosa and the Tegesta if they were not true?"

"I do not think that we will ever know," Rebet said as she approached the ladder.

Teeka's face looked pleasantly puzzled. "If it was so, if once the Kahoosa and the Tegesta were one, then it is not so strange a thought that they could be one again."

Teeka walked to the edge. "We will begin our lessons soon. I think Tosa would also like to learn. She asks many questions."

Rebet had already begun to descend. "Yes, Tosa was always a curious one. I think she can be trusted to keep our secret."

Each day Teeka felt more and more secure. Kuta had not harassed her, and she had more time to herself. She constantly seemed to think of Auro. She found it difficult to concentrate on anything other than Auro. That obsession mixed her emotions. She wanted to think about him, but she also wanted to think about other things. Perhaps there was something wrong with her. This was not normal.

Teeka turned onto her side and looked into the far distance. The night was clear, the stars glittering in the sky. Each celestial body was the hearth of a spirit or a man who had crossed over, and they looked down on the People, watching, protecting, and guiding. But they also sparkled in the Kahoosa sky. She crept to the edge of the open side of her platform. Drawing her knees up, she propped her head and hands upon them. *Tomorrow,* she thought, *I will ask Kaho to return me to my people. He is grateful and will return my deed.*

When morning came, she took extra care in tending to herself. She wanted to be at her best when she met with Kaho. By the time she reached him, the people of the village were busy with their morning work.

"Kaho looks well this morning," she began.

"The limp is improving."

"The spirits have found favor in you. You are a fortunate man."

"I am not just any man. I am Kaho, who deserves their favor. My people pay the spirits great respect, and I offer them all that I have."

"Yet they do not take from you," Teeka commented.

"They take," he retorted.

Teeka wished to move the conversation more toward her goal but did not want to risk being too brazen.

"Let me have a closer look at the wound to make sure

that my medicine has finished its work."

She moved closer to inspect the leg. Kaho sat and extended it for her.

"Your medicine has cured me. We will find the bear, and she will not live out the day."

"My medicine is not so strong that it can cure all sicknesses from wounds. You must be careful. You may find yourself slower, and that will make you vulnerable."

"Do you always give advice to kings?"

"No," she said with a smile, "just those whom I have healed. I do not like to see all my hard work go to nothing."

"Will I always have to listen to your advice, or can I end my indebtedness with some gift to you?" he asked, partly in jest.

"Do you think you are indebted to me?" she asked, opening the door for her request.

"The Kahoosa believe that if a man is injured by another, he must take the earliest opportunity to retaliate. That ends the matter. If a man's life is saved by another, he owes that man his life, or he must repay him with something to end the debt. Did you not save my life?"

Teeka now fully understood the episode she had witnessed between the two young boys, Boro and Nakosa. Even a friendly, accidental injury required immediate retaliation.

"Yes, I saved your life, but I do not expect anything in return. What I did was simply the way of the Tegesta," she said, baiting the hook.

Any offer would have to come from him. He was not one to meet the demands of anyone, especially a woman.

"But it is not the way of the Kahoosa, and you are now with the Kahoosa, or have you forgotten?"

"No, I have not forgotten."

"Then name the repayment. Do you wish special clothing or adornments?"

"No, I wish nothing."

"I can confer special status if I choose to. Is that what you wish?"

"No, I do not wish for special status."

Kaho was becoming irritated.

"I will not be indebted to you. If you like nothing I offer, then you name the payment that will cancel the debt. The only thing you may not ask is that I return you to the Tegesta."

"I can think of nothing," Teeka answered, feeling dizzy with disappointment. He would never let her go.

As soon as she had spoken, she walked to the ladder and climbed down.

Kaho threw his long stick crutch across the floor. How had she gotten the upper hand? She tempted him and yet personified innocence. She manipulated him with her kindness and left him frustrated with her eeriness. She had healed him and requested nothing in return. He had stolen her from her people, and she offered no resistance. She had done nothing, and she had done everything. The last thing he wanted was to be obligated to her. How was it that she made him feel so inferior? He would end this quickly.

Teeka left to meet her friends. Later she would think of something. Rebet and Tosa were already at Teeka's platform and had seated themselves on the floor. They had begun to lay out the contents of the baskets they had brought. The top layers were simple, edible plants. Just beneath was the substance of their lesson for the day.

The first to be discussed was an evergreen vine. The leaves were dark forest green on the top and pale green beneath, and the flowers were fragrant and yellow.

"Where did you find them?" Teeka asked, knowing that they had had to travel a distance to find the climbing plant.

"To the east, growing around a tree," Rebet answered with pride.

The jessamine was just coming into bloom, and Tosa held it to her nose, breathing in the sweet fragrance.

"Do not be fooled by the sweetness of the fragrance," Teeka instructed. "The flowers, leaves, and root are poisonous, but the root, when prepared properly, is a medicine for the old and failing."

She sliced off a fingernail-sized bit of the rootstock. "Grated and steeped in a large amount of water, small doses will make a slow heart beat faster. But too much of this medicine will kill a person. Use this potion only when you have no other choice."

The two women examined the plant, turning it and taking note of its shape. When they had finished, they put it aside and chose another from the basket.

"We already know of this one," announced Rebet. "It is good for pain in the stomach. It is a common medicine among the Kahoosa. It is not a secret of Kuta."

"That is true," Teeka agreed, "but I have another use for it. When a woman has borne many children, her body is tired. She may not wish to carry any more babies for a while. She may need a rest. It does not work for long, and it does not always work. But sometimes it stops the woman's body from having another child."

Rebet and Tosa had never heard of such a thing, and Teeka read their faces.

"It has given many Tegesta women a rest. Only the shamans know the way to keep a woman from not having a baby forever."

Rebet and Tosa were nervous about such talk. Their

eyes stared with worry, and Tosa bit her bottom lip. Rebet translated to Tosa everything that she did not understand. Teeka's last sentence still plagued Rebet as she retold it in her own language. When she had finished, Tosa put her hand to her mouth.

"Does this medicine not make the spirits angry?" Rebet asked.

Before Teeka could answer, Rebet blurted out another of her concerns. "Are women not punished for even thinking that they do not want another child? Such an attitude is unheard of among the Kahoosa."

"There are certain times when a woman does not need to have another child—when she is in poor health, if she does not deliver babies very well, or when she already has a sick child who requires all her attention. The Tegesta believe that the spirits have given us knowledge of this medicine so that we may use it."

Rebet began to pack her basket. "I do not want to learn how to prepare this medicine. I am afraid," she said, fumbling with the plants as she lined her basket with them.

Tosa began to gather her plants, but more slowly than Rebet. She stood and watched Rebet walk away and then sat again.

"Teeka," she whispered, "I want no more babies." Her eyes glistened with the promise of tears that did not come.

"You are not so old, Tosa," Teeka said, "and you are healthy."

"No more babies," she said again very softly, as if someone might be listening. This time Tosa's eyes filled with tears, and one spilled down her cheek before she could wipe it away.

The Kahoosa did not understand women very well,

Teeka thought, as she sat across from her friend and demonstrated the procedure for preparing the medicine that would keep her infertile for a while.

When the lesson had ended, Tosa put her arms around Teeka and then wiped her eyes.

"Thank you, my friend."

Chapter Eighteen

TEEKA HAD MANY DREAMS. The moon was again growing larger, and the phantoms slipped into her head. Obscure pictures, like paint running and smearing, interrupted pleasant visions, and then disappeared. Scenes appeared and melted before she could make sense of them. They darted into her sleep, jarred her, and then left, as if they enjoyed playing a tormenting game.

Teeka's eyes snapped open. Relieved that she had only been dreaming, she sighed deeply and looked into the night sky. The gibbous moon taunted her. It saw and knew all that happened in the night, and Teeka felt a jealous pang. If only she could see things so clearly.

She was certain that Kaho was not going to free her, and she knew he would come for her soon. A fleeting thought rushed through her. That was it. She would be what Kaho wanted. She would make him want her more than anything, and when he finally got his way ... She stopped short. It was brilliant. How had such a perfect plan ever come in her head? The spirit of Tamuk must be with her, she was certain. At last she knew that she would be free.

One other thought kept flitting in and out of her mind. She had pushed it away many times before. It was another option, and she knew she had to confront it sometime. With the plan she had already worked out, it did not seem so scary to face this idea that she had tried to ignore.

Kaho did not frighten her anymore. He was not Auro, but she did have some feeling for him. And she wondered if she could ever really go home again. Many of the things she had done and thought made her unacceptable to the Tegesta. Maybe she could give up and deal with what the spirits had given to her, just as Teges had told her to do. Perhaps a marriage to Kaho would help bring about a lasting peace between the tribes. It was something to consider. She wondered if she could even attempt it. Would she ever be able to let go of the commitment she had made to Auro? No, she concluded. She should not think these things. She already had a plan that could bring her freedom. She must put these other thoughts away. They were betrayals.

Later that night, while she slept, Kaho stood at the edge of her platform, his curiosity aroused. She tossed and groaned as her small body, beaded with perspiration, twitched and then lay still again. Repeatedly, he watched her shift from the heat and humidity. A light breeze rustled the leaves and caused the grasses to lean, blowing a slender wisp of her blue-black hair across her face. Even in sleep she intrigued him, teased him, and aroused him.

From the edge of the platform he called her name.

Teeka's eyes opened, and she tilted her head to gain better focus.

"I am in need of a woman," he said softly.

The timing was perfect. If he had come for her a day earlier, she would not have been ready. But now everything was clear. What she was going to do was not acceptable for a Tegesta woman, but she was not with the Tegesta, and she would do what she had to. She would deal with the rest later.

"Walk closer that I might see the face of the king who needs this woman," she said to him in a voice tinged with both innocence and titillation.

Kaho stepped forward before he realized that he was obeying her command. He stopped before he reached touching distance.

Teeka leaned forward, drew up her knees, and folded her arms across them. She laid her head on her wrists. Her eyes were wide and her lips pouty, like a scolded child's.

"What makes you stop?" she asked.

If he continued to stand still, he would owe her an explanation; if he moved toward her, he would be submitting to her. He chose to stand still. "This bed is not the one I prefer."

Kaho motioned for her to descend the ladder, and Teeka moved across the platform, brushing her hair from her face. Both men and women always walked behind unless told to do otherwise. But this woman he wanted to watch. Walking next to her would confirm her equality. She would walk in front, another necessary insult that he would have to tolerate.

When Kaho reached the bottom of the ladder, he waved the sentries off. There would be no witnesses to the order of their procession to his bed.

Her graceful movements were shaded with subtle oscillations and undulations that suggested her sexuality. Her back was straight and proud, and she faced directly ahead, never looking down.

If the moon had been full, he would have seen more clearly the incline of her head and the shine of her skin from the youthful oil that kept her skin soft and supple. Perhaps he would also have seen an unexpected smile.

But the moonlight was only bright enough for him to see how she tantalized him.

Teeka walked to the foot of the ladder that ascended to his platform and paused. Kaho stood for a moment, looking at the body that waked him. Her breasts were covered by her long hair, which fell to the front, and her skirt covered her from the waist to the tops of her thighs. She was more desirable dressed and hidden than any woman he had known nude.

"Because you are a maiden, are you afraid?" he asked.

"I am not afraid," she answered calmly. "You come to me with desire, not with intent to harm."

"You are very perceptive," he spoke. "This king enjoys bringing pleasure, not just seeking it," he said, taking her hand and leading her up the ladder.

At the foot of the bed, Kaho removed his minimal clothing, and Teeka swept her hair to the back, exposing her breasts. Every woman he had ever had had stood motionless before him at a time like this. This woman was not aggressive, but she was also not intimidated, a combination that confused and aroused him.

Teeka slid her moss skirt to the floor and stepped out of it. The night was warm and humid, as it often was at the southern end of the peninsula, and her skin was moist. The breeze touched her back and puffed strands of her long hair into her face. Her slender fingers brushed them away. The rotation of her shoulder as she did so was almost an overture, and Kaho replied by stepping close to her and wrapping his arms around her small waist.

She could feel his arousal pressed against her. Kaho reached behind her neck and lifted the cord that laced her medicine bag to her. He raised it over her head and lifted it free. Again his hands found another leather necklace strand, and he started to lift it off. She pulled his hand away and held the pendant close to her heart.

"No," she said shyly. "Leave this."

"It may be a nuisance," he argued, going after it again.

"Please leave it."

It was not that important, he decided—not important enough to spoil the evening, and so he let it drop.

She placed both of his hands on the curve of her hips. He would never forget this night with her, she thought as she drew him down with her on the soft bed.

Kaho lay on his side next to her, letting his hands wander the length of her body. He raised his head so that he could see all that he touched. There was a sexual animal inside her that he was going to loose for the first time, he thought. Once she had had this experience with him, she would need him. Tonight would end the obligation.

His hand stroked the inside of her thigh, edging its way up teasingly. Teeka bent her leg, giving him better access, but then turned onto her side, guiding his hardness between her thighs. She did not allow penetration, but moved her hips to simulate the act. The dampness and warmth of her skin, combined with her movements, caught him off guard, and his hips jerked. He needed to pull away, take control, but the sensation was so pleasurable that he did not want her to stop.

Teeka relaxed her legs, freeing him, and slid downward. Her tongue drew smooth circles on his belly, then moved into the hollow of his groin. Kaho arched his back, and pulled her up to him. His mouth found hers waiting, lips parted and inviting.

Again he assumed the dominating role, tasting and touching hidden parts of her. Suddenly he felt her warm hand wrap itself around him. The throbbing he felt was a warning that he was too close. He tried to push her hand away from his pulsating erection, but she resisted.

Suddenly she released him and put herself on top of him, gyrating her hips against him. No woman had ever sought to please him the way she did. Without allowing entry, she was taking him. The sensation was too much, and the convulsive contractions that spilled his seed began, leaving the gush of his pleasure between them, rather than inside her.

When it was over for him, Teeka raised herself and rolled off him. Her face was flushed and hot, her body tight and wired. She lay next to him, heaving for breath. He waved her away without speaking. She dressed herself and left, having accomplished the task for the evening. She was pleased with her efficiency. Yes, she thought again, she had been very successful. But she did not feel the elation she thought she should. She had just taken the first step toward securing her freedom, but somehow she felt melancholy. She took no pride in her deed and had found no joy in humiliating Kaho. Those were the true and honest feelings she had. If nothing else, he would want to be rid of her now. He would not tell anyone about his performance, and the best way to be sure no one would ever find out was to send her back to her people. Maybe this evening alone would secure her freedom. If not, she knew what she would have to do. The amulet felt especially and uncomfortably warm against her skin. Unconsciously she lifted it, holding it tightly. Her work would not be finished until she was home again.

She wandered through the village unwatched and made her way to a spot in the stream where she could clean herself. She dropped her skirt on the bank and waded in, washing away the sticky fruit of Kaho's pleasure. Since she had come to this village, this was the first time she had been completely alone, unguarded, and she reveled in her freedom. When clean, she stretched out on the shore and watched the moon. She wished Auro could be by her side. "I will be back," she said aloud.

The episode with Kaho had left her feeling incomplete. She still trembled. She needed to have the gift of joining. It was a need inside her so strong that she could not deny it, even though she was certain that it was improper. But perhaps the Tegesta spirits did not see her while she was with the Kahoosa. Maybe she was not Tegesta under the Kahoosa sky. Then she had a bizarre thought. Perhaps both the Kahoosa and the Tegesta spirits watched her. Perhaps she had been sent here for a reason. Maybe she was both, the old half of her still Tegesta and a new half becoming Kahoosa. Or maybe there was no design by the spirits, and she had been abandoned by them all. Maybe she was a woman with no tribe and no guide spirit. She would have to rely on herself alone. She would not count on or depend on anything else. The thought made her feel that she was in control of her fate.

Finally she dressed herself and began her walk back to her platform. She could escape now, and no one would know until morning. But Kaho would be vengeful to her and to the People.

She finally reached her platform and found the guards sleeping. With her eyes open and alert, she lay down on her mat. At last she had developed a plan, but now that she had put it into motion she doubted it. She felt some anxiety about returning home. Neither Teges nor her sister Illa had encouraged her to return. Why would they tell her not to let her heart ache too much? Maybe there was nothing to go home to.

"No," she said aloud as she sat up straight. Tonight had been the prelude. Tomorrow she would begin.

The snoring of one of the guards below her platform was in disharmony with the silence of the night. Teeka lay on her stomach and leaned her head over the side of the platform. She still felt the little quick spasms in that part of her, as if she were trying to draw something inside. She watched the guards sleep and thought how easy it would be to lure one of them up to her.

Her body slowly untangled, and she began to relax. And then she saw him, lurking in the shadows. Did he think she would not see him? Did he never sleep?

Kuta edged closer, carrying fetishes and mumbling words she did not understand. One guard awakened and nudged the other sleeping sentry. Kaho's directions were to send any man away. They were not to allow any man to ascend the ladder. They hoped Kuta would not insist. They did not want a confrontation with the shaman.

Kuta stood below, speaking with the guards. She hoped they would send him away. Had he also stood beneath Kaho's platform earlier? The idea that he had listened or watched made her flesh crawl.

Finally, and obviously unhappily, Kuta walked away, grumbling and fidgeting with the fetishes. Before he vanished in the night, he turned and shouted up to her, "I will be rid of you."

Teeka waited for him to return. She watched in the darkness, straining her eyes until she could no longer fight off sleep. Without realizing, she closed her eyes.

———

Beneath her, one of the sentinels elbowed the other.

"Do you hear that?" he whispered.

From somewhere in the distance he heard a humming,

a droning.

"It must be Kuta."

Veins of lightning crossed the sky, followed by a distant rumble.

Chapter Nineteen

BEFORE THE SUN ROSE, Teeka went below, took a coal from the central hearth, and started a small fire to make an aromatic pomade. After it cooled, she scooped the pomade into a shell and took it with her to the pool where she attended to her morning bathing.

When she stepped out of the water, she retrieved the shell with its precious contents. Gingerly, she dipped one finger into it and rubbed the collected residual in the creases and folds of her body and at the nape of her neck. With one smooth stroke she drew a line from her throat to her navel, painting herself with the aura of spring.

Quickly she dressed in a fresh moss skirt and laced a shell-beaded thong through one side of her hair. The juice-laden pulp of one small wild strawberry, the last for the season, added a faint highlight to her already rosy lips. She dipped her little finger into the pomade again and lubricated her lips, leaving them soft, moist, and tempting. She picked up the small, thin twig that she had charred in the fire, and then she knelt by the water to look at her reflection. Carefully she dotted the charcoal in the empty spaces between her heavy black lower eyelashes. With upward strokes, she darkened the sun-bleached ends of her upper lashes. When finished, she stared into the pool, evaluating her appearance. Her dark eyes flashed back at her. They looked different somehow from the eyes she had seen so many times in the water near her village. The shape and color were the same, but there was more depth, more woman, less child.

Rebet and Cala passed her on the path that ran between the village and the women's section of the stream. They nodded at one another. Rebet paused, sniffing the air as Teeka passed, and then continued down to the water.

Tosa was busy feeding the children and stood with a wide grin when Teeka approached her fire.

"Good morning," she said in the language of the Tegesta.

Teeka returned the greeting in Kahoosa. Tosa's husband nodded to her and then wandered off.

Near the fire she saw the white elixir made from the milkweed sitting in the hollow of a small shell near Tosa's breakfast bowl. Tosa saw that Teeka had noticed. She picked it up and drank it down, tossing the shell into the fire.

"No babies," Tosa said.

"Maybe," Teeka corrected.

"Maybe," Tosa repeated.

Tosa sprang to her feet and retrieved a small gathering basket filled with some of the plants Teeka had described.

"Lesson?" Tosa eagerly asked.

Teeka shook her head. "Later."

Tosa breathed deeply, trying to place the fragrance that she smelled. Soon she realized that it was coming from Teeka.

"You smell of the spring."

Teeka was pleased that the aroma was pleasant and noticeable.

"Teach Tosa that fragrance?"

"Later, with the lesson, I will teach Tosa."

Teeka was anxious for time to pass. She wanted Kaho's belly full when she went to him. Tosa continued to chatter, combining the Tegesta and Kahoosa languages and filling in the gaps with signs, but Teeka wasn't hearing or seeing. Finally Tosa waved her hand in front of Teeka's face.

"I am sorry," Teeka said, trying to turn her attention to Tosa.

Maybe this visit to Tosa had been a bad idea. Teeka needed to be alone to make some final decisions. She stood and patted her friend on her shoulder.

"Stay?" Tosa asked.

"We will have a lesson later," Teeka said.

"Is Teeka sick?" the woman asked, concerned about her friend's obvious distraction.

"No, Kaho is on my mind."

"Kaho? Why?"

Teeka took the opportunity to lay the foundation. She put her hand over her heart, signing "love."

"Teeka loves Kaho?" Tosa asked in disbelief.

Teeka did not want to start too dramatically, and so she shrugged her shoulders as if she was not sure. This was easy and convincing because there was some truth in what she said to Tosa. She looked confused and unsure because she was. She was having a hard time distinguishing between that which was real and that which was part of her performance—part of her plan.

"No," said Tosa and then signed "lonely."

"Yes, maybe I am lonely," Teeka agreed.

"Tegesta man?"

"Yes, Tegesta man," Teeka answered, taking the pendant in her hand.

Tosa's eyes fell to the ground, showing her empathy.

"Tosa," Teeka began, "do not know or ask too much about me."

Tosa's puzzled face stared at her, but she did not pursue the issue.

"Are you my friend?" she asked.

"I am your friend," Teeka answered as she turned to leave.

She could feel Tosa's eyes on her back as she walked away. Holding the pendant with both hands, she closed her eyes. She did not like deceiving her friend. Like so many things she had thought and done lately, being deceitful was not the way of the People. She wondered if there was any of Little Doe left in her.

Teeka sat inside her platform, going over the fine details of her plan. She would have Kaho take her as his bride. She would make him live only for her. And on the wedding night she would leave him. He would not be able to go back to his tribe and tell them that his bride had left the wedding bed. He would have to make up some tragic story about her death. She would be safely home, and the Kahoosa would not come for her. Decisions made, she brushed her hair, added a fresh gloss to her lips, and then climbed down.

The guards followed closely as she crossed the top of the mound and stopped at the foot of the ladder to Kaho's platform. She started to climb the ladder, but one of the guards grabbed her arm and pulled her back. She would not be allowed to enter Kaho's quarters without an invitation.

Kaho, having heard the small scuffle, came to the entrance and looked down, then walked out of sight.

"Kaho," she called out, "this maiden needs to speak with the man who has made her a woman."

The guards smiled at each other, hearing the intimate

revelation. She had given Kaho no choice; he would have to see her now. He came to the opening and ordered the guards to release her.

Teeka gracefully climbed the ladder. When she reached the top, she waited for him to signal her so she could approach him. Kaho motioned to her with his hands and then turned his back to her.

"I have come to beg your forgiveness," she began. "I do not understand joining, and I am fearful that I spoiled it because I am so inexperienced. You stirred a new and wonderful hunger within me. You have had many women, and you know the things that make a woman feel the pleasure."

Kaho's chest puffed up as she inflated his ego.

"Sometimes it is difficult for a maiden to join with a man of experience," he said, turning to face her. "For some it may be impossible."

Teeka stepped a little closer, her scent wafting in the air.

"Now that I have had a taste of you, I will long for you forever. If you will give me another chance, I will try to learn. Is it this way with all men?" she asked innocently.

"No, not with all men. I told you before that I seek not only my own pleasure. I like to make the woman feel the full pleasure of joining."

"Perhaps you need not touch me so much with your hands and your mouth. You found places that I did not know about. Is there something wrong with me?"

"There is nothing wrong with you," he said with more softness in his voice. "You are right; I was too strong."

"Will you give me another chance? Will you teach me the ways of joining?"

The trap was set, and the bait was irresistible.

Kaho reached for a handful of her hair, and she took another step forward until they stood close but not touching. She lowered her eyelids shyly. He moved the rest of her hair to her back and then placed his hand on her breast. She whimpered softly, and Kaho chuckled.

"There is much to teach you," he said.

His hands roamed over her, and he delighted in the shudder that visibly crossed her. He would let her think about it all day.

"I will come for you tonight. I will begin to teach you how to enjoy a man like me."

"But the night is so far away."

"Tonight," he reiterated, leading her to the ladder.

She turned back to him with pleading eyes and then climbed down to the waiting guards.

She walked past her shelter and continued on.

————

"Do you want your lesson now?" Teeka asked Tosa.

Teeka found an empty basket and then led Tosa into the brush, following old trails made by medicine men and women. For hundreds of years, feet had trod upon these paths, preventing grass and other plants from growing and leaving a depression as the soil had been tamped down. Often the land was so low that they waded through knee-deep water before reaching drier earth.

The guards followed, bored with the chores of the women. They thought that Teeka and Tosa were collecting plants for food. Men were not the gatherers, and so they did not know that the flowering plant, which Teeka pointed to a few yards off the trail, was never used for food.

The large white trumpet flowers of the jimsonweed did not smell sweet to Tosa, and she wrinkled her nose.

Teeka pulled up the whole plant, exposing a large whitish root from which sprang the yellowish green branching stem.

"Teeka, you take the thorn apple?" she asked, wondering why she would choose such a fetid plant.

"One is enough," was all that she answered.

Teeka would not include this in the pomade she would teach Tosa to make. This one had special powers. Only Tegesta brides used this. When the fresh plant was crushed and the juice extracted, a small drop added to a perfume was a powerful aphrodisiac. It was also given to the man and the woman in a diluted tea during the marriage ceremony. It ensured a happy wedding night for both. When she had first seen it used like that, she had not understood. Explanations were vague, and the person she asked always seemed embarrassed. As she had gotten older, she stopped the questioning, realizing that it was part of the forbidden talk. Now she understood.

Teeka pointed out other fragrant flowers for Tosa, and Tosa had a few of her own favorites but let them be. She wanted to duplicate the scent that Teeka wore. The combination had to be exact; she knew that.

Teeka stopped for a moment, scanning the landscape. There was one other plant that she wanted for herself. It was one that was often used to draw water off the body, but its flowers, when steeped alone, increased the sexual appetite. The men of the Tegesta often gave it to their wives, and wives slipped it into their husbands' tea if their interest seemed to be waning. Until the night with Auro, she had not understood the potion that was whispered about by her people.

In an area of flat, moist meadow, Teeka spotted the tall plant she sought. It could be identified by the purple color where the leaves joined the stem. Tosa followed and watched Teeka pluck the purplish white flowers that grew in clusters. Tosa reached for some, but Teeka nudged her hand back.

"This is not for Tosa's perfume," she explained.

The walk back was just as boring for the guards, who chatted and laughed, often mocking the two women. Tosa would catch some of their conversation now and again and showed her disapproval by glaring back at them. They would be silent for a while, but soon enough they would begin again.

"I hope they do as much to their wives as they say they would like to do with us," she tried to tell Teeka, but the thought was a bit too complicated to express using both languages and signs, and Teeka did not understand.

When they arrived back at the village, they went directly to Teeka's platform and began sorting the plants. Teeka showed Tosa which ones would be included in the pomade that she would make. She also sorted out the ones that she would have special use for this night.

By the fire they worked on their preparations. First, they melted some fat and measured the petals in the correct proportions, so that the sweet smell Tosa liked so much would be exactly the same.

While Tosa was making her perfume, Teeka filled a shallow pot with water and waited for it to boil. She hurried it along by adding hot heartstones that sizzled and hissed when dropped into the pot. When the water began to rumble slightly, she moved it to the end of the spit that held it just above the fire. The heat was not as direct there, and she added her chosen petals. On top of the steaming pot she placed a pottery slab, black as the earth, with the glitter of the quartz sand that had been used to temper it. This would hold in the heat, preventing the steam from escaping. The moisture collected on the underside of the slab and dripped back in, stopping any of the fragrance from escaping into the air. A few moments later, she removed the pot from the fire and set aside the slab, letting the liquid cool. Tosa leaned over it and sniffed the contents. The unusual aroma whirled upward, and Tosa breathed deeply through her nose. The smell was not sweet like the perfume she had just made. Teeka's scent was deeper, earthier, but very pleasant just the same. Somehow it reminded Tosa of the night. She preferred her own.

Teeka's next task was to prepare a tea from saw palmetto berries, juice of the jimsonweed, and the purplish white petals of the flower known as queen of the meadow. The infusion had to be prepared very precisely or it could be dangerous. Satisfied that she had succeeded, she set it aside.

"Tosa, will you help me prepare a special meal? I want to make something to take to Kaho."

"You cook for Kaho?"

Teeka nodded.

"Only Kaho's wives prepare his food," Tosa said.

"Am I the woman of Kaho?" Teeka asked.

"Yes."

"Will you help me? I have no meat."

"The hunters have brought some deer. I will get a small piece of venison and some bread."

"Good. I have made the drink," she said, looking at the tea she had prepared.

She would not wait for Kaho to come to her. She would take him his food before the rest of the village ate. She would watch him sip his tea and watch his desire grow for her. He would be full and satisfied in all ways but one.

Tosa left, carrying her fragrant prize. She would be

back later with the food that Teeka had asked for.

The afternoon sun made Teeka feel tired. She had no chores to do and no handwork like the other women of the village. A nap would help pass the time, and then she would not feel the lethargy that came with the night.

She carried her things up the ladder, making two trips. Almost everything was ready.

Chapter Twenty

THE SUNSET WAS NEAR. The heat of the sun was weaker, and a thunderhead rolled in the west, waking Teeka. The wind began to whip, scattering leaves on the floor of her platform.

The people of the village kept watch, knowing they might have to postpone their evening meal if the storms came. They stirred their brews, shielded their fires, and waited.

It turned out to be an empty threat. Big thunder-heads often formed and then dissipated before they reached the village. The weather was unpredictable and could radically change from hour to hour.

The butterflies sought the shelter of the trees for the night, and the mosquitoes ventured out. The women lit the smudge pots filled with garfish oil, which were scattered about the village. The smoke that came from the pots repelled the hungry insects. The gar was an ugly fish, but very useful. It not only provided smoke that kept the insects away but also kept the alligators' bellies full.

After bathing, she splashed the prepared contents of her bowl over her whole body. The guards watched, eyeing her naked body. She stared back at them. As she passed, the scent that she left behind made one of them think of lying in the grass with her, but the fantasy quickly passed when he thought of Kaho.

Teeka climbed back up to her platform, brought down the basket of food, and warmed the contents over the fire. People were beginning to gather at the central hearth. Her timing was good.

When the food was warm enough, she placed it in the basket and headed toward Kaho's platform. As always, the sentries followed. When she began her ascent up the ladder, one of her watchmen reached out to stop her.

"I have a surprise for Kaho," she said.

The guard did not understand. Teeka spoke again but used some Kahoosa words. He searched the basket, then looked back at her. She smiled, almost suggestively, and he stepped back so that she could ascend the ladder.

Kaho appeared in the doorway. "The man I have assigned to watch you should take his job more seriously," Kaho said as she reached the top.

"Do not be angry with him. I persuaded him to let me bring you this surprise."

"You are a very persuasive woman. What brings you here? Could you not wait for me to come for you?" He was pleased with himself.

Teeka walked closer with the basket. He could smell the warm meat and bread, but the aroma of food was mixed with another scent that called upon his senses more strongly. As she stood very close, his nostrils flared. As he breathed in, he felt a flood of warmth, much like the one that swept him when he drank the ritual black tea.

"I have made you a Tegesta tea," she said, holding the bowl close to his lips. "I hope you will like it."

Kaho sipped and let the flavor roll in his mouth for a moment.

"It is different, but I find it pleasing."

"Sip again. I am sure that you will like it even more."

Kaho let her put it to his lips. He took a mouthful and did find it a savory drink.

"Now I know two things that the Tegesta do well. They raise their maidens pure, and they make a fine tea."

Her lips curled into a faint smile, and then she asked permission to sit by him.

"Have you thought again about what you want me to give you in order to end my obligation to you?" he asked.

"I have thought."

"Then tell me what it is."

"My desires and wishes have changed since when you first brought me here. I have learned that I should not be frightened of you, and I do not feel that you are obligated."

"Is that all?" he probed, wanting to hear her admit her need for him. "I insist on granting your request."

"Must I embarrass myself again before you?"

"I do not wish for you to be embarrassed. I just want to do something for you in return for my life. It should not be so difficult to think of something now that your feelings have changed."

"There is only one thing that I have thought of, but it is too much to ask of you."

"Tell me."

"I want to be with you. I want to be Kaho's woman. I want you to ..." Teeka's voice trailed off.

"Can you not finish?"

Teeka lowered her eyes. "I want to join with you. But I should not feel this way."

"Many women never know the pleasures of joining because their husbands do not know how to excite them. Some men think only of themselves, but I find no pleasure in that. That is the way of the animals. I have brought the desire alive in you. It is good."

"You have awakened something in me and in my heart. My fear has turned to something different."

"Do not mistake passion for affection of the heart."

"Perhaps I shall make a fool of myself before you again, but this thing that has softened my heart began when you were ill. Maybe it even began during the canoe journey to the village of the Kahoosa." Teeka paused for an instant, realizing that she was close to speaking from the heart. "When I saw you standing in the canoe, so near to me, and you did not harm me, I felt an attraction. You, who are so strong and brave, chose me."

Teeka lifted the bowl to his lips again, and as she did so, the breeze carried more of her perfume to him.

"Last night when you sent me away, there were no guards. I could have run, but I chose not to," she whispered.

Kaho reached for her face and drew it to his, letting his lips find hers, moist and receptive. His tongue sought entry, and Teeka parted her lips, allowing it.

As he pulled her to him, the sun disappeared beneath the earth, and the noises of the village began to subside. He turned her sideways, and she lay in his arms as he sat. Tenderly he moved her hair away from her breasts, exposing them to his touch.

She was more passive than she had been the night before, but she gave him clues with the movements of her body and the rhythm of her breathing. Softly she exhaled, sighing with his touch. She curled in his arms, turning her head and covering his chest with quick soft kisses.

Kaho turned her around, pressing her shoulder gently to the floor. His hands trailed down her sides, and he pressed himself against her, making full contact with her body. Teeka bent her head back, offering more of herself to his touch and searching mouth.

Suddenly a voice interrupted their explorations. Rebet and Cala stood at the entry.

Kaho rose sharply and spoke to them in their own tongue with a hard and angry voice. The two women made their way down the ladder, but Kaho seemed disturbed that the moment had been soured by them.

Teeka grasped the opportunity to tease, took him by both hands, and tugged him to his feet.

"Tomorrow's moon," she said, implying that she would leave and that they should wait to be together until the next night.

"Do not let them spoil this for you," he told her.

"But they are your wives. They have more of a place here with you than I."

"They are my wives only to satisfy a custom."

Teeka could see the worry on his face. He did not want her to leave. The aphrodisiacs had enhanced her desirability, and he could not resist her.

"I told you that I would teach you the ways of pleasure, and I will do so."

"Do you have a special place for us to be alone?"

"I know of a place. Not too far, but away from the village," Kaho said, leading her down the ladder and waving off the guards.

As they walked, Teeka remembered the night under the sky with Auro. The moonlight bounced off the amulet and into Teeka's eyes. Spontaneously she wrapped her slender fingers around it. Nothing would ever be like that for her again, but she would recall how it was and perform for Kaho as if he were Auro. She did not like the realization that her heart had softened toward this man who caused so many unwanted changes in her life, but she admitted that perhaps she would enjoy this night with

Kaho. Her body did hunger. That would make carrying out her plan a bit easier.

"Have you never loved a woman?" she asked as they walked. "Have you never lived your days to be with her, be near her, touch her, lie with her?"

"I have enjoyed the pleasures of many women. But I have never considered marriage other than to Rebet and Cala. It silenced the old ones, and they are good wives. They have produced many children from my seed."

Teeka stopped. "Something confuses me. You said that Rebet and Cala have produced many children from your seed. I do not understand what that means."

"Do you understand joining?" he asked as they again began to move along the path.

"I am confused. What does your seed have to do with Rebet and Cala having many children? The spirits give babies to women after they marry."

"Babies grow from the seed that a man spills during the joining. How do you know so much and so little at the same time?"

"Does a baby really grow from a man's seed?"

Teeka was astounded at the revelation. The milkweed potion could interfere with the woman's body accepting a baby, but she had always thought that the spirits made babies, and no woman could always control the ways of the spirits. That was the doing of the shaman.

"The spirits have to want the baby to grow inside the woman, but, Teeka, it is the man's seed that makes the baby begin to grow. Without joining there can be no baby."

"Then it takes both the spirits and the man?"

"Now you understand."

"How do I know that what you say is not just the belief of the Kahoosa? How do I know that it is so?"

"You have admitted that your people do not speak of these things, so how do you know that I am wrong?"

"I would have been told after I married."

"But you are not married, and I have told you so that you know. The Kahoosa do not have taboos like the Tegesta."

She could see in Kaho's face that he enjoyed revealing secrets about joining. It was his way to be the teacher.

At last they reached a clearing on the bank of a small tributary stream. He stood her next to the bubbling water and stepped back a moment, taking in all of her. He moved closer to the still and wide-eyed Teeka, loosening the vine belt, sliding her skirt down. Her body was perfect. Her bosom was not too big, and her hips were not too wide. He backed into the water and led her forward to meet him.

The effect of the drug was at its height as he disrobed. She stood waiting. She would not be aggressive this time. She would let him bathe her in his passion. She would be very responsive, and he would be successful in what he saw as his task.

The water rushed over their feet as Kaho reached for her and rested his hands on her warm, soft shoulders. The night wind carried the choral sounds of nature as he drew her to him. She could hear his breathing, deep and even, and her body yielded, giving up its stiffness to assume more pliant contours, melding to his. Every recess of his masculine body flooded with her flesh.

Teeka ran her hands up the sides of his thighs, beginning as low as she could reach, and then slithering upward, ending at his buttocks. She pulled him even closer to her. Kaho's knees went weak with the increased pressure of her hips. He wrapped his arms around her and lowered her to the ground.

He sat up, straddling her knees, watching, taking in all that his senses could hold as he touched each part of her. She raised her arms, encouraging him to lie atop her.

"In time," he told her. "Slowly. Very slowly."

Moving off her, he lay next to her, exploring her with his mouth and hands. Teeka's back arched as he teased near that part of her that ached to be touched and filled. She let him wander, nipping and stroking. She thrust her pelvis upward when he finally did touch her there. His strokes were light, driving her wild with frustration. She reached for his hand and pushed it down more firmly. A throaty sigh gushed from her, and then he moved over her, probing for entry. Gently, he found his way. She met him at each stroke, driving him deeper, swallowing all of him in the warm cavity that tightly embraced him. His pace accelerated until both of them gasped the last breath before the waves of orgasmic pleasure shook them.

Both lay heaving with exhaustion. A film of perspiration glossed their skin, making them shine in the moonlight. Kaho nuzzled beneath her chin, cushioning himself with her breasts. He started to move off her, but she held him tightly and began to move her hips ever so slightly.

"Again," she whispered.

With eyes closed she rose up to him, touching her lips to his and drawing small lines with her tongue across his mouth. At the same time she tightened and relaxed the muscles that held him within her, and she continued to move her hips in small circles.

She had allowed him no respite, and he found that he did not need it. What was it about this woman that made him insatiable? He was as hungry for her now as he had been a few moments before. Would he ever have enough of her?

Within minutes they were again at the door of ecstasy. He pumped into her, and she rose to each thrust, taking him, absorbing him, until nothing was left in the world except the pleasure that she brought him. Again he fell against her, drained and heaving for air.

"Was I better tonight?" she whispered breathlessly.

Kaho let his head drop back down on her chest as he breathed out a low sigh.

Teeka trailed her finger down his spine. "Will you stay with me for a while? I do not wish to go back to the guards. I want to be with the man who has shown me the Gift of joining."

Beneath his heavy body, she wondered about the wedding night. When she left him, what would he feel? Anger? Humiliation? Hurt? And what excuse would he make up to tell the rest of the Kahoosa? How would he explain why she had not returned with him?

She did not like to think about those things. They made her feel guilty and ashamed. She wondered if she could bring herself to carry it off. She even wondered if she really wanted to. She raised her hand to the back of his head and stroked his hair.

Kaho rolled to one side and rested her head against his shoulder. Teeka closed her eyes and drifted off to sleep as Kaho watched her. He was content and marveled at the woman who lay in his arms. There had never been a woman like this one, a woman who could take all that he could give, and then more. Lovemaking was instinctive to her.

The moonlight drenched the pendant, and its high luster shone brightly. Curiously he picked it up, but dropped it immediately, drawing back his hand. It was hot to the touch and burned his finger. That was more than strange. He had disliked that amulet the moment he saw it. How could she stand to let it touch her chest? Didn't it burn her? He would have to ask her about it. Kaho nudged her, making her awaken.

"We must go back now."

Teeka sighed and stood. He kept his arm about her shoulders as he walked her back to the village. She did not walk behind or in front. She walked next to him.

When they reached her shelter, he watched her climb the ladder. She never turned to look back at him. He poked one of the sleeping guards in the shoulder.

"Wake him," he said, pointing to the other guard. "How often must I tell you? Do not ever sleep when you watch her. I want her to go nowhere without you. Tell the others, when it is their duty, that I want her watched even more carefully than before."

Kaho's stride was full and intimated arrogance and pride, but anyone who saw his eyes would have known he was fighting an invisible net that tangled inside his head. His mind told him one thing, and his body contradicted it. He wanted Teeka near him. He wanted to have her again and again throughout the night. As soon as he thought his passion had abated, a new wave of insistent desire nearly drowned him.

Teeka had known the turmoil that was twisting inside him when she heard his feet meet the ground as he departed. He was like a blind warrior, not seeing the battle. It was all hidden and masked by the brush of physical needs. He did not even recognize the weapon.

Chapter Twenty-one

TEGES SMILED AT THE YOUNG MAN, Macota. He was happy to hear the request. Ever since Macota had brought Azlee and her family to the village, Teges had been watching them. Macota was certainly smitten by the maiden's almost childlike but alluring face and shapely body. She was young and could not have entered her first moon cycle very long ago. But then, Macota was not much older. For some, love happened early and quickly, he thought. For others, it came later. His own love and marriage had come early in his life. But sadly, before the seasons had had a chance to repeat themselves, Laxa, his beautiful bride, had crossed to the Other Side. She had not screamed or cried in the pain of childbirth. She had been brave to the end, finally delivering their lifeless son. And then she had breathed her last breath as he gently caressed her small cold hand. He had mourned, but now he remembered only the love they had shared. Over the many, many seasons he had found that he could not love another. He had had the love of his life even if it had been for such a short time. It pleased Teges to see that love alive in other young people.

Teges had found himself chuckling quietly as he watched Macota's pitiful attempts at courtship. The young man's tongue was often tied, it seemed. He stumbled over his words, his face became flushed, and his body grew weak, nearly causing him to swoon before her. But Azlee had not seemed to notice.

Young love was always refreshing to Teges. Macota's plea had been predictable. Teges, lost in his thoughts, hardly even heard him when he spoke.

"I wish to take the maiden Azlee," Macota repeated, awaiting Teges's response.

"Azlee. Yes, Azlee from the clan of the People whose village lies one day to the south," Teges finally answered.

"Yes, Cacique, that is correct."

Teges smiled at Macota. "She is young."

"I know that, Cacique. I am young also. Who can attempt to understand the decisions of the spirits? The Great One has put such love in my heart. I cannot deny it."

"And Azlee? Has the Great One put love in her heart for you—with the same fire, the same passion?"

Macota grinned. "Her heart is full, Cacique."

"A lifetime is a long time, and you are still young. Are you certain that you wish to spend the rest of your life with her? And is this what she wishes?"

"I would not have come to you if that was not our intention. After we become one, only the spirits will be able to separate us."

"I think your heart has guided you to the woman who will make your life full. I give my consent. Now you must take your request to Auro, the shaman. He will consult with the spirits to be sure that your guide spirits are compatible."

Teges did not miss Macota's anxiousness. The young man fidgeted, waiting to be dismissed. Again Teges smiled at him.

"Go, then," he said, dismissing him with a hand signal.

Macota backed away and then trotted off across the mound. Teges laughed softly, filled with the joy that he knew Macota and Azlee felt. This was one of the things that made him glad he was Cacique. It tempered all those less desirable responsibilities.

"Love is alive, Laxa, and I know you are here to feel the same joy," he whispered before pushing himself up with his walking stick.

It did not take long for Macota to reach Auro's hearth. No one saw much of the spirit man. Most of the time he stayed in his platform, taking advantage of the thatched sides of his shelter to hide and brood in its gloom, letting his mind be eaten away by his preoccupation with his misery.

"Auro? Shaman?" Macota called out.

There was no reply, but Macota could hear shuffling inside the platform.

"Shaman? Please come down. I have need of you."

Auro used a small piece of deer hide to wipe the beads of sweat from his forehead. His face was streaked with dirt that had settled in his perspiration, and his body reeked with the stench of uncleanliness. His muscles had lost their tone with lack of exercise, and his once clear brown skin was almost a pasty yellow. Dark moons circled his glassy eyes. His black hair was matted close to his head and had picked up small bits of leaves and other litter.

Who could be calling him? Who was the worm, the slug, who wished his favor? The last thing he had done for this clan of cowards was to warn them of the impending big storm. Later he had rebuilt his shelter with no help. Oh, they had offered to help, but he would not allow their filthy hands to touch it. What had they ever done for him? Nothing.

"Shaman, are you there?" Macota called again.

Auro walked to the head of the ladder, squinting in the brightness of the day. His head wobbled as he leaned against a post.

"What is it that you want?" he asked.

"Please come down. It is Macota, and I need to speak with you."

"You do not wish to speak. You have come to ask a favor of the shaman. Is that not so?"

"I have great respect for you, Shaman, and I want you to consult with the spirits."

Auro perked up at the small compliment and descended, finally stepping onto the ground and facing Macota.

"How do you want me to intervene for you?" he asked.

Macota was almost afraid to ask, but the request had to be made. Auro's apprentice, Olagale, was not ready, and Teges would not declare Olagale Shaman. Not yet, even though everyone realized that Auro was no longer himself. Teges had told the Council that the day would come. For now Macota had no choice. He would have to be careful of the way he worded things. For the marriage to take place, he needed Auro.

"Shaman," he began, lowering his head to display his respect. "You are from the pure line—the line of Tamuk and his father, and his father before him. And so I come to you with the greatest respect."

Macota looked up, quickly glancing at Auro's face. Some of the harsh lines had smoothed. He would continue in the same vein.

"Only you can speak with the spirits. I can pray to them, thank them, but only you can hear their voices so clearly. And only you can understand their messages. You are the link between the People and the spirits. That is why I am pleased to ask about a marriage, my marriage, to Azlee. I need you to ask the spirits if we are compatible." Macota swallowed hard, feeling his teeth bite the inside of his cheek with nervousness. "Will you do this for me?"

There was a moment of silence that made Macota feel disheartened. But then Auro spoke. "Give me the names of your guide spirits."

Macota fought the smile that would have told of his relief. "Tamuk gave me the guide spirit of the red-tailed hawk. Azlee's is the brown rabbit."

"Yes," Auro commented. "I see your spirit, Red-tailed Hawk. I will do this for you. Come again tomorrow, and I will give you an answer."

Macota thanked him and left. When he turned away, Macota closed his eyes in thankfulness. It could have gone badly, but it had gone well. He was forever indebted to the spirit that had helped him. Maybe Teges was right. Maybe the People should be patient with Auro.

Teges saw Macota stop and speak with Azlee. The maiden reminded him so much of his Laxa. She looked into Macota's eyes as he spoke, seeming to lose herself there. Gently he touched her cheek and then held her hand. Teges knew how they both must ache to hold each other and whisper wonderful things to each other in the night. He knew that Macota would give her the Gift gently and tenderly, teaching her the sweetness of the Joining Spirit. Without question, this union was meant to be; it was a marriage destined by the spirits.

Teges inferred that Auro had consented and had not given Macota a rough time. Perhaps Auro would heal. Though the Council had begged, in Auro's absence, to denounce Auro as the shaman, Teges had objected. He had agreed that Auro was unbalanced, that he was lost inside himself, but if his position was taken from him also, he would have no chance of recovery. Teges insisted that the spirits themselves would take care of the matter. They would not forsake the People, and it was not man's job to interfere with the work of the spirits. He directed the clan to be patient, to wait for the spirits to finish whatever had begun. Auro was more than just a man. He was a holy man, a man who dwelt with the spirits, and he should be left to the spirits. The Council finally backed down, but with strong reluctance.

———

By nightfall the clan members had finished their daily chores and settled onto their mats for sleep, but Auro was just about to begin his work. Often he found that he communicated with the spirits better during the darkness. Beside his fire he chanted softly until his body dripped with sweat from sitting so close to the hearth. This was part of his purification. He continued his song until his mouth was dry.

Auro lifted the bowl that held the potion he had prepared earlier. His father had taught him the ingredients and their measurements. At first, after his father's death, he had often heard Tamuk's voice in his head, directing him, helping him when he was called upon to perform the duties of a shaman. But as time passed, the guiding voice had gotten softer and softer. Now, tonight, there was no voice at all.

Auro poured the bitter liquid into his mouth and then swallowed. He could feel it slide warmly down his throat, and he sensed the heaviness of it as it reached his stomach. In a moment the purification would be complete, and he would be allowed into that other world.

The shaman walked into the brush and scratched a

small depression into the earth, and then the elixir gripped his stomach. Auro retched, ridding his body of all the remaining impurities.

Beside his fire again, he was prepared for what came next. His eyes rolled back as he fell backward. It began with only small tremors of his hands and feet but grew to violent quakes that seemed to batter his whole body. In a moment he went limp. The visions were blurred at first, just rapid and distorted images, but they soon cleared. He could now call upon the spirits.

When it was over, Auro was exhausted. It took much from a shaman to visit the spirit world. The spirits had confirmed that Red-tailed Hawk and Brown Rabbit were compatible spirits. He would tell Macota in the morning. But now he would sleep on the ground, not having enough energy to climb his ladder.

Auro dreamed. He saw Teeka stepping into Kaho's canoe, her back to the People. He was above the scene, looking down. He saw himself and he saw Ata take him by the arm to keep him still. Then there was darkness until another dream crept in.

He heard his father's warning: "Only the spirits from the Darkside answer such pleas. They will also collect a debt. Are you willing to sacrifice some part of her to pay the debt?" Tamuk's words were loud and echoed inside Auro's head.

His father's face floated in the dark clouds of the dream. "Auro," he called to his son, "I am with you."

Auro turned in his sleep as if trying to waken. "Do you hear me?" Tamuk asked, calling him back into his dream.

"I hear."

"My death was not all of the price that is to be paid. There is more."

"I have suffered enough, Father. Leave me."

"It is not you alone. Do you not understand that? You made Teeka a part of this. Did you not think that she would also suffer?"

"All I asked is that she love me forever."

"And what life did that leave her? You robbed her of her will. Her life is filled with the torment of her obsession with returning to you. That obsession will make it impossible for her ever to come home to stay. As I told you, there is always a trade-off. The Darkside will take something in return."

"They have already stripped me."

"They are not done, Auro."

Again Auro shifted. He wanted to leave the dream. These were not words he wanted to hear. Without opening his eyes, he was awake and thirsty. Sluggishly he climbed the ladder, sipped some water from a bowl, and then lay back on his mat. It would be morning soon. Maybe the dreams were over for the night.

But they were not over. This time he left his body and soared above the earth to the village of the Kahoosa. His spirit eye saw through the roof of Kaho's platform. He saw the naked king inside. Auro came closer. Kaho was moving, groaning, and beneath him was a woman writhing with pleasure. Kaho arched upward, throwing his head back and then letting his head fall forward onto the woman's heaving chest. The woman's face was covered with her hair as Kaho rolled off her. She reached up, brushing her hair back, sighing with the glow of satisfaction.

Auro sat straight up on his mat, awake. The woman was Teeka. He thought he was going to vomit. He pounded his fist into the floor of his platform and shouted.

Auro chose not to sleep. It was nearly dawn anyway.

He sat by his hearth drinking some tea that he brewed. He decided not to go and wash in the water. It was too much effort. He would clean himself some other time.

He watched the sun come up. It was going to be a clear day according to the early signs. Maybe in the afternoon there would be a brief thunderstorm. He tried to think about other uncomplicated things, but the vision of Kaho joining with Teeka kept flashing before him, and in the background was his father's voice telling him about the price to be paid.

Auro put his hands to his temples, holding his head as if it might explode. He squeezed hard, trying to rid himself of the images that haunted him.

Macota stood nearby, hesitating to encroach. Perhaps he should wait until later. He started to walk away.

Auro suddenly let go of his head, looking across the village, trying to orient himself. He saw Macota turning away.

"Macota," he called in a scratchy voice.

Macota stopped and looked back.

"Come, Red-tailed Hawk. I have an answer for you."

The young man stood still, afraid to move.

"Come, I said. Come closer so that I may speak to you," Auro said.

Macota began to walk slowly toward the shaman. A few others watched from the distance. They had heard Auro call out to him and were curious.

"That is better," Auro announced as Macota stood in front of him. "Now sit."

Auro paused, waiting for the man to comply. "I spent the night in the spirit world," he whispered. Macota strained to hear him. "I went there for you."

"I thank you, Shaman," Macota said in normal volume, hoping that Auro's bizarre whispering would stop.

"I told them of the marriage request. I told them I spoke of Red-tailed Hawk and Brown Rabbit," Auro continued to whisper.

Macota was uncomfortable. "Have you had your morning meal, Shaman?" Macota asked. "Why do you not let me get you something to eat and we can discuss this later?"

"No!" Auro shouted, grabbing Macota's arm as he started to stand. "You must hear this now," he muttered again.

Macota sat back down. He wished Teges could see how peculiarly Auro was behaving. Macota did not want to hear the shaman's answer from the spirits. He was certain that Auro was demented, and anything he said would come from his insane mind.

"I went to them on your behalf," Auro reiterated. "I asked for their favor, but, Macota, they would not agree. The spirit of the Red-tailed Hawk and the Brown Rabbit are not compatible. I am sorry."

Macota could not believe what he was hearing. "I am also sorry, Shaman, but I do not believe you. I think you have lost your way, and because you cannot have happiness you do not want anyone else to be happy. You are stuck inside, in your misery. Azlee and I will not be part of it."

Macota stood and left, stepping hard on the earth with his anger. He walked straight to Teges.

"I have been to see Auro. He consulted the spirits last night."

Teges expected good news. "When will the wedding be?"

"There will be no wedding. Not here in this village. Auro says that the spirits told him we are not compatible.

He speaks in whispers. He is unclean and he stinks. I refuse to take his word."

Teges was still in shock. This was unbelievable. In many generations there had been very few spirit denials. And those few had been justified. "I will speak to him," Teges said. "I will have him set this straight."

"Do not bother, Cacique. I would not have him call the spirits for our wedding anyway. I am going to take Azlee and her family back to her clan. They have a shaman. He is not of the pure line, but he can consult with the spirits, just as Auro does. He can also call them to a wedding."

"But that shaman is sure to ask why you have returned. He will not interfere with Auro's decisions."

"The word about Auro has reached all the clans of the Tegesta. Everyone knows he is deranged. I will have no problem."

Teges looked sad. "You will do what you must."

"I have great respect and admiration for you, Cacique, and for the line from which Auro came. But I will not let him destroy my chance at happiness."

"Of course not," Teges answered. "When all this tragic dust has settled back onto the earth, when the spirits resolve this, I hope you will come back to the clan of Teges and make your home with us again."

"When the dust falls on the earth."

Macota walked away, and Teges felt his heart wrench. He had been right when he had told Teeka to accept what the spirits had decided for her. He hoped that she would let Auro's memory slip from her heart because the man she missed and loved truly was only a memory.

Chapter Twenty-two

KAHO CAME TO TEEKA as she sat sorting plants with Tosa.

"Leave us," he ordered Tosa.

Tosa quickly stuffed the plants into her baskets, mixing those she had taken so long to sort and categorize.

Kaho grew impatient. "Leave it!"

Tosa dropped a handful of leaves and backed to the head of the ladder. She nodded good-bye to Teeka and sank from sight.

"What makes Kaho so short-tempered this day?" Teeka asked.

"I have not decided if I should take you as a wife. The trials must continue so that I can make my decision."

"Why do you rush? I go nowhere. Maybe you will decide that I am not suitable. I do not press you."

"You press me without knowing."

"I am here for you when you want me."

"But the trials must continue. I cannot make a decision without all the proper trials."

"What is it that you wish?"

Her patience and unconcern further snarled his emotions and drew telltale lines on his face.

"I will come for you this night," he said, turning and leaving.

Teeka curled herself over her knees as she sat and faced him. Her smile was faint and intoxicating.

———

Kaho came for Teeka that night and every night thereafter. She had become a narcotic that he craved and could not do without.

Rebet had come less often for lessons since she found Teeka in Kaho's arms. The situation was too awkward for her. She liked Teeka, and she really did not love Kaho, but every time she saw Teeka, she was reminded of that scene. It made her uncomfortable and uneasy with Teeka. It was something she should not have witnessed. Cala had taken it better. It had not seemed to disturb her.

Kuta continued to stare at Teeka whenever she was in sight. There were nights when she could hear his voice near her platform, and she was certain that she had seen him on several occasions.

One evening, as Kaho covered her tingling body with hot kisses, he stopped suddenly and went to the door of his platform.

Teeka grabbed a blanket made from rabbit fur and bundled herself in it.

"Who is there?" he called.

"What did you hear?" she asked.

Kaho stood silently, looking out into the night. Moments later he walked back to her side and stretched out beside her.

"I thought I heard a noise. It sounded like Kuta."

"Kuta?"

"I could barely hear it, but I thought it was his voice whispering something, almost like a chant."

Kaho soon put the incident out of his mind, but Teeka could not. As he walked her back to her platform, she scanned the shadows. *Kuta is there, hiding and watching,* she thought.

She greeted the guards who stood at the base of her platform. She was actually glad they were there.

At the last moment, before Kaho left, she called out to him.

He quickly turned, waiting for her to speak, but she did not.

"Nothing," she finally said.

She could not tell him that Kuta wanted to be rid of her. She could not cause discord. Her task was to win Kaho's heart and the affection of the Kahoosa. This was something she would need to take care of herself.

The bright sphere of silver light had finally entered the cycle during which it exposed all of itself. Teeka's belly cramped. It was time for her moon cycle.

Kuta constantly followed her, gave her evil looks, and whispered things under his breath. One morning he had even dared to stop her as she walked to the water.

"You are not wanted here," he said, clenching his teeth and talking so quietly that no one else could hear.

"You are the shaman, Kuta. I do not want to take that away from you. Why do you do this to me?"

Kuta turned on his heel and left, mumbling.

Teeka decided that she had to speak with him, to win his favor. But Kaho and the rest could not know it. That would invite too many questions and bring an open rift. She had to confront the spirit man and end his jealousy before he spoiled everything. Kaho had to make her his bride—take her to the wedding bed. Only then could she leave. To save himself from the humiliation of his bride fleeing the wedding bed, Kaho would have to make up an excuse about her disappearance—some tragic tale of her death. There no time to waste. Every day Kuta threatened her plan.

Teeka felt the cramp again. Her moon cycle was coming. The timing was perfect. She would see Kuta while in isolation. No one would ever know.

She began to pack some of her things in her basket and then stood holding the pendant, deep in thought. With precision she selected a few leaves, flower petals, and roots, placed them in the bottom of her basket, and covered them with the other articles.

At the base of the ladder she hesitated. Should she tell Kaho? No, he would be informed soon enough. The guards followed her across the mound and up the edge of the burial mound to the isolation shelter. Pansar was there, but she offered Teeka no greeting.

Teeka set up her area with the comforts that she had brought. At midday she walked to the stream and filled a bowl with water. There were no provisions for fire in the isolation, so the sun would have to do the brewing. From the pouch she carried at her side, she withdrew a handful of plant parts and sprinkled them into the bowl of water. Pansar's watchful eye prevented her from carefully measuring each component, but the mixture would be good enough.

With the bowl hidden at her side, she walked into the bushes, as if she were going to relieve herself. In the center of a patch of grass, she placed the bowl in a position that the shadows did not hover over. The heat of the sun would brew the tea she would use on this night.

She reappeared from the brush, smoothing her skirt as if she had used the area as it was intended. It was time to begin.

"Teeka," she said, pointing to herself.

One of the young sentries seemed flattered and was anxious to relay his name.

"Geros," he said.elbowing the other guard, to prompt his response.

"Melet," he answered, a little less vigorously.

She batted her eyelashes slowly and then signed "strong man" at Geros, whom she judged more vulnerable.

The words that Tosa had taught her were enough to convey her messages. Combined with universal signs, she could talk with him. There was even an advantage in her lack of fluency.

Geros flexed his muscle. "Hunter," he said.

She reached for his burgeoning biceps. "Good hunter, very strong," she said in a voice that made her seem impressed by his boyish display.

She turned her attention to the less interested sentry and touched Melet's shoulder, following the outline of his muscle.

"Very strong and brave," she cooed.

Melet showed a bit more interest with the personal attention. She began to walk away, but knew and used the motions of her body that would hold their attention. She would be the subject of their conversation the rest of the day. They could not have any intimate contact with a menstruating woman, but she could taunt and tease their imaginations.

Late in the day she returned to the grasses that hid her secret. She swirled the sun-warmed liquid with her finger, stirring all the leached herbs to the top. With her hand cupped, she scooped the residue from the top and discarded it. Then she carried the bowl out in full view of the sentinels.

"What do you carry?" Melet asked.

She understood but pretended not to. She stopped and faced the interrogator, cocked her head, and looked questioningly at him.

Melet touched the bowl. "What is this?" he asked again.

"Tea. Good Tegesta tea," she said, holding it to his nose to whiff.

The tea had a bouquet that was as soporific as its contents truly were. After he had sniffed it to his satisfaction, she took it away, stirred it with her finger, and then traced the liquid that remained on her finger over her lips.

"Good tea," she said somewhat huskily and moved away.

She would wait until nightfall. If Kaho's pattern remained unchanged, these two new young sentinels would be with her through the night. The older ones he changed more often, but youth had to be tried for endurance and stamina. Kaho tested everyone.

Pansar stretched out on her mat and napped. Teeka moved to the side of the platform and dangled her legs over it, attracting the attention of the young men who watched her. Slowly she pulled her hair away and romanced them with her coquettish smile.

The sun continued to hide itself beneath the cypress that pricked the sky of the western horizon. The last of the orange clouds drained of color just after her evening meal arrived. She put the food aside, too nervous to eat.

In the darkness, Teeka reclined on her mat, waiting for Pansar to sleep. When she could hear Pansar's slumbering breaths, she sat up, the pendant warm in her hands. She stood and paced, waiting for the fires of the village to burn out. She was like a cat, taut and sleek. She padded back and forth liquidly as if she had melted into the night.

The last fire seemed to die, and Teeka looked over the edge of the platform at Geros and Melet. They could not come to her; it was forbidden for men to encroach on this unclean place, but she could go to them. In her hands she carried the bowl of tea. She was more than a silhouette on this brightly lit night. It was apparent from her gait that she was not attempting to escape. Both men relaxed into friendlier postures.

She stood directly in front of them. "No sleep," she said, hoping they understood her broken Kahoosa. "Lonely," she signed.

The two men looked around and, seeing no one, invited her to stay.

Again Teeka flattered the two, calling them strong and brave. Deliberately she touched each of them ever so delicately, admiring their muscles. Then she held the bowl to her lips, pretending to drink some of her tea. She held it out and offered a drink to Geros. He accepted.

Melet was next to ingest the drug. She relaxed even more, the hardest part done.

They continued with their trivial attempts at conversing. Geros was the first to show the effects, swaying slightly on his feet. He sat down on the ground, bracing himself with his hands so that he sat erect. Melet also sat, listing to one side. Teeka watched the signs and offered them another drink.

When the bowl was empty, she bade them good night and returned to the platform.

She waited a little while longer, fidgeting with anticipation. She could not be too quick. Again she paced, wringing her sweaty hands. Finally, when she could wait no longer, she climbed down and soaked up the direct moonlight. She walked past the two sleeping guards. The drug would keep them deep in sleep until the morning.

She crept silently across the ground. At the far end of the village, Kuta's platform stood alone. She had not seen it before, never having had a reason to go so far in that direction. A fog hovered around it, almost seeming to weave in and out of the thatch. Teeka stopped and looked at it. She shuddered. Maybe this was not such a good idea, she thought.

She grasped the pendant, as if asking for strength from it. She scraped her bottom lip against her top teeth, and then took a deep breath. She had to settle this with Kuta.

Slowly she approached the base of Kuta's platform. The crickets and frogs seemed to roar in her ears as she filled with fear. Just as she opened her mouth to call up to him, a deep voice called to her from behind.

"What have you come for?"

It was Kuta, his face twisted with anger.

"I need to talk to you—to end this distrust between us."

"There is no distrust you can end. You are not wanted here. I have warned Kaho. He does not know the things that I know and is easily fooled by a woman who knows how to use her body to get what she wants."

The description of her tore at her heart with the truth. Kuta was right about some things. But she was no threat to him. She wanted to leave as much as he wanted her gone.

"Do you not think I would leave if I could?"

"You will not leave until you have ruined me in the eyes of the Kahoosa. And you will take our cacique, also."

"What is the matter with you? I do not want anything from any of you. Why can you not understand that?"

Kuta began to chant, ignoring her.

"Listen to me," she said again. "Hear me."

But the shaman continued as if she were not there. He sang softly, shaking his rattle. The deer hooves at the end of his stick clacked together, and the shells that dangled from it hit one another in rhythm with the old man's chant.

"Kuta. Please!"

But the medicine man was not to be interrupted. He was alone in his other world, undistracted and determined.

Teeka gave up, now even more frightened of what he might do. He would never let her have Kaho. He would keep the distrust alive in all the Kahoosa.

When she finally reached the platform, she was sobbing. Kuta had it all wrong. She was out to discredit neither him nor his medicine, but still he was going to ruin everything.

Teeka reclined on her mat. Her belly still ached. She had come to the platform too soon, too anxious to have the chance to talk to Kuta. The bleeding had not started yet. Soon enough.

By the end of the fifth day Teeka had done a lot of thinking. Her cycle had still not come, but she expected it any time. She would have to leave anyway and hope that she would skip this moon cycle or that she would be able to stay away from Kaho when it did come. It would be difficult for her to explain why she had stayed these five days. If only her body would cooperate with the cycles of the moon. Would she never adjust to her new life? she wondered.

She had decided that if Kuta went to Kaho about their meeting, she would deny it. No one else had seen her. The guards had slept through, but they would never admit it. They would declare that they had watched her all the night.

She was safe.

When she left the platform, no one was there to meet her. She walked to the circle and, with no complicating thoughts, performed the purification ritual with the ease of a Kahoosa woman. Then she walked directly to the hearth of the king.

Kaho stood when he saw her approaching and dismissed Kuta with a simple wave of the hand. Kuta hunched over, walked away, and scowled at her.

She did not dare hesitate in her steps for fear that Kaho would know there was truth in whatever Kuta had been telling him. She walked straight and directly.

Teeka laid her basket at Kaho's feet, reached for his face, and ran her fingers across his cheek.

"I have missed you."

Kaho stepped back.

"What makes you shrink from me? Have I offended you with my boldness?" she asked.

"Kuta warns me that you possess evil spirits. He says you wish to destroy us both. He still blames you for Wintu's death."

"I did not come here. You brought me here. Kuta is foolish and frightened. If you think it is so, why do you not send me away and end your trouble?"

Teeka turned away from him, waiting for his response. She felt his hand on her shoulder, encouraging her to face him.

"I think my trouble would increase if I sent you away. I believe as you do that Kuta is old and frightened. Let him shake his rattles and call to the spirits for an answer."

Teeka smiled at him and again touched his cheek.

"Let us begin again," she said. "I have missed you."

"Come with me," he said. "I wish to show you something."

She followed Kaho up the ladder of his platform. When she reached the top, her eyes widened at what she saw.

234

Chapter Twenty-three

ALL OF TEEKA'S THINGS had been placed neatly around Kaho's large platform.

"Does this not please you?" he asked, seeing her face.

"But I do not understand."

"I do not want to have to go and seek you when I want you near. The trials cannot be completed that way."

"But even Cala and Rebet do not live at your hearth, and they are your wives. Will this not anger them and the others?"

"The king of the Kahoosa may do as he chooses without consulting his wives. This is what I choose."

"Then I am pleased," she said, smiling.

Kaho reached for her and pulled her close to him.

"The Kahoosa do not accept outsiders easily. It does not upset them for their king to have a woman from another tribe, but marriage is sacred. It comes from the spirits. Time will help them to accept the idea."

"But I am Tegesta, and I know how your people feel about my tribe. They may never accept me, and they may poison your mind toward me. Kuta has already tried. Of that I am afraid. If you are displeased with me—"

"No one makes decisions for me."

"Then if you wish me to stay, I will. But I do not know what you expect of me. Do I perform the chores of a wife?"

"There is only one duty of a wife that I ask of you."

Teeka ran her hand down his chest and feathered her fingers on his bare stomach.

"That is not a duty. It is my pleasure."

Kaho smiled at the only woman he had ever known to find as much excitement in joining as he did. He desired her right now, but he had many things to attend to this day, and she would be here for him later.

———

After he left, Teeka gathered a few of her plants in a basket and went to the fire of Tosa.

"Do you wish a lesson?" she said, catching Tosa by surprise.

"I did not see you coming," she said, startled by her friend's appearance.

"Kaho has put my things at his fire," Teeka said, almost nonchalantly.

Tosa looked up, uncertain that she had heard correctly. "What?"

"Kaho has taken my things to his fire," Teeka repeated.

Tosa looked back in the basket, fingering some of the contents before she spoke. "All of your things?"

"All but my mat."

"Does this make Teeka happy?"

Teeka touched her heart and signed love.

"What of the Tegesta man?" Tosa asked, looking down again.

"He is a dream from my past."

"Kaho has never had anyone live at his fire. Has he told you that you will be his bride?"

"He wishes to finish the trials first."

236

"Perhaps his heart reaches out for the first time."

"Perhaps," Teeka said, hoping the seed of the falsehood had fallen on fertile ground.

"Follow your heart, Teeka, but do not let yourself be fooled. His is a wrath like no other's."

"I wish to please him with all that I do, but I do not think that the Kahoosa will permit the marriage."

"Kaho has broken many customs," Tosa quickly replied. "He will do as he wants."

"What will your people think when they see that I live with Kaho?"

"It may anger them at first that he has chosen a Tegesta. They do not know you as I do. He has taken other Tegesta women from other villages, but no one has lived at his fire."

"This will be a difficult time for us."

"The trials are no longer to see if you suit him. The trials are to test the Kahoosa."

The lesson was short. Teeka described the qualities of the dually common plants. There were slight differences in their preparations, but basically the uses were the same.

Teeka lived at Kaho's hearth. The moon turned in the sky. The trials continued.

During one of the lessons with Tosa, Teeka's stomach rumbled, and a wave of nausea overtook her. Her face grew pale.

"Can we stop the lesson for today?"

"Have I said something that upsets you?"

"No, no. There is just so much strain. Perhaps it is something that I ate."

Teeka picked up her basket and walked back to her home. Her stomach continued churning until she knew that she was going to vomit. She ran out into the wild, bent forward, and retched until tears ran from her eyes.

Finally she stopped and sat down, rubbing her face with her hands.

Her guards stood back and turned their faces away. No matter how closely they were to watch her, they did not need to subject themselves to watching her vomit.

She walked more slowly than she had before, and the climb up the ladder taxed her. Her skin was clammy, and the bitter taste left in her mouth made her feel even worse. Teeka reached for the pendant. She could not get sick now. There was too much to do.

The nausea left as abruptly as it had come. The perspiration that collected on her skin began its cooling work as the breeze filtered through the platform.

"What is wrong?" Kaho's voice rang out from the top of the ladder.

"I must have eaten something that did not settle well."

He walked closer to her and touched her skin.

"There is no fire in your skin. It is cool, but I will send for Kuta."

"No, do not send for him. The nausea has passed. I feel fine."

"I will be leaving, and I want Kuta to attend to you in case you are becoming ill."

Teeka looked up sharply. "Leaving? Where are you going?"

"We are going to hunt. I will not be gone long."

"Do you go to hunt the bear?"

"We go to hunt for food, but I will find her."

"You must be careful. She is angry and will know that you have come."

"She will not have two chances at me. If the spirits had intended for her to have me, it would have been done."

"Must you go? Can you not stay here with me?"

"We need more food. Our supply is low. And there are young men who need the opportunity to learn the ways of cooperative hunting. Most of the men, except the old ones and Kuta, will be going."

"How long will you be away from me?"

"Only the passing of two moons—a day to travel, a day to hunt, and a day to return."

"I will think of you all the time you are gone."

"Tonight we will be together," he said, touching her breast.

"Must we wait for the darkness?" she asked, holding his hand to her.

"You are a woman who keeps my attention, but there are many preparations that must be made today if we are to leave in the morning," Kaho said, walking over to his cache of weapons. "The hunters are waiting for me so that we can discuss our plans."

Teeka stood and followed him to the corner.

"There is enough time," she said, stroking his legs. "There is nothing that cannot wait a little longer."

She knelt and touched her lips to his thighs. Her hands wandered, finding those places that excited him.

"They await me," he weakly protested.

"Shh," she said, putting her hand over his mouth.

Kaho went down on his knees and put his arms around her, pulling her on top of him. His hands flew over her back and body, trying to feel all of her at once.

The weight and magnetism of her body against his was suddenly gone. She moved as if borne on the air. Kaho stared with glazed eyes, feeling as if he were rummaging through some strange and erotic dream.

In the shadows of the platform, she beckoned for him to come to the bed. When he was close enough, she reached out and touched him. Her touch was magical, the essence of a man's imagination. She urged him beneath her. He was a willing subject, letting her work her miracles on him. She was giving him the Gift, asking nothing in return.

She sat astride him, her hair falling against his chest. When she moaned with pleasure, he exploded inside her.

He lay beneath her, still breathing hard from the exquisite ecstasy that only this woman could bring him. Voices from beneath the platform shattered the moment. The word had spread rapidly that Teeka now lived at the king's hearth. The people were not happy, and his delay only aggravated them. The Council of men waited for him. There was much to be done, and their leader had been distracted by a Tegesta woman.

Kaho finally rose from her, called by the disharmony that festered outside. Teeka stood next to him, wrapping her arms around him.

"Go now. Your people need you."

He nodded, and she nuzzled her face in his neck, tickling his ear with her tongue.

"The night will not be long enough," she whispered.

By evening, the ceremonies that attended the hunt had begun. Teeka was not permitted to take part, but she watched, standing on the platform.

Kuta wore a carved wooden mask strapped to his head with leather thongs. It was a fierce mask, with shell eyes and feathers cresting the top. Most of the hunters held wooden staffs topped with intricately carved animal heads.

All of the hunters were painted with the pigments of different berries. The tattooed Kaho stood in the center, chanting hunting songs that spurred the excitement of the others. The ceremony was much more elaborate, in both sound and color, than that of the Tegesta.

After watching for a while, Teeka began to feel tired. The sickness that had assaulted her earlier had sapped her strength and energy. She moved to the mat and lay down, listening to the hypnotic voices of the throng. She hoped her cycle would come while Kaho was gone. It would make things so much easier.

Her mind wandered until it found its way into sleep. The voices were the lullaby that sang to her of more time alone to rest. She did not hear when they ended, nor was she aware when Kaho lay down next to her. It took his touching and stroking to awaken her.

Kaho was awake when the sun rose. "I have released the guards," he whispered in her ear as he got ready to leave.

She opened her eyes and pulled his face to hers, touching her lips to his.

"You are testing me, but you must know that the guards will not be needed. I will be here waiting for you when you return," she told him.

He bent closer, feeling the warmth of her sleepy body.

"I would stay longer, but the hunters gather already."

"Bring me the head of the bear that almost took you from me."

She watched him walk to the ladder. He was full of pride, and for an instant Teeka felt a pang of —love?

———

She did not open her eyes again until she heard Tosa calling her. Slowly she went to the top of the ladder and looked down.

"What is it, Tosa?"

"Do you know how late it is? I was worried."

Teeka looked at the sky, judging the time of day by the position of the sun. It was indeed late. "I have slept too long."

"May I visit you?"

All she wanted to do was go back to sleep, but she allowed Tosa to come up.

Tosa held her palm in front of her own face and lowered her hand, asking Teeka why she looked so bad.

"I was not feeling well yesterday, but I am better today."

"Let me get you something to eat."

The thought made Teeka's face drain of color. "I do not have an appetite. Maybe later."

Tosa looked at her, thinking. "What has made you ill?"

"It must have been something I ate. Kaho said there was no fire in my body."

Tosa put her hand on Teeka's forehead. Still unsatisfied, she touched her mouth to Teeka's forehead.

"He is right. There is no fire. Your skin is cool, but you sweat."

"So you see, there is nothing seriously wrong."

"I am not so sure. Have you ever been sick like this before?"

"No. Never. I am strong. This will not last long."

"Are your breasts tender?"

Teeka glared at Tosa for asking such a personal question.

"Are they?" Tosa asked again.

"Yes, but they always—"

"Teeka, why did you go to the isolation when it was not your time?" she asked bluntly. "You have not had your cycle. Is that not the truth?"

"Tosa, what would make you say such a thing?"

"Because you have been with Kaho. Your cycle has not come because you have a baby inside you."

Teeka jumped to her feet. "No, that cannot be."

"It can be, unless Tegesta babies come from somewhere else."

What if Kaho and Tosa were right? What if babies did start from the joining? But she had no husband—this had to be impossible.

"The spirits would not permit it without a husband," she said, feeling better.

"But you have been with Kaho as though there were a marriage. You have joined, and so in the eyes of the spirits you are married."

Teeka sat and put both hands over her face.

"What will I do? What will I do?"

"You will tell Kaho. He should know."

"No. Not yet. I need to be accepted by your people first. Then I will tell him. Will you help me, Tosa?"

"I will introduce you to the women now; while the men are gone."

Teeka evaluated Tosa's suggestion and decided it was a good strategy. "Let me freshen up first. I will come for you when I am finished."

Tosa left, and Teeka sat in the middle of the floor staring into the distance. She had never considered this possibility. What would Auro think when she returned to him? The Tegesta would never forgive her. They would not understand what she had had to do in order to be free. They knew only the way of the Tegesta. They would not understand.

There was a medicine that might bring on her cycle, but it was dangerous. If she did carry a baby, the potion could kill them both.

One step at a time, she decided as she finished preparing herself to meet the women of the village. She had taken herself this far. She would finish and then worry about the Tegesta.

Her stomach had settled by the time she reached Tosa's.

"Are you ready?" Tosa asked her.

"I have done all that I can do."

"Then the first place I will take you is to the fire of Liset. She has many friends, and the women listen to her. It is a good place to start."

"I am ready," Teeka said, holding the pendant tightly in her hand.

―――

Tosa had made a good decision. Teeka was difficult not to like. She was unassuming, pretty to look at, very sincere, and a curiosity. By the end of the day, Liset and most of the women of the village were talking about how wonderfully nice the Tegesta woman was—all except Pansar, who waved her off when Tosa took Teeka to her platform.

―――

Both Teeka and Tosa missed the evening meal. Teeka could not eat at the central hearth, and Tosa was enjoying her company too much to leave her. Instead, they ate the last of Tosa's coontie bread and talked of all the women Teeka had met that day.

Tosa suddenly changed the subject. "Have you decided to tell Kaho when he returns?"

"In time. We must adjust to each other first. When the time is right, I will tell him."

"Why did you go to the isolation if it was not your cycle?" Tosa asked.

Teeka looked at her with eyes that begged.

"As I have said before, do not ask too many questions about me. I tell you this because you are my friend."

She said no more and left, with Tosa watching the apparition of a woman disappear into the dusk. There was a part of Teeka that she knew well and a part that she knew nothing of, and she suspected that if she did, it would sadden her.

Chapter Twenty-four

THE DAY HAD BEEN PRODUCTIVE. She had met many of the women, and whether or not the men believed it, the women did influence them. The men made the obvious decisions, but the women talked to them alone in the night.

The next morning her stomach rebelled again, and she refused the food that Tosa offered her. Now that she knew the problem, she knew the solution. She gathered some herbs that would settle her stomach, and she prepared the elixir. She had much more work to do before the men returned.

She roamed through the village with Tosa, greeting the women. She divulged more of the intimacies that confirmed that she loved their king. When their husbands, sons, and brothers returned, there would be gentle talk. Liset would probably be the first to initiate such a conversation.

Pansar and Kuta worried her. They stared at her when she passed by. Pansar was just disagreeable, but Kuta sneered and spread bad thoughts and doubt. Because he was the shaman, people would listen to him.

When the others gathered at the central hearth for the evening meal, Teeka sat alone at her fire. The smoke from the spoked hearth curled into the air, and the laughter of those who sat by it seemed more distant than it was.

When she had finished her meal, she rinsed the bowls and threw the waste into the fire. She would sleep early tonight, she thought.

The moon was rising in the sky. Each night it grew smaller and smaller, marking the time. She stood, fascinated by the celestial body as she combed the tangles from her hair with her fingers. Sleepily, she climbed into the shelter. Her back was to the ladder, so she could not see it, but she heard hands grasping the rungs and feet advancing up the ladder.

She turned swiftly to see the head of Kuta emerging over the edge of the platform. As his whole body rose up, she could see that he was dressed in a ceremonial costume. His head was banded with quills from the eagle, and he wore a cloak of bearskin. In one hand he carried a small lance that dripped with feathers, and he wore a necklace of antler tips and a vest of shell beads. In his other hand he carried a rattle.

Teeka's stomach balled into a sick knot. "What makes Kuta visit this woman in Kaho's absence?" she asked, hoping to intimidate him.

"Who is this woman?" he said, stepping closer with a handful of sacred objects.

"You know who this woman is. I am Teeka, woman of your cacique."

"But who is the spirit of Teeka?"

"My guide spirit is that of Little Doe. Why do you come to ask as the moon rises in the evening sky?"

"I do not see the spirit that you tell me. I see something else. The pendant you wear has been touched by something black and foul."

She grabbed at the columella amulet. She did not want to hear this. "Stop it," she cried. "This is a gift of love, no more."

"There is no love in that pendant."

"Then your magic is weak, and you cannot see things for what they are."

"I have come to rid the Kahoosa of a woman controlled by the Darkside."

"Do I really look so threatening?" she asked, still not believing the shaman's unbending convictions.

"It is not the body that a shaman sees."

"Tamuk, who is a most powerful shaman, gave me my guide spirit. Do you challenge his magic?"

"I have heard that Tamuk is dead. Is that not so?"

"Why do you not ask the spirits of the Kahoosa, if they see all?"

Kuta propped his lance against the wall of the platform and flicked water from a pouch, spraying her.

"What is this that you do?" she asked angrily.

He began to chant and call out the names of different spirits. As he walked around her, chanting, he came closer, drawing the circle tighter and tighter. The powder he sprinkled as he walked seemed to confine her to the center of the circle that he paced. Suddenly she felt trapped, and her body tensed. Still clutching the pendant, she turned in circles, following him with her eyes. She tried to speak, but when she opened her mouth, there was no sound.

Kuta stopped and looked. He had her confined. His magic was strong. He reached inside the circle, a sharp knife in the palm of his hand. Kuta severed the leather necklace that held the pendant and jerked it free.

The columella hit the planks and skittered outside the powder circle.

"Please, Kuta," she screamed. "What are you doing? It is nothing but a necklace."

Kuta's hands trembled, and he began to shake the carved wooden rattle that was shaped like the head of a hawk.

Teeka bent forward, reaching out, but her hands could not pass over the circle.

"Give it back to me," she pleaded.

Again he pitched droplets of that liquid at her. It sizzled on her skin. She wiped at her burning eyes, trying to protect her face from him. But no matter which way she turned, he was there. His rattles and chants grew louder and louder, his voice pealing, hurting her ears.

She turned and turned, spinning in circles.

Faster!

Covering her ears!

Swatting at the spray!

Falling to the floor!

Giving up!

Crying!

"No...no ...no."

Dizziness.

Blackness.

———

She was stiff and sore as she began to awaken. She had slept on the floor, and there was a trace of some type of powdery circle around her. The last she remembered was Kuta splashing some hideous liquid on her that burned her skin. She sat up, finding that her body reeked of old perspiration, and her hair was matted. Crawling on her hands and knees, she brushed away the fine white grains on the floor. The circle confined her no more.

Teeka crawled outside the circle and picked up the pendant. She propped herself against the wall of the platform, squeezing the necklace in her hands.

"Kaho!" she cried.

Stunned that she had not called for Auro, she let her head droop, and she began to sob.

"Auro," she cried angrily, "why have you let this happen to me?"

She was tired of the planning and plotting. She was not the same person she had been when she was brought here. She had compromised the values of the People. The spirits did not even see her anymore, or else they ignored her. She was exhausted from the fight—the constant lie. She wanted to let it all go.

She remembered her dream and how Auro had stood on the bank, not rescuing her. Now the dream at last made sense. The alligator was Auro, and Tamuk had tried to stop him. What Auro had done had led to Tamuk's death, and she was being swallowed by the same thing. The Auro she saw on the bank was the real man, the one who had made her sacrifice herself for him. He had no intent to rescue her from the water in the dream. The water was his magic, and he wanted her to drown in it.

There was nothing to go home to. Teges was right. Auro was from a past she could never reclaim. She remembered him tying the amulet around her neck and making her promise. She had loved him with all her heart. Why had he done this to her? Why was the love she gave him not enough? If he had loved her, how could he have stolen her life, her will, her chance to be happy?

In anger, she hurled the amulet across the room, watching it hit the opposite wall and bounce off onto the floor.

"Always!" she screamed.

Teeka covered her face with her hands, whimpering, crying, weeping loudly, finally venting all the fear, resentment, betrayal, and depression she had felt for so many passing moons.

Later, she gathered her things, tied the necklace, and put it over her head. The bond between Teeka and Auro was not something she could sever on her own. She was a woman of honor and she had made a commitment. But he did have the power to end the relationship, to set her free, and she would deal with that. Now she knew where she belonged. She was Kaho's woman. She was amazed at all the revelations she had had since last night's moon. Now her direction was guided by a different force—her own. Her heart belonged to her, and she was free to give it. She was no longer trapped or held against her will. She was where she wanted to be.

It was not that she had forgotten the People. The Tegesta were still very much a part of her, but now so were the Kahoosa. The spirits did things according to their plan, and she was an instrument they were using. She saw that clearly now. There was something much bigger going on, and she was to be a part of it. Because she was Tegesta, she understood the implications of the People's visit to the village of the Kahoosa. She was here to nurture the seed they had planted.

It had been a long, long time since she had felt so good. Her thoughts were clear, not confused, not complicated. She walked to the water to cleanse herself. Many of the women had already gathered there for their morning ritual. She separated herself from the rest, not wanting to engage in trivial conversation.

——

Teeka looked into the water, amused at what she saw. The face was the same, but the innocence of her youth was completely gone. She studied the face, trying to decide if she liked it or not.

She entwined flowers in her clean hair, and perfumed herself with the light fragrance of spring. Kaho would return this night.

Tosa followed her back, calling her name. Teeka turned.

"Yes, Tosa, what is it?"

"Will there be a lesson today?"

"Perhaps tomorrow," Teeka answered.

Tosa smiled at her, but her voice sounded disappointed. "Yes, maybe tomorrow."

Teeka continued to Kaho's platform—her platform. During the afternoon she replaced the grasses in the mat with other soft grasses, which she sprinkled with a musky perfume. Late in the day she prepared another aphrodisiac tea and laced it with an extremely mild hallucinogen. The marriage proposal would come soon. The amicable relationships she had established with the women would help to quiet any objections that might arise over the Kahoosa king taking a Tegesta woman as his bride.

Teeka fondled the pendant. She recalled throwing it, screaming, feeling so resentful. It had felt good to release all that anger. She had not confronted those feelings until this morning. Kuta had actually done her a favor. She had let go of Auro, and in so doing she had severed his magic. There would always be a place for him in her heart, but that precious space was for the Auro she had loved, not for the man he had turned out to be. They had been so young, so overwhelmed by their love for each other. It was the passion of youth, which one only experienced once, she thought to herself. She would always love his memory. How oddly things had changed. She no longer was the girl she had been then. Now whenever she closed her eyes, it was Kaho's face she saw. It was Kaho she missed, and she was eager for his return.

Just before dusk she heard a clamor in the village, trumpeting the return of the hunters. On travoises they carried the spoils of their hunt. Kaho led them into the village, carrying the head of a bear.

The villagers scampered to meet the returning men. Teeka waited, standing in the doorway of the platform. She watched him approach the crowd and then look for her. She stood tall and proud. Kaho stopped, halting all the others.

"Woman, come down. You are the chosen woman of Kaho, and I request that you come to meet me as I return."

It was an invitation to a rite that was reserved for the Kahoosa king. Every man and woman stood still. This was a precedent, and despite their excitement, the clanspeople did not overlook the importance of the moment. Teeka reached for the necklace. It irritated her, as it had at the beginning. She started to lift it, then let it fall back against her chest.

She descended the ladder and walked through the crowd, which parted for her. Pansar alone stood her ground, blocking Teeka's path. Teeka walked up to the scowling woman and stopped. Kaho found the display of hostility intolerable and angrily ordered Pansar away.

When Teeka stood directly in front of him, he handed her the head of the bear.

"This is the beast. I give you its head in gratitude for saving my life. It was your medicine that made me well again."

The sucking in of breath from surprise stirred the air. Kaho had just publicly insulted the shaman, giving credit to the Tegesta woman for returning him to health after the bear's attack.

Kuta clamped his teeth together, and no one dared to look at him.

"This woman whom I have chosen prepared special medicines that cured me. Kuta's medicine did not work, and she risked her life to save me. For this deed of courage I reward her with the head of the bear."

Teeka had not expected such an open declaration. Surreptitiously she watched Kuta back out of the crowd. He was filled with rage and humiliation, a very dangerous combination.

Proudly she carried the bear's head by the fur on the top. When the center of the ceremonial plaza was reached, Kaho removed the skin and fur, which would be saved. The bear was a respected animal known for its strength and perseverance. The jaws were left in place, but Kaho extracted one of the canine teeth and showed it to Teeka.

"This should go into your medicine bag. It marks the beginning of your new life." It was also a new beginning for the Kahoosa, he thought. Perhaps his joining with Teeka was symbolic of how the Kahoosa and the Tegesta might also one day merge. This was a very different thought for him. His way had always been to conquer through might, but Teeka had shown him a different way, and maybe a more effective way. The unification of the Kahoosa and the Tegesta would create a powerful nation. Though Kuta was the only one who was supposed to have visions, Kaho also had prophetic dreams, and because of the Tegesta initiative to visit his village, he thought they, too, must see the same kind of things. There were new ideas riding the winds.

Kaho looked at the woman in front of him. The Kahoosa would have to accept her. He held the huge bear canine up so that all could see. "You shall possess this totem, and it will give you the bear's strength and courage."

Proclaiming and giving totems was the right of the shaman. The clanspeople watched, holding their breath at the breach of tradition. Kaho had often transgressed custom, but he had never presumed to have the power and gift of the shaman. This woman definitely had the heart of the mighty Kaho, and from the look in her eyes, he had hers. The men stirred, but the women, knowing Teeka better than the men did, were more accepting and found some romance in this unashamed infraction.

Kaho raised the large tooth and drew a cross on her forehead with the bloody end. As he placed it in the pouch around her neck, in front of all the Kahoosa, she reached out and gently touched the back of his hand. It was obvious that Kaho would soon announce his intent to take this woman as his bride.

Kaho sensed the mood of the clan, reading the messages in their postures and faces. Many were clearly reluctant to accept his decision. A little more time was all he needed.

Teeka had also been studying the people who surrounded her and watched, but she was careful not to let the happiness that rose inside her show on her face. It was a solemn moment that needed to be sanctified with sober expressions.

Teeka's mind whirled. The future of the Tegesta and the Kahoosa was entrusted to her. She had won Kaho's heart, and the spirits had known that she would. They had even known that Kaho would win hers. Now she was to share that trust with him. They were to blend, to take the best from each tribe and braid it into one. Inside her she held the key to the future. It had begun with only two people and would spread to make a new nation, one that was full of the Tegesta gentleness and the Kahoosa strength. The plan that had been set forth by the spirits continued to unfold like some bright star coming out from behind a cloud. Her direction was clear. She would follow the path that was bathed in the light of the spirits.

She touched her medicine bag, which had become tangled with the pendant.

Chapter Twenty-five

TEEKA WAS NOW THE WOMAN whom every man wanted. Kaho had elevated her to a place that Kuta could not reach with his slanderous accusations. Teeka had built the foundation so well that even the advice of a shaman could not undermine it.

She hoped.

By the rising of the crescent moon, which promised the coming of another full moon, the men of the Kahoosa had yielded to the soft talk of their women, and Teeka ate at the central hearth. She was Kahoosa.

Kaho led her to the gathering for the evening meal. She was the object of every man's imagination as she moved about the hearth. She was polite and courteous but spoke to none of the males, not wanting to endanger her position with the women.

At the end of the meal, Kaho rose before his people and addressed them.

"I have chosen Teeka to be my bride. The trials are completed, and she pleases me."

Kuta suddenly emerged from the crowd of huddled bodies.

"But the shaman has not conferred with the spirits. You speak too soon, Kaho."

Kaho reached for Teeka's hand and helped her to

stand next to him.

"This woman is Kahoosa, but her spirits are those of the Tegesta. She is out of your domain," Kaho contested.

Kuta's face contorted with frustration. The heat of fury started to boil inside him. He could feel the blood hammering in his temples. His mouth suddenly went dry. His heart sped up, tumbling in his chest, and he broke out in a dripping sweat.

"But I should still seek the wisdom of the Kahoosa spirits," he said with a weak and trembling voice. Kuta's tongue felt swollen, and the words were coming slowly. "You cannot take her until the spirits agree. Can you not see past this woman?"

Kuta felt a sting in his nostrils, and he felt a warm and thick liquid draining from his nose. He wiped it away and saw that the back of his hand was smeared with blood. He tried to speak again, but he was cut off by a strangling, until he made no sound but a gurgle.

Kuta fell to his knees, eyes wide and staring in fright. Suddenly there was a pressure in his chest and a sharp pain down his left arm and across his left jaw. His lips turned blue as he collapsed and lay still on the ground.

No one moved, unsure of what had happened. He was a spirit man, capable of incomprehensible demonstrations when taken over by those he called. They waited for Kuta to rise up, but he did not.

Finally Pansar stood and crossed the circle of people. She crouched next to Kuta, pulled at his shoulder, and turned him over. His face was frozen in the fear he had felt at the moment of his death.

"He is dead," she announced.

The Kahoosa stood dazed and bewildered. A low mumble began as they tried to make sense out of what they had just seen. They looked to Kaho.

Kaho appointed two men to carry Kuta's body back to his platform. The apprentice shaman followed. It would be his duty to sit with the body all night and be certain that the spirits recognized Kuta so that he could cross to the Other Side. He would prepare Kuta's body for burial, smearing it with red and yellow ocher. One small triangular piece of bone would be cut from his skull. A hole would be drilled at one of the points, and the new shaman would wear it around his neck.

The people dispersed somberly. They had seen many men die, but they had never seen one die this way. Kaho was the last to leave, overseeing the orderly procession of his people.

"Put this from your mind," Teeka told him.

"What could he have done to anger the spirits? Kuta's death causes me pain and worry. Through most of his life he was a good shaman, even if at the end he became confused. He did not deserve such a gruesome death."

"It is done, and you cannot undo it," she said as they reached the base of their platform. "Only another shaman can try to interpret Kuta's death. It is over. Let me soothe you," she said, pressing the palm of her hand to his face.

Kaho pinned her back to the ladder. His hands grasped at all the curves of her body, and his mouth plundered hers. He was consuming her, folding her into him.

He suddenly jerked away. A thin line of blood oozed from a small cut on his chest.

"Your pendant," he said.

Teeka looked down, watching him lift the necklace over her head. She froze, waiting for the pain in her head and the dizziness, but it did not come. A different feeling was sweeping through her.

She touched her finger to the tiny rivulet of blood and

wiped it away. Lightly she touched her lips to his chest. His hand lifted her chin so that he could look into her face. His eyes were gentle and caring, and they looked at her deeply. His face was etched with lines of passion.

Kaho whispered her name, and she heard the tenderness in his voice.

Teeka pressed her lips to the injury. Her mouth left damp circles on his chest as she relished the taste of his skin. A rush of warmth splashed over her. She ached to enfold him, to lessen his pain and worry.

"Come," she whispered again, grabbing a rung of the ladder.

Kaho groaned as he released her. Very slowly she ascended, stopping now and again to let him touch her, until she finally reached the top. At the head of the ladder, Teeka sat on the edge of the platform, and then lay back, resting her back on the floor, leaving her legs dangling over the side. Kaho continued up, until his waist was just above the level of the platform. He leaned forward, touching his lips to the flesh of her belly and to the crest of her hips.

He entered her almost immediately, feeling himself burn with the need to release himself inside her. Teeka met each drive, crying out with the pleasure of him filling her. He fell forward, and she held him to her by his shoulders until his thirst for her was quenched.

She let the fire extinguish itself slowly and then led him onto the platform and the mat they shared. She floated in his warmth, feeling him wrap his arms around her, even as he slept. His ragged breathing finally turned to the long and deep rhythm of sleep. She could feel his heart thumping against her back as she snuggled even closer.

Teeka woke during the night and sat up. She touched

his face and then curled herself against him, his breath falling welcomed on her neck.

———

Their marriage was to coincide with other ceremonies. The new shaman would be officially named, and on that special evening, he would give totems to the new babies and greet each clan member's spirit. The Kahoosa would thank the animal spirits for the success of the hunters and the safety of the clan. Kaho had invited the caciques and representatives from the other Kahoosa villages and had already sent runners to extend his invitations. Many new mothers would bring their babies for the spirit-giving ceremony. The shaman from their home village, if they had one, would accompany them. This would be a special honor, for both the babies and the shamans, to have the totem-naming ceremony in the village of Kaho.

Rebet and Cala were charged with making Teeka's marriage costume. It was elaborate, tediously made from the pale white and pastel feathers of the wading birds. The feathers were bound together to make a cloak that flowed to the ground.

On the day of the ceremony, Teeka went to Rebet's platform to don the wedding cloak. It would have been unfavorable for her to touch it before the day of the wedding, and so this morning she was eager to see it and touch it. Rebet lifted it and set it on Teeka's shoulders.

"You look beautiful, Teeka," Rebet said.

"Thank you," she responded politely. "Your hands have made this so lovely."

There was a strained silence for a few moments, but then Teeka spoke. "I know all of this has been awkward. I wish we could get past that and be friends again."

"I also think it would be nice." Rebet drew in a noisy

breath and let it out. "Kaho has never really been my husband—or Cala's. He really is yours alone, and I have no bad feelings about that."

Teeka took Rebet's hand. Both understood the gesture.

She removed the cloak from Teeka. "Kaho will lose his breath when he sees you," Rebet remarked as Teeka left.

———

The village began to flood with visitors, and Kaho was away from Teeka much of the day greeting them She took advantage of the time to rest and prepare. From the corner of the platform, she reached into one of her small baskets. From it she retrieved the columella amulet. Teeka held it up, watching it dangle and spin at the end of the fine leather necklace.

There was one large basket that Kaho and Teeka would take with them to the wedding shelter. It was filled with food and herbs to help feed them for half a moon cycle. They would supplement the staples with plants that grew near the wedding hut. Teeka reached through the contents of the basket, easing the amulet to the bottom.

By twilight the central hearth was heaped with so much wood that it blazed high in the sky. The usual evening meal was replaced with a later feast. Rebet delivered the marriage costume. Kaho was to wait away from Teeka from sunset until the time she was presented to him. She had no family to stand with her, and so she would go to him alone.

Teeka threaded fresh flowers in her hair and stained her face with a wash of clay pigment. She had prepared another special fragrance for this night, and she splashed her body with it. She applied an emollient to make her skin soft and smooth. She chalked her lashes with charcoal and lightly glossed her lips with a pomade.

From the height of the platform she could see the crowd gathering about the fire. After a ritual proclamation, the new shaman danced and chanted, showing off his charismatic skills. One at a time the women presented their babies to their new shaman. With the most animated gestures and expressions, each baby was given a guide spirit. Each child now had two names—one common name that his mother had chosen, and one animal spirit name that would guide and protect the child through life.

All the other ceremonies were at last completed, and Kaho stood near the shaman, close to the fire. Teeka's time had come.

All eyes looked in the direction of Kaho's platform, seeing the distant and exquisite form of the bride. Her steps were unhurried, and her body seemed to flow with the land and air. The bride of the king captivated her audience, and the Kahoosa stared in awe at the ethereal figure. The light of the full moon and the firelight played off each other, flashing their light upon her just long enough to enrapture those who watched.

Every man felt a stab of jealousy and envy as she made her promises under the direction of the shaman. She had practiced the Kahoosa words, and they flowed like warm tea from her tongue. Kaho searched for the depth of his voice as he said the marriage words. She saturated his senses and suffocated him with her beauty.

The joviality of the crowd had turned to wonder. Her countenance and symmetry were sorceresses that held the wedding guests spellbound. If she had been a spirit, they would have worshiped her.

Kaho picked up the basket and led her away from

those she enchanted. She followed him to the canoe. She sat facing him as he poled out into the water. In the moonlight, he feasted on her beauty.

The marriage bed was far enough away from the village that none of the wedding night sounds could be heard. Here the couple had a chance to be alone, uninhibited, undisturbed. It was a sacred time and deserved the seclusion. The women of the village checked on the special shelter periodically, so that the plants and vines that grew so rapidly would not overtake it. Just before a marriage, a group of older women cleaned the camp and made it ready for the new couple.

Kaho extended his hand, helping her from the dugout. He led her up a small trail bordered by tall grass and plants. As the brush cleared, Teeka saw the camp. The open path to it was laden with garlands of sweet-smelling flowers, and bracken fern draped over the roof of the platform.

"A Tegesta woman has stolen the heart of the king of the Kahoosa, and he thought he had stolen her from her people. One can never understand the ways of the spirits."

The low platform held a bed of soft grasses, but he wanted her here on the soft earth that brought forth all life. His mouth found hers waiting, welcoming him. She clung to his powerful shoulders, returning pleasure for pleasure.

His hands lightly caressed the fullness of her breasts, delighting in their feverish answer to his touch. His mouth nipped at her neck as he pulled her down onto the earth. Teeka clutched at his back, moaning with the ache of her body.

The splendid contours of his taut body rode beneath her hands. She stroked and explored all the ripples and definitions of his lean, simmering body. She could feel the tension that coiled within him, and she smiled as his hungry mouth made its way down the graceful curve of her neck.

She arched her back and spread her arms, offering all of herself to him. Kaho raised his head and looked at the magnificent woman who lay beneath him. Her skin was covered by a veil of perspiration, and she looked luminescent in the moonlight.

"I tell you what I have never told anyone. I love you," he murmured. "The spirits made me see you that day."

She sighed as his deliberate and expert touch found her warm, moist softness.

"Yes," she purred. "It must have been the spirits."

There on the damp earth the Joining Spirit recognized them as one.

———

The wedding bed was soft. They lay on their sides, Kaho's arm over her, his nose nestled in her sweet hair.

Very carefully she slid out of his arms, not waking him. She reached inside the basket, curled her fingers around the columella pendant, and pulled it free.

Chapter Twenty-six

SHE WAITED OUT THE NIGHT, exploring the virgin territory around her. Traveling through her was a current that made her pace. At times she would sit next to Kaho as he slept, studying him, finding something new to treasure each time she looked. Once she even dared to touch her fingers to his lips. She did not want him to wake because when he did, she would have to tell him.

Too soon, needles of sunlight pierced the branches. Teeka lay next to him, waiting for his dark eyes to open.

She felt his lips touch her forehead and his hand brush across her cheek and then her throat. As he wandered on, delighting in her soft flesh, his hand stopped at the slick hardness of the amulet.

Surprised, he propped himself up on his elbow. "You wear that pendant again?"

"Yes."

Kaho's stomach tightened. She had not worn the amulet since he had taken it off of her the night Kuta died. He had never liked it, and he knew that in some way it tied her to her people. As long as she wore it, there would always be a part of her that was not his.

"Can I ask you about it?" he asked.

"Not now," she whispered. "Let me lie in your arms a little longer."

"Stay in my arms forever," he told her, feeling a sudden chill. They lingered there, entwined, afraid to let the moment end.

Teeka finally moved away. "Let me get my husband something to eat. You must have an appetite this morning."

"Mmm," he answered, "indeed I do have an appetite. Come with me," he said, rising to his feet and taking the basket in his hand. He wrapped his free arm around her waist as he led her to the water.

He carried her into the chest-deep water. Flesh to flesh, Kaho held her in his arms, her legs wrapped around him. He tasted the hollow in her throat and her soft shoulders. Her lips were warm and inviting.

She returned his kiss with fire. Kaho's knees bent under him from the flaming desire she kindled inside him.

"You nearly drown me with your passion," he said.

Teeka blushed and smiled. If the moment had not been so intense, they would have laughed.

Kaho carried her to the shore and fell against her, soaking her body with his.

"Kaho," she whispered.

He was a brave warrior, a king, and for the first time felt fear—fear of losing her. Maybe if she did not say it, it would not come true.

"Kaho," she started again, but he put his hand to her mouth, gently, to silence her.

She fell to his expert touch, to his kisses. He was a master, knowing all those things her body could not resist. Within moments she was lost beneath him, accepting and giving the Gift.

Kaho rolled his heavy body to one side, reclaiming his breath. "You take all my strength," he murmured. She turned onto her side, still with her eyes closed, and reached out to touch his face.

He sat up next to her, taking berries from the basket and putting them in her mouth.

"The bride of the Kahoosa king should smile."

"Yes, she should," Teeka answered.

He brushed his lips against hers. "Then smile for this man."

Teeka turned her head and sat up. "I …"

"Can it not wait?" he asked, hoping for another delay. "Put it from your mind, whatever it is, at least for this day. Just be here with me, my bride."

"I have put it away too long," she answered, standing and looking away.

He stepped up close behind her, put both hands on her shoulders, pressing his lips to her ear. "Then make me a part of it."

Teeka turned to face him. "I have something I must finish. It eats at me from the inside."

"If it haunts you and causes you so much pain, then end it. Let me help you."

"You cannot. It is something I must do alone."

"Tell me."

Teeka walked away, finally turning to him. "I have to go home."

Kaho felt a stab of pain. There was a space inside her that he had not been able to fill.

"To the Tegesta?" he asked, even though he knew the answer.

"Yes."

"Then I will go with you," he offered. "Let me take you."

"No. Alone. I need to go alone."

"I will not interfere."

"Kaho, this is something I must do alone. I want help

268

from no one else, no other influence. I need to find all the strength inside me. It is important to me that I do it this way. Please trust me."

"I cannot let you go alone," he argued, standing closer. "It is too dangerous. Besides, you do not know the way."

"I remember the way."

"Teeka," he said, looking squarely into her eyes, supporting her chin in his hand. "Nothing I say is going to change your mind?"

Teeka shook her head and then pressed her face to his chest.

"Are you coming back to me?" he asked in a low raspy voice.

"Yes, I will be back before it is time to leave the wedding hut, before the moon passes through the last half of its cycle. I will come back to you here."

Kaho looked hard at her face. If there were signs of betrayal, he did not see them. Perhaps because he did not want to.

"Am I a fool to let you go? I cannot let myself distrust you. The thought is too painful. I will be here, waiting, counting the moons."

"Then I will leave this day. The sooner I leave, the sooner I will return."

Kaho kissed the top of her head. "You must take the basket. You do not have any food to take with you."

"But what will you eat?"

"Am I not a hunter? And the earth yields its fruits. Do not worry about me."

Kaho stood on the bank, watching her until the bends and curves of the water and the lush drapery of foliage took her from him.

"Before the moon is full," he called out.

———

She was better at maneuvering the canoe this time. She dipped the paddle into the water and pulled it to her, directing the bow out into the water.

The current carried her sometimes, and at other times she exerted all her strength to win the argument of her direction. The sun was hot, but the breeze kept her cool. The sweet fruits in the basket held off hunger.

The water moved slowly under the canoe. Teeka's arms were tired, so she enjoyed the slow drift that let her rest for a moment. She looked over the edge at her reflection. Each time she saw herself recently, she was surprised. The young girl had vanished without a proper good-bye.

She poked one finger into her reflection, watching the ripples and distortions it caused. When the image cleared, she stared at the woman in the water, and the beautiful amulet that dangled around her neck.

While the current was kind, she leaned back in the canoe, watching the clear blue sky. She was going home.

Chapter Twenty-seven

The mist of early morning had disappeared and been replaced by the low, massive, and woolly cumulus clouds that promised a fair day. They hung in the sky, waiting for a wind on which they could ride. Teeka paddled the canoe down the twisting river. When she was close to the shore, she poled her way. The sun scorched her back. There was no breeze.

Often she reached into the water and splashed handfuls of it up and down her arms, but with no wind it did not provide much relief. As the canoe moved through the water, the air passed over her skin. It did not make her cool, but it made the heat tolerable.

In the late afternoon, she found a spot to put ashore. Her body ached, and there was a constant nagging in her belly. The sky began to cloud up, turning dark with the threat of a thunderstorm.

She cleared away the debris from beneath a low-branched cypress. This was where she would wait out the storm. Before the rain came, she needed to gather some dry wood and grass, so that she could start a fire later. She gathered twigs, dry grasses, and a few large pieces of dead wood. She broke down the larger pieces and folded the grasses in half, bundling them. With the knife Kaho had put in the basket for her, she cut away green cabbage palm fronds and used them to wrap the firewood and tinder. She propped the package in her basket and hoped the contents would not be drenched. Making a fire was difficult under any circumstances, but without dry wood and tinder, it was virtually impossible. How easy it had been just to take a coal from the central hearth.

The rumbling of thunder came closer. The sky

blackened. When the birds fell silent and disappeared, Teeka retreated to her shelter beneath the cypress. A flash of lightning and the loud crack of thunder that went with it heralded the approach of rain and the wind. The wind whipped the branches and even the soil, whirling up dead leaves. The small canoe rocked against the shore as the wind and water slapped at it. Teeka pulled the basket closer to her, crouching over it, desperately trying to keep it dry.

The whole earth seemed to shake as the thunder rolled on. Zigzag streaks of light struck the earth nearby, making Teeka close her eyes. When she opened them, she looked toward the river. The canoe was being battered. The slender trunk of the young sweet bay magnolia, to which she had tied the canoe, was being stripped of its limbs. The canoe yanked at the vine rope, bending the sapling, raking away the small branches. The loop threatened to slide off the top.

Teeka crawled out from under the tree, squinting in the rain. She stood, fighting the wind and the rain that stung her skin. She had to secure the canoe.

Suddenly a raging burst of wind hurled a broken limb into her side, knocking her to the ground. She scrambled to her feet and slid through the mud until she arrived at the bank. Just as she reached for the line, it slipped over the top of the bent tree. The canoe began to back into the water. Teeka lurched for the canoe, grabbing it with one hand. She tried to hold on, but her footing gave way. The canoe dragged her with it as it moved sideways through the water. She could no longer touch the bottom. She sputtered as a blast of water went into her nose and mouth.

She let go, realizing that she could not save the canoe. When she reached the shore, she clambered up the bank, coughing a few times from the water she had swallowed. Only after collapsing beneath the cypress did she realize how bruised and exhausted she was.

The storm finally subsided. Teeka was soaked and chilled. She lifted the palm-wrapped wood, and water drained out. There would be no fire to dry and warm her and brew her tea.

The dreary day gave way to the night. The dull ache in her belly tugged at her, and the bruises hurt when she lay down. The palms of her hands stung from the scrapes, and her head ached.

Though she doubted she would sleep, her body gave in.

———

Teeka shifted as daylight danced through the leaves. The earth had swallowed the rain, and the sunlight had dried the last evidence of a storm. The mud cracked on her skin as she moved to the river. The scrapes and cuts stung as the water touched them. When she finished bathing, Teeka took a small bowl and used some leaves and berries from the basket to make tea. She checked the twigs and other tinder that lay nearby. All of it was still too wet to burn. The bright sun would have to warm the water enough to make a weak tea.

———

While the brew steeped, she sought some moss for a new skirt, since hers was now shredded. She shook the gray-green air plant vigorously to dislodge small spiders and mites. If she had had a fire, she would have heated the spidery plant in a bowl of water, or smoked it, driving out all the pests. But this would have to do for now. She worked the moss around a vine belt. It was not her best work, she thought.

The tepid tea slid down her throat to her stomach. She held the bowl under her nose, swirling the liquid so that she could enjoy the scent. She had no appetite but hoped that the tea would make her feel better. It did not.

She tossed out the rest. It had done nothing to relieve the soreness or the nagging ache. She did not have any more time to spend trying to ease her pain. The journey home would take more time on foot. She loaded the basket with all that she had taken from it and walked to the water. On the shoreline across from her, a tree hung over the river. One large broken branch trailed on the water's surface. She remembered seeing the tree before. She was going in the right direction.

Other landmarks that she remembered popped into view, until she came to a fork in the stream. She scanned the landscape, trying to locate something familiar, but she saw nothing. Maybe from the shore she could not see the thing that would tell her how to proceed. She waded into the water, sliding each foot in front of her, feeling for any sudden dropoff. Turning slowly in a circle, she surveyed the trees and rocks. Finally, just around the curve, she saw the protruding end of a log that stuck out into the water. A strangler fig had taken root on top of it and grew up, as if it sat on fertile ground. That she remembered. Everything in this land struggled for its life.

By dusk she noticed that she had traveled for a long time without seeing anything special. Surely she had not erred. She could not have turned in the wrong direction since there were no possible turns to make. It would be dark soon, and she knew it would probably be best if she stopped for the night.

The constant crampy feeling still took her appetite. She sucked the juice from a few berries and then put the basket away. She made a bed of young tender blades of grass and tried to sleep, but the night was torturous. As soon as she fell asleep, the tugging ache would pitch to a quick sharp pain. It lasted only long enough to bring her out of sleep, and then it would be gone.

She was glad when morning finally came. The activity of the day would keep her mind off her discomfort. She was quick to pack her things and begin again. She walked much of the day, still not locating any signs. Perhaps she should backtrack, she thought, stopping to make a decision. She must have missed something. She stared in all directions, and then upstream on the opposite bank she saw a clearing. It was the one where they had stayed on the way to the village of the Kahoosa.

Teeka searched the water for the shallowest part. She stripped and placed her skirt in the basket, which she balanced on top of her head and steadied with one hand. Slowly she walked out into the water, scanning the river for alligators. With caution, she continued in. Near the middle, the water reached her neck. Holding the basket overhead with one hand, she sidestroked until she could walk out onto the opposite shore.

From the village of the Tegesta it had been a one-day trip by canoe to this campsite. She should be able to make it home in another day and a half.

Her fatigue was transformed into energy. Suddenly a sharp pain pierced her belly, and she bent double. It took her breath away for a moment, and she couldn't move. Just as quickly it eased, changing back into the dull ache.

————

She kept a steady pace the rest of the day, but by sunset the pains had become more frequent, causing her to freeze until they passed. With the onset of evening, she was glad to stop. Without any preparations, she fell onto the ground and slept.

The short sleep gave her the strength she needed to endure the rest of the night. She was awakened by a stabbing pain that felt like a hot stick ramming through her back. It started in the small of her back and wrapped itself around her middle like a tight, hot band.

She felt a warm gush between her legs, sat up, and looked. She was lying in a puddle of blood. The world began to spin, and she felt nausea grip her as she lay back down, terrified. Was she dying? Were the spirits battling inside her? Were the Tegesta spirits punishing her?

The bleeding continued, and Teeka drifted in and out of consciousness. Sometime near morning she realized what was happening. Her body was expelling the baby. She had seen it happen to women before. She reached down, touched her belly, and cried.

She had lost so much blood during the night that each time she tried to raise her head, she was overcome by dizziness. Her mouth was dry, and her lips were parched. She was so thirsty. She was close to the water but could not move to it. And she was still bleeding.

———

When she opened her eyes again, the sunlight made her wince. Large dark shadows of turkey buzzards circled in a deathwatch. The day passed with her fading in and out of a haze. She welcomed the coolness that came with the evening. The bleeding had slowed, so that it was more like a normal moon cycle, but she was weak. If she was going to survive, she would have to fight. She was alone, and her life depended on her will.

Teeka turned onto her belly and began to crawl toward the water like a snake. The exertion made her heart flutter arrhythmically. It startled her. She froze until it passed, then tried again. The effort was exhausting, and after a few feet she stopped to rest. She could see the water and even smell it. A few feet at a time, she struggled toward the life-giving river.

At last she was close enough to touch it with her fingertips. She lay flat on the ground, arms outstretched. She drew her wet fingers to her mouth. The moisture burned her lips and only tempted her thirst. She needed to move nearer so that she could cup her hands in the water, and bring it to her mouth. The skin on her stomach was abraded, and the muscles of her body ached. She felt her throat close as she began to cry, but there was no excess moisture in her body to be given up to tears. She was so very close but could not make her body move the short distance.

When she looked up again, she saw the water under her hands, almost to her face. It was clear and sparkling, and she could hear it bubble as it traveled with the current. Somehow she had been wrong. The water was here within her reach. She raised herself on her elbows and cupped her hands in the water. She parted her lips, opened her mouth, and sucked up the fresh clean water.

Her mouth was filled with the dry earth, and she spat it out. Her mind was playing tricks. There had been no water so close. There was no water in her hands or mouth. She had scooped up the earth and had tried to drink it.

Again she dragged herself across the coarse ground on her belly, edging her way until the water washed over her hands, and across her forearms. She stretched herself with a final lunge until her face landed in the edge of the stream. She opened her mouth and drank, coming up for air and sputtering.

Slower this time, she lowered her head and sipped, carefully swallowing small amounts at a time. Her stomach wouldn't hold as much as she desired to drink, so she stopped and eased herself backward, just out of the water, and slept.

She awakened periodically to sip water and then slept again. She had no judgment of the time passing. Her unrelenting thirst seemed to be the only thing that could rouse her. As soon as she had satisfied the immediate need, she slept again.

The last time she awakened, she felt more strength in her muscles and she stayed awake and alert a little longer than she had before. She was going to survive.

———

The sky filled with dark and ominous clouds, but the shadows of the scavengers did not hover above. As her strength returned, her mind found other things with which to occupy itself.

She cried, surprised at what a feeling of loss she felt. The baby was suddenly real. Though she had not been able to think much about the child she had carried, she now suffered from the emptiness inside. She had thought that the time would come to enjoy carrying the child. She had never expected this.

Teeka thought about the time that had been lost. She would not be able to mourn now. She needed to concentrate on her task. The sorrowful thoughts only cluttered her mind. She needed to prepare medicines that would strengthen her. Her body lacked the energy she had to possess in order to continue. Teeka also made a deliberate effort to not dwell on the past. She was close to home. Knowing that, she slept soundly through the night.

———

Cold needles of windblown rain pricked at Teeka's face, waking her. Quickly she hid herself beneath the canopy of trees and leaned against the trunk of a greening cypress. Clumps of moss hung from the ends of the branches and wild pine bromeliads wrapped their roots around the limbs. The stiff, tapering gray-green leaves of the air plants huddled around the bases of the spikes that grew upward, ending in bright red bracts. Behind her was a tall dahoon tree heavily laden with the berries that could be brewed into a tasty hot tea. Everywhere she looked, the earth was ripe with color. It was the wondrous season when the spirits replenished the earth.

When the weather cleared, she packed her basket and discarded all those things that she could do without. She added herbs that she could use to help her recover.

In the fading afternoon, she made a camp. This time she decided to build a shelter. If it rained again, her sleep would not be interrupted. She found a long branch and wedged the ends into the forks of two low-limbed cypress trees that stood close together. Then, finding more fallen branches, she propped them against it. She built two sides and left the ends open. She would be well shielded.

By the time twilight came, she had finished and stood back admiring her work and resourcefulness. She had built a small but sturdy lean-to. She was amazed at what she had learned to do, and had made herself do, since leaving the Tegesta. Whatever the challenge, she had managed to meet it. She was independent and resourceful. She would never be the same.

Chapter Twenty-eight

SHE WAS AGAIN TROUBLED by the dream. Tamuk was destroyed by the alligator, and then she was being swallowed by the mud. Auro watched. Teeka called to him, but he did not answer.

"Auro," she called angrily, "how can you love me and let this happen to me?"

Auro still did not answer. She felt herself being sucked under the mud. It was tugging at her throat, pulling her head under.

It was the amulet, she realized. It was weighing her down, dragging her beneath the sludge. She grabbed it, pulling it up. She had to get if off. But her mouth was already filling with the mud. She was panicking, trying to remove the necklace that had tangled in her hair.

The mud oozed over her nose and then her eyes. She was choking, suffocating. In one last effort, she gathered all her strength and yanked the necklace free. With its removal, the weight was gone, and her head popped clear of the mud. She drank in the air, filling her burning lungs with it.

Auro was gone.

When she awoke in the morning, threads of the dream stayed with her. It did not frighten her as badly as it had before because this time the mud had not kept her under.

The spirits were kind. They had shown her the dream again so that she could confirm its meaning. It added to the intensity of her conviction that she was doing the right thing.

Teeka was ravenous, devouring more than she normally did for a morning meal. She felt strong and full of energy.

She walked briskly all morning. Finally she needed no more clues to direction, the land was familiar, and the village was almost within sight. She would be there soon. Knowing how close she was seemed to give her strength and endurance. At last she pushed aside the last spray of unfriendly stalks and blades. She could even smell the scents that meant home and she flooded with memories.

Teeka bathed in the water, washing away the mud, dirt, and perspiration. She waited until darkness. Her people did not need to know she was home. It would only complicate things for Auro and also for her. She crept through the underbrush until she could see the shadowy outline of the village. Dark silhouettes busied themselves about the village with preparations for the night. She watched, trying to make out the identity of each. But she was too distant. One last straggler crossed in front of the fire, and then disappeared in the blackness. Though the central hearth glowed brightly, almost all the small, individual fires had been extinguished. Only a few glowing coals dotted the mound. She waited a little longer and then made her way to the far end of the village where the shaman's platform stood. Quietly she approached it from behind.

Carefully she set down the basket and then walked to one of the supporting poles of the platform. She leaned against it, trying to quiet her breath. Auro was just above her.

Without a sound she started at the bottom of the ladder, applying her weight slowly so that the rungs did not creak. As her head rose above the floor of the platform, she called to him..

"Auro, it is Teeka." She reached the top and stood on the floor of the platform. "I am here."

"Teeka," he blurted, standing. "It is you."

"Yes," she answered him.

Auro came close and embraced her. He lifted Teeka's face and touched his lips to her forehead. "How have you done this?" he whispered as his hands stroked her back, feeling the softness of her skin. He pressed even closer, breathing in her scent and letting it set off the memories of their night together.

Auro bit softly into her neck. He grabbed handfuls of her hair and clutched at her shoulders.

"Auro," she said, twisting her head away, "there are many things I need to tell you."

"Lie beside me and whisper those things that I long to hear," he said softly, urging her to his mat. "Rest your head on my chest," he told her, brushing her hair from her face. "Was it terrible for you?" he asked.

"Yes," she answered, "but not all of it. Things change. People change."

In the dim light, she had seen enough. Auro had changed, and whatever had happened inside him was reflected in his appearance. The once strong lines of his jaw were now slack. His dark eyes held no depth, and even his voice had been touched with madness. It hurt her to see what he had become. Any resentment she had once felt melted away. She would be as gentle as she could. She wished him no more pain.

"Auro, there are things that need to be settled. Things that I need to tell you."

He held her, feeling the warmth of her radiate to his body. "You do not need to tell me anything. Just rest here with me. Tomorrow will be soon enough."

He seemed to sense that this was the end. He wanted time. He did not want to hear what she had to say. But Teeka knew that the longer she waited, the more prolonged the agony would be. It would be better to be swift. Like any wound, the cleaner, the quicker, the less pain.

"My journey has been long and tiring, but it is not finished. Auro," she said, sitting up, "sit and face me. I need to look into your eyes."

Auro sat up, his face carved with worry.

"When Kaho first took me, I was obsessed with returning. I would have done anything—anything to come back to you."

"And you have come back," he said.

"Yes, I have. But I am not the same as when I left."

"Neither of us is the same. Each of us has changed. But my love for you has not changed. Are you trying to tell me that you no longer love me?"

"I will always love you. The part of me that I gave to you is always yours."

Auro straightened. "But there is more, is there not?"

Teeka looked down at the necklace. It was as beautiful as the day Auro had given it to her.

"Tell me about the amulet," she said.

"It was my wedding gift to you. Look, I still wear the match. It is a symbol of my undying love for you."

Teeka looked deep into his eyes. "Did you use your father's magic when you made it?" she asked bluntly.

Auro stood up and walked away from her, facing the entrance of his platform. "My love for you has nothing to do with magic."

"You made me promise never to take it off. You told me that if I did, I would betray our love. My hands can never take it off. The guilt that I feel—even if I think about taking it off—makes me sick. I made a vow, a promise to you. Through everything that has happened, I still honor that commitment. I can never end it. I cannot take off the pendant."

Auro turned quickly. "You have wanted to take it off? Does it not mean anything to you?"

"I only want it to mean what you told me it means—a wedding gift of love from you. But there is more to it than that. As long as I wear it, my life has a single direction. I have no choices. When Kaho took me, you knew that he would never release me. You knew that I would never really be your woman. But you gave me the amulet so I could never forget. As long as I wear it, I can never get on with my life. It takes from me any chance of joy or happiness. It fills my existence with sorrow. It allows me nothing but to always grieve for you."

"No! That is not what the pendant was for. No!"

"Maybe that is not what you meant to do, but that is what has happened."

"But you are here now, away from Kaho. You have come home to me. Why does that not bring you joy? Do you fear that the Kahoosa will come for you?"

"Kaho will not come, but I cannot stay. Because I could not let go of you, Auro, I have done things ..."

"Teeka, I never meant to hurt you. I used Tamuk's magic only because I love you, and I could not bear to think that you might one day forget me," he said   .

"I am not Tegesta anymore. In my need to come home to you, my obsession, I have broken the ways of the People. I am not who I was."

"Do not tell me more," he said.

"I have to tell you. You need to understand why I cannot stay. The spirit of Little Doe is gone forever. If the amulet was to ensure my love for you, it also took away my chance to come home again—to be with you. I can never be the woman of a Tegesta man. The spirits of the People find disgrace in me."

Auro put his arms around her and held her. "What have I done? Tamuk was right." He paused before he began again. "I never meant to cause you so much pain. I was desperate. You were stolen from me. I was so filled with hate for Kaho. I let that hate get confused with my love for you. If I could not have you, then I wanted no one else to ever delight in having you. What man finds pleasure in a woman if he can never have her heart? I wanted to sour Kaho's wedding bed. It was the only way I could retaliate. I was so blinded that I could not see how selfish I was being. It was not supposed to be this way. It was not supposed to hurt you."

Teeka backed away from him and touched her fingertips to his lips. "I need you to end this for me. It can never end by my hand, or by any other hand. You must let me go. I need you to take the amulet off."

"My heart will always be yours," he whispered, taking the leather necklace thong in his hand.

"We will never forget each other." She gently touched her hand to the top of his. "Love me enough to free me. Make it right for us both, Auro. Take the amulet."

Auro slowly lifted it from her throat and over her head.

"I am sorry," he whispered from his heart. He remembered the night he had given it to her. How beautiful she had looked—like tonight. Countless memories spilled through his mind.

"Always," she whispered.

Chapter Twenty-nine

AURO WALKED HER TO THE CANOES.

"Take one. It will be a faster and safer journey for you."

Teeka reached for his hand. "One never knows the way of the spirits. It is strange how things end."

Auro pulled her hand, making her step closer to him. "You are beautiful in the moonlight," he said, smiling. He was fighting the terrible pain that he felt inside. He would not let her know. It would be too selfish.

He placed one hand behind her neck and the other on her waist, drawing her face and body to his. The kiss was languorous, filled with emotion but not the fire of passion. Whatever they had not been able to say to each other was told at that moment.

He helped her into the canoe and shoved it off the bank into the black water. He had once thought that he had done a brave and courageous thing, but now he knew it was an act of weakness. He would suffer the pain of losing her twice—another price to pay. He wished he had listened to his father's words. He was not fit to be of Tamuk's blood. He was unworthy of being the shaman of the People.

Auro left the bank and returned to the village. He suddenly felt old and tired. There would be much to do tomorrow.

Inside his platform, he felt through all the storage areas. His fingers guided him through baskets that lined the walls. Finally, beneath some large baskets of pokeberry and button snakeroot, he felt the deerskin.

Carefully he pulled it from underneath the other baskets. Auro sat on the floor with it in his lap. Without unwrapping it, he began to chant, not certain that the spirits would even hear him.

When light began to stream into his dark platform, he stopped his song and peeled back the deerskin. The wooden bowl was warm and smooth. The inside felt slick to his touch. The fluted edges had been chipped, but the original carved design on the outside was clean and distinct. After all the generations, the expert craftsmanship was still evident.

Auro placed the bowl near his mat, covering it with the deerskin. He went down the ladder and walked to the central hearth for coals to start his fire. Then he returned to his platform, brewed some tea, and warmed some coontie bread. He cleaned himself in the river, soaking the days and days and days of neglect from him. He would redeem some respect for Tamuk and his ancestors. They were a proud line, and he had shamed them. He could never right the disgrace that he had brought about, but there were some things he could do and some things he should tend to before it was over.

———

Auro looked about the village. The men would have to go hunting soon. Even though they smoked and dried their meat, the warm humid climate made it spoil quickly, and so they stored it but a few days.

Some of the young children had already scurried

down, one still clinging his soft coverlet of rabbit fur. Their mothers worked at their cookfires while the children laughed and played.

Auro wandered, stopping to speak with friends and family. They were glad to see him. He had washed and seemed to have more spirit in his gait. Many of the villagers stared as he walked by. Teges had been right, they thought. It appeared that they had their shaman back.

Shala was especially happy to see her son looking so well. Her health had deteriorated since Tamuk's death, and after Auro's apparent decline she had found no reason to persevere. But now her son had some of the fire back in his eyes.

Auro stayed a long time with Shala. They reminisced, recalling Auro's childhood and Tamuk's life. At times they laughed and at other times the tears streamed down their faces as they embraced each other.

He also sat with Selo and Illa. With Auro, they talked of Teeka and remembered many of the happy times.

Teges sat by his fire, sipping his warm tea. He looked up when Auro sat across from him. He was pleased to see Auro looking so well, but this posed many questions. He did not wish to insult Auro by commenting on his surprise at Auro's appearance.

"Some tea?" Teges offered.

"I have already had my morning meal," Auro answered, "but I will enjoy your company."

The two sat, watching the other members of the clan go about their daily chores.

"Everyone is well," Auro commented.

"The People have good fortune," Teges agreed.

Auro pointed toward his apprentice, Olagale. "He learns very fast. I have no son, but I have trained Olagale well. He will make a good shaman."

"In time." Teges nodded.

"He knows enough."

"He will never know enough. He does not have the blood. The knowledge ends with you."

"Perhaps it should," Auro said.

"Everything is changing. I watch Yagua. He seems so young and impulsive. When I cross over, Yagua will take the name of the People, Teges, the king of the Tegesta. How will he lead? How many traditions and customs will be lost in the new generation?"

"I fill Olagale's ears with the legends. I tell him of the lessons our fathers, and their fathers before them, have learned. I tell him to listen to those lessons, but I think my words do not find a suitable place in his head. With your passing, and Tamuk's, many of the old ways will be lost forever."

"The spirits direct our fate, Auro, but we are not relieved from the responsibility of passing on all that we know. And there is a new wind blowing. Olagale tells me of his dreams. There is something big coming, a threat to all the tribes. I hope the peace we started will grow."

Auro shook his head. "I have not fulfilled all of my obligations as shaman, and it is time for me to turn over the responsibilities. The things that Olagale sees I have forbidden my own eyes to see. I have not allowed the visions. Even so, I wonder if I have passed on enough to my successor. I am not as wise as Tamuk. My advice to Olagale is weaker than Tamuk's advice to me."

"Your thoughts are troubled this morning."

"Teges, what would happen if I *met* with an accident? Olagale would have to assume the responsibility of shaman."

"The People would survive. Olagale will take seriously

his obligations. Why do you have such morbid thoughts?"

"I just wonder," he answered. "Do you see the People as sound? Do you see Olagale as ready?"

"The People are sound. Is any man prepared for the responsibility of becoming the cacique? Is any man prepared to become shaman?"

Teges sniffed at the air. "It will rain," he said. "My old bones will ache tonight."

Auro stood to leave. "I have things to do before the afternoon rain. I am glad we have had this time to talk. Tamuk would like it."

Auro extended his hand, helping the wrinkled old man to his feet, then walked away. Teges stood still. Though Auro looked better and seemed more coherent, there was something that worried him. The madness had been replaced with something even graver. Teges tottered a few steps, starting to follow so that he could speak with Auro again, but stopped.

Auro continued to visit. This day he would speak with all his friends. He would not have another opportunity, and so he wanted to leave all loose ends tied. Disagreements would be settled and bonds of friendships ensured.

Most of the Tegesta were enjoying the noon meal when he poled the canoe away from the village. Later, when he reached a place to beach his canoe, he did it with the quiet of a hunter. He wandered the area with a purpose, gathering plants. He stopped by the blue-flowered lobelia and cut away a few of the stems, watching the poisonous, milky sap ooze from the cut ends. He placed them in a pouch and walked on.

A woody vine climbed the trunk of a slash pine. It had bloomed earlier, and now the pods had split, exposing the glossy scarlet seeds with the shiny black eyes. Just one, chewed well, was enough to kill a man. From the pods he stripped the seeds of the crab's-eye and dropped them inside his pouch.

The last thing he chose was another vine with beautiful yellow flowers—the yellow jessamine. When he put it inside his pouch, he checked the other contents. These were not the ingredients of the noble recipe. He did not deserve that. This was his powerful potion. Death would be swift, but not painless. He would use the bowl so that all would know what he had done. He owed that to the People.

By late afternoon, Teges's predicted rain had begun to fall. By nightfall, Auro had returned to the village. At the base of his platform he crushed the ingredients in the wooden bowl. He ground them with a stone, then scraped the powder into a bowl of hot water that was suspended over his fire. The mixture made a colorful, deadly stew.

As the potion simmered, Auro called to the spirits. He asked that they forgive him for what he had done and what he was about to do.

When he looked down into the fire, he saw his amulet. He lifted it over his head and threw it into the flames.

With his magic he released all the spirits from inside him. He was only a man—a man not worthy of the Tegesta spirits. He was prepared. Auro lifted the bowl off the skewer by its leather strap and set it next to him. From a small hide pocket at his side, he took Teeka's pendant and clutched it in his hand. Afraid that in the throes of death this would not be secure enough, he looped the necklace around his wrist several times. He hoped that Teges would know that it was important to him.

When the brew had cooled enough, he poured it into

the wooden bowl. There were no songs to be sung, no chants, and no prayers. He was an empty man with no spirit. He lifted the bowl to his lips. At first he sipped it, but then he drank it down.

Auro stretched out under the stars. That he would have no hearth in the heavens was his last thought before he began to sweat. Suddenly his vision and hearing became acutely sensitive. Small tremors began in his limbs and spread inward until his whole body shook violently; foam bubbled out of his mouth, and his eyes rolled to the back of his head.

His body collapsed and went limp, sweat gushing from his skin. Then the convulsions began again—and again—over and over until he stopped breathing.

———

Teges could not sleep. He was worried about Auro. He shifted his weight, hoping to ease some of the discomfort his old body felt when trying to sleep. It did not help. Slowly he pushed himself up until he sat on his mat. He decided to go and talk with Auro by the fire. He would tell him stories of his father, tales of Tamuk and Teges as boys.

"Ah," he said aloud, seeing Auro's fire still bright in the night. He was not sleeping. But as he got closer, he saw Auro on the ground. He hobbled faster, grunting with the effort.

He looked down on the body of the young shaman. Teges knew immediately that the shaman was dead.

"Why?" he asked, looking at Auro. He saw the bowl and knew what he had done. He shook his head. Why would Auro do such a terrible thing? Taking one's own life was punishable by the People and the spirits. Because he had done this, Auro could not even be buried with the

People. He would have to be interred away from the others in dishonor. How would he tell Shala?

Teges bent closer, balancing himself with his walking stick. What was that object around Auro's wrist? There was a leather strand wrapped around his wrist, and he clutched something in his hand.

Carefully, Teges lowered himself to the ground. He pried Auro's fingers from around the amulet. At first he thought it was the amulet that Auro usually wore, but when the fire and moonlight bounced off of it, he realized that it was not. This one was much more beautifully polished. In fact, Teges had never seen such a luster. Whatever it was, it must have been very important to Auro and his choice to end his life in disgrace.

Teges walked haltingly across the village to the platforms of Olagale and Yagua. Together they went to tell Shala.

———

By the next day, all of the village knew. Word spread to the other clans. Olagale and Teges prepared Auro's body. The line of pure shamans had abruptly come to an end. When they had finished, they wrapped his body in a hide funeral wrap.

After the others had gone, Teges slipped the amulet beneath the wrap so that it rested on Auro's chest. No grave goods could be buried with Auro because of his disgrace. But because of Teges's long friendship with Tamuk, he broke a small tradition that did not seem so important anymore. He knew that Tamuk would have wanted it so. Obviously, Auro had trusted that Teges would understand. That was why he had bound it to his wrist. It was all he had asked from this world, and Teges honored his request. No one would know.

———

Only Shala, Teges, Yagua, and Olagale attended the burial. The men dug the grave, and then they lowered Auro's hide-wrapped body into the hole in the earth. Teges stumbled with the labor. Auro's body tumbled into the grave. The funeral wrap flapped open.

"What is that?" Shala asked, catching a glimpse of the amulet before it slid down the slope of Auro's chest and out of sight. Teges squeezed Shala's hand. Yagua and Olagale looked puzzled. In their struggle for balance, they had not seen it.

"I am sorry," she said. "There is nothing. My eyes see things that are not there, and my ears hardly hear what is there," she said. "I am old and should not trust my senses anymore."

After they had covered Auro's body with soil, they marked his grave by laying a small hump of stones on top. They placed a turtle shell on top of that, and Teges brought out a dead rattlesnake, a large diamondback, which he coiled around the stones. It would tell anyone who passed that a man with no spirits lay there.

There were no words or chants at this burial, but Shala rested her hands on top of the marker and closed her eyes. If she offered prayer, she did not share it. Yagua touched her shoulder, discouraging her.

"He was my son," she said, looking sharply at Yagua, fighting back the tears that welled in her eyes.

Teges frowned at the man who was to be his successor. He indicated with his head that they should leave. Shala deserved a chance to grieve alone.

The men walked away, and in a few moments Shala followed. The land was still and silent with their departure. Even the wind did not blow.

Chapter Thirty

THE DARKNESS FORCED Teeka to travel slowly. The small canoe bumped into knuckles of land that buckled up beneath the water, seemingly detached from the shore. The water level was still elevated and occasional spots that usually stood erect out of the river now hid just beneath it, sometimes scraping the bottom of the cypress dugout. The canoe had not been made so long ago, and the smell of the cypress wafted to her nostrils. One of the men had felled the tree and then burned it out. What the fire did not take was scraped out with a columella gouge, the same part of a conch or busycon shell from which Auro had made her pendant. The moon and the stars were just bright enough so that Teeka could almost see her reflection in the water. The frogs and the crickets made friendly night sounds. Now and again she heard the grunt of some irritated alligator. Perhaps her boat had threatened to come too close to a nest on the shore.

She closed her eyes, concentrating on the harmony of the creatures around her. As the canoe moved up the river, she listened to the water ripple, tickling the side of the boat. Even the breeze stroking her cheek and then brushing her ears was a familiar sound and a comforting sensation. In her solitude, she envied the men the freedom they enjoyed in being able to venture out alone into the land among all the animals, as she was this night. It seemed that this was a natural state. She felt attached, a part of the world around her. She belonged here. This was her land, her home, and she was just as much a part of the grand design as were the mosquito, the turtle, the deer, the bird, and the bear. All of them—the plants, the animals, the air, the water, the people—were woven tightly together like a well-made basket.

With her eyes closed she sank deeper into thought until those perceptions became strands of a web, spreading out, losing their point of reference. She was asleep.

———

A sudden bump jarred her, jolting her awake. The canoe abruptly stopped, and she lurched forward. She was grounded. Teeka stood and sank the pole into the water. She pushed on the bottom, but the canoe did not move. She spread her feet apart and rocked back and forth, hoping to dislodge herself. Probably without her weight inside, the canoe would move easily. Once she was out in the water she could dig away the silt, then push the canoe free. It should not take much effort. If she could get some footing, she might be able to lift the bow end and slide it over.

Just as she started to leave the dugout, she heard the bellow of a large male alligator. He was not right upon her, but her action in the water would attract him. She decided to stay where she was until morning. She needed a good night's sleep anyway. She was safe in the canoe. It would not drift, and so she did not fear waking up lost.

Teeka curled herself in the bottom of the dugout. The sides of the canoe cuddled her, and the current rocked her to sleep. She raised one hand to her neck but not for the pendant. This time she fingered the bear's tooth that Kaho had put in her medicine bag. Everything had at last been put right. The nightmare had ended. Finally there was a future to look forward to. There was work to be done. The spirits counted on her.

The sensitive canoe rocked from the small wake left by the alligator as it passed by, curious. The large male went beneath the water and swam to the canoe. The bright moon in the sky made it easy for him to see what was above him, floating on top of the water. After passing by, he surfaced and turned to face the object that had his attention. His nostrils flared, catching a scent, which he interpreted as food. Slowly, cautiously, the alligator moved his tail from side to side, propelling himself quietly, like a dark ghost, half submerged and half above the water. When he got close enough, he paused. Had his prey seen him? Nothing moved. He did not even blink.

The object showed no evidence of fear or attack. He had not been noticed. Closer. Sucking in the air. He paused, confused by the facts. He smelled animal—meat, food—but that scent was mixed with something else. Closer. He barely nudged the canoe with his nose. Disappointed, he moved away, pumping his muscular tail from one side to the other, making a small wake, a series of ripples that passed beneath the canoe.

Teeka's hip ached from the hard surface of the canoe. She turned, catching the rough splinters. In a moment she had drifted back to sleep. The moon watched like a guard sent by the spirits until the sun argued its way over the eastern horizon.

———

The birds quickly noticed the new day's light and began their morning songs. Teeka stretched out on her back and opened her eyes. She would get an early start, and instead of stopping at the campsite, she would travel on into the night. She would arrive late. Kaho would most surely be sleeping, but he would not mind her waking him. He would be expected to stay at the wedding platform for only a few more days. She knew he would be worried already. She hoped he had believed in her.

Teeka splashed water on her face, thinking of all the things she needed to tell Kaho. The baby would be one of the most difficult. For the first time since she had lost the baby, she allowed herself to think about it. The child she had never known held a special place in her heart. Death seemed so unfair a destiny for such a little spirit. Teeka pressed her fingers to her mouth as if that would stop the tears that burned her eyes. She would have to trust the spirits' decisions. Such things were not for her to question.

Again she splashed her face with water. She did not need to dwell on the past; there was too much ahead that would require her attention. She did have a mission. For the first time in a long time, she found herself eager to begin the new day. There were no shadows and no secrets.

She looked at the water, searching for a sign of the alligator she had heard in the night. She did not see him. Teeka eased herself over the side of the canoe. She had bathed in this river. She had walked in this river, and she had swum its breadth. She had drunk from this river. But this morning she felt uncertain about entering the water. It was brown and cloudy, which made it impossible to see the bottom. In other parts of the river, the water was so clear that one could hardly tell it was there. Every pebble, every stone that rested on the bottom, was clearly visible. But not here.

Slowly she lowered herself. She felt vulnerable when the water climbed up her legs as if it were alive. She held on to the side of the dugout, gradually letting herself down. A coot rustled the reeds near the shore, then broke from cover, flapping its wings, and cracking the unnerving silence. Teeka jerked herself up, scraping her rib cage against the side of the canoe. When she realized what had startled her, she was not sure if she wanted to cry or laugh.

To her surprise, the canoe started to move, drifting down the river. Her sudden motion had set it free. She pulled herself over the side and flopped into the bottom of the dugout. It would be nice to be home. Home. What an extraordinary thought. She realized that she now considered the Kahoosa village her home. She lay in the bottom of the canoe smiling and wiping away the tears that ran down her face.

——

The day continued to evolve passively, giving her time to rest, to drift, to be alone with pleasant thoughts. It was a good time. It was a time to revitalize. The river wound and twisted, but Teeka followed the clear landmarks. When night fell, the moon provided the light. The journey back had been uneventful and easy.

Carefully, Teeka drew her paddle through the water, turning the bow, forcing the canoe to follow a small stream that flowed out of the bigger river. Each new tributary had its own mark to guide her home. Finally, beneath the bright moon, she turned the canoe again. The lilies huddled together, nearly choking the small stream. The canoe left a trail of insulted water plants behind it as Teeka moved steadily toward her destination.

The clearing was just ahead. She moved the canoe into

the brush, short of the landing. Stepping out of the bow, she pulled the canoe aground and tied it to a lonely cypress knee. In the shallow water that had flooded over the shore, Teeka bathed, rinsing the soil of the journey from her body. When she was finished, she stood naked on the bank, drying in the breeze. She leaned her head to the side so that all her hair fell over one shoulder. She twisted the long black cluster, wringing the water out. She thought about making a perfume but decided that it would take too much time. Instead of the long process, she found some aromatic flowers, pulverized them, and rubbed the residue in the creases of her body.

She chewed a sweet leaf from a plant that grew close to the ground. It left her mouth feeling cool and refreshed. Quickly she reworked the moss around the vine belt of her skirt. Her hair was still wet, but it did not drip. She could not wait for it to dry.

Swiftly she freed the canoe and pushed out into the water. Ahead she could see the clearing. In moments her canoe was beached. Her heart swelled with affection as she trotted up the path to the wedding platform.

Many of the garlands that had been made by the Kahoosa women to decorate the wedding hut had browned, and dead petals of flowers littered the trail. Teeka remembered how beautiful it had been when she had first seen it.

Up the path she saw the shelter. Quietly she stepped on the floor, creeping up on the beautiful sleeping man. Her stomach fluttered with nervousness. On her knees beside him, she breathed in deeply, closing her eyes, enjoying his scent. Softly she pressed her lips to the side of his neck and whispered to him.

"King of the Kahoosa, your woman has come home to you."

Her voice was so soft she was not sure it would wake him, but Kaho turned from his side to his back, opening his eyes. His lips formed a word, maybe her name, but she touched her finger to his mouth.

"Say nothing except that you love me."

Kaho raised his hand to the back of her neck. He felt only one necklace strand as he pulled her toward him, drawing her mouth down to his. Teeka closed her eyes before their lips met, and she heard him murmur to her.

"Woman of Kaho, this king gives you his heart."

The sound of his voice, the touch of his hand, and the warmth of his lips filled her as her body melted into his.

Kaho carefully picked up his knife from the floor beside his mat. Gently he pulled her body over his, wrapping his arms around her. Easily he glided his hand and the knife down her spine until he felt the waistband of her skirt. He slid the sharp edge under the belt and, with a quick turn of his wrist, cut it.

She lifted her head and looked into his face.

"I hope this skirt was not too much work."

Teeka lifted her hips, slid the skirt to one side, and tossed it across the shelter. Kaho skimmed the knife across the floor and moved her beneath him. He would give to her all that he could. She was his bride.

———

In the morning, they were both surprised to see the lateness of the sun's position in the sky. Even after they had satisfied their passion, they had held each other, enjoying the feel of the other's body so close. When they did awake, Teeka felt Kaho's arm still over her hip. Her back was pressed against his chest, his face against her shoulder. She felt so content that she hated to move and break the magic. She turned over so that she faced him, touching his chest with slow, sleepy kisses.

"Where do we start this day?" he asked.

"We have started it as we should—together."

"Every new day will begin the same. Every new day I will be thankful to wake and find you next to me."

"The spirits are smiling on us."

Kaho kissed her forehead. "Which spirits? The Kahoosa or the Tegesta?"

"Do not ask such difficult questions so early in the morning," she responded. "Later I will say much to answer your question."

Kaho sat up. "Stay here. Take more time in waking. I will bring your morning meal."

"No," she answered. "I wish to serve my husband."

Kaho's face imitated a boyish pout. "I had planned this for your return."

Teeka grinned at him. "You always know just what to say and how to look at me."

Kaho disappeared quickly, and Teeka stretched and yawned. The wedding mat was large and soft, and her body resettled comfortably back into it. It was not long before she smelled the smoke from the fire Kaho had started. The aroma of the berry tea made her stomach growl with hunger.

Teeka finally got up and went to him. She stood behind him as he squatted by the fire, turning the skewer that held the fresh fish. She rubbed his shoulders while he stirred the tea.

Kaho patted the earth next to him, asking her to sit with him. He poured some of the hot tea into a smaller drinking bowl and offered her some. She sipped at it, rolling the flavor over in her mouth.

"It is not as good as the teas you have made me," he commented.

"It is delicious," she contradicted. "Besides, it was made by my husband's hand."

"And you say that I know what to say." He laughed. "Perhaps you wish me to prepare your morning meal every morning. What would the Kahoosa think of their king?"

"They would think that he loves the woman he took as his wife."

"Ha!" he said with a chuckle.

Teeka took a big swallow of the tea. Today he was going to hear a lot of things he would think strange. She would start with the question he had already posed.

"Which spirits do you think are smiling?" she began.

"You have not let that thought leave your head?"

"I told you I would have much to say later."

"And it is later?"

"Yes, and I really do have much to say about it, but I am not certain what you will think."

"Well, then, why do you not begin?" he asked, taking the fish from the skewer and laying it on a wooden slab, prying it apart to expose the white flesh inside.

"I am Tegesta by my birth, but I live under the Kahoosa sky. Inside my medicine bag I carry totems from the Tegesta spirits that were given to me by a shaman. Inside that same medicine bag I carry another totem. It is not Tegesta."

"The bear tooth? Is that what you mean?"

"Yes, the bear tooth. You gave that to me, and it is Kahoosa. Then to whose spirits do I belong? Which spirits watch over me? I carry totems of both."

"You are Kahoosa now."

"Yes, but I was born Tegesta. A person cannot give that up just because she decides to. But you are also correct. I am Kahoosa. The Kahoosa spirits recognize me, and so do the Tegesta. I carry totems of the Tegesta and the Kahoosa. The totems do not argue inside the bag. They rest next to each other. Together they tell my story. Together they make me stronger than I was before."

Kaho looked at her, puzzled.

"I am certain of this. Kaho, there is more. When I left you here, I took with me a secret that I wish I had shared with you. Inside of me I carried our child. The Kahoosa spirits recognized me. Your spirits knew me as your wife, a Kahoosa wife. They did not turn from me. As you told me, it takes both the man's seed and the spirits to make a baby grow."

"What do you mean? You say you carried the child. And why did you not tell me?"

"I did not tell you because I wanted everything settled first. I thought that when I came back to you, I could tell you about the child, and then we could rejoice. I did not want anything from my past to interfere with that joy. But on my way I lost the baby. My body turned it out from me."

"Then what you say is incorrect. The spirits battled over the child. The baby was part of me, Kahoosa, and part of you, Tegesta."

"The baby was both in one. I lost the baby because of the ordeal I went through. The journey was difficult, and I had been under much strain. And if the spirits did take the child away, it was because this was not the best time for it to be born."

Teeka's eyes teared as she argued the last point. Her voice cracked, and Kaho wanted the conversation ended.

"Teeka, it does not matter to me about the spirits. It is not important. And we will have other babies," he said, putting his arm around her shoulders and pulling her to him so that she rested her head on his shoulder.

"The spirits do matter, and what I have to tell you is important. It is why you chose me that day. It is why you were injured by the bear—so that I would heal you and fall in love with you. The spirits designed it all. The Tegesta and the Kahoosa are different in the way that they do things, but really there is not much difference. Their words and legends are much the same. The Tegesta and the Kahoosa are one to the spirits. I know that it is so. They are the same spirits. Our joining is the proof. And the children we will have will also be the proof. The spirits look for the Kahoosa and the Tegesta to unite."

Kaho stood up and paced. "I do not think that could ever be."

"But it will. The spirits have even moved the Tegesta to initiate the first step. They did not come just to see me. That was only an excuse. As I told you, this is all the grand design of the spirits. When we return, speak to the shaman. Ask him to talk with the spirits."

Kaho again sat next to her. He looked at her face, which was flushed with excitement. "You did have much to say. It will give me many days of thought."

Chapter Thirty-one

The seasons came and went. Teeka and Kaho went back to the village, and the Kahoosa celebrated their return. Tosa continued with her lessons, and Teeka had also shared what she knew of the Tegesta medicine with the Kahoosa shaman, who listened carefully, intrigued with all that she knew.

Early one morning Teeka awakened cold. She shivered, pulling her deerskins around her and snuggling up to Kaho's warm body. The air in her nose was chilly and dry, and it made her throat hurt. She held her hands over her nose and breathed into them, warming the end of her nose.

Kaho pulled her closer, wrapping his arms around her. It had been a few complete moon cycles since she had last been to the isolation area. Though she had no illness or weakness this time, she knew the child had begun to grow inside of her.

Kaho rested his hand on her belly as if he might feel the life inside of her.

"It is still too early for that," she told him.

"It is not too early for the son of a Kahoosa king and a Tegesta woman."

Teeka laughed at his proud remark. "I suppose it is not," she answered, "but it is too early for the mighty

Kahoosa king to feel him."

"You spoil my fun," he complained, moving his ear to take his hand's place on her abdomen. "Shh," he whispered.

"If you hear anything, it is my hunger this morning," she said, touching the top of his head.

His lips left a damp kiss on her stomach before he moved his face to her breasts.

"Keep me warm this morning," she murmured as his tongue drew smooth, wet lines along the curves of her body.

He was gentle and tender, gradually building her desire.

"I do not want to hurt you," he managed to say.

"Never," she answered, her breath catching.

The hide covers were soon too heavy, and the air delightfully cold. Next to each other they lay breathless.

Teeka turned to her stomach and propped herself up on her elbows. She looked across to the packed basket.

"You have not consented to do this just for me, have you?" she asked.

"You know that I would do anything for you, but this is what the future holds. Shaman has told me of some of the visions that are beginning to concern him. It is my responsibility as cacique to consider and act upon those things he suspects."

Teeka felt relief. The journey they were to take to the village of Teges was a response, a show of good faith, that the Kahoosa were willing to live with the Tegesta peacefully. Teeka at the side of the Kahoosa king was a symbol. She did want to see her mother and her sister, especially now that she carried a child. She wanted to share this joy with them. She also hoped to find Auro well and happy, recovered from the sickness that had overtaken his mind. She wanted to see the Tegesta pay him honor as their shaman.

"I have everything prepared so that we can leave in the morning," Teeka told him. "I am pleased that it is just the two of us. It will show the Tegesta the side of you that I know. Teges will see the real king of the Kahoosa, and he will respect you because you allow yourself to be vulnerable in the face of the Tegesta. That is the true mark of courage."

Kaho looked at her; something in the back of his mind still bothered him. Though he felt sure there were no other motives for the visit, he often wondered what it was that had made her leave their wedding bed and return to her village. He had no doubt that she loved him, but there was always that shadow. Perhaps he would understand with the visit. He would not ask her. If it was something she wanted to tell him, she would.

The Kahoosa appeared pleased with the decision Kaho had made. It had become difficult for them to remember the young Kaho, who had taken everyone and everything with his powerful reign. Now they saw him as a man. They did not fear his wrath but respected his leadership. He had always envisioned a united people— just his method and approach had been wrong. It had taken the Tegesta woman to show him the way.

——

In the early morning, Teeka and Kaho pushed off into the river, traveling toward the clan of Teges. The landmarks were familiar. By the edge of the water, a raccoon looked up from the crab he had been pursuing. The canoe traveled slowly and steadily.

They camped along the bank where the high marsh grass cleared. Kaho built a small lean-to that would keep the cold north wind from blowing on them. Before nightfall Teeka watched Kaho stand on the rocks with his spear lifted level with his shoulder, waiting for a fish to pass by. She shivered from the cold breeze and went back to the fire that he had started when they first arrived. Throwing some grass and twigs on top of the coals brought it to a blaze. Teeka held her hands out to it, rubbing first one and then the other. Cold weather did not often come, and she did not like it.

Kaho returned with a fresh bass. He skewered it and sat with her by the fire, turning the fish so that it cooked evenly. There were no berries to pick; they had all gone to seed, though she did find some leaves, which she brewed into a tasty tea.

As the sun continued to go down, Kaho banked the fire with some hardwood that would burn like coals through the night. They stretched one of the hide covers over the fire until it was warm, and then crawled inside the lean-to. Together they huddled contentedly through the night beneath the warmth of the blankets.

The next morning was not quite so cold, and Teeka was grateful. At least when the cold air did come, it did not usually last very long. That was especially good for the old and ailing. It was difficult for the Kahoosa to cope with the cold weather because all their strategies were planned to be effective in very warm weather. The spirits saw to it that even though the icy air from the north sometimes surged over them, it was soon chased away. The only good thing that Teeka could see come of it was a reprieve from the pesty mosquitoes.

Kaho was careful to extinguish all the coals from the fire before they left. The cold season was also a dry season, and a small spark from an unattended fire could cause a wildfire that might burn for days and days, turning the land to ash and perhaps even ruining their village if it came that way.

Along the way they ate from the basket that Teeka had prepared before they left. Kaho's strong arms moved them swiftly toward the Tegesta village. At last they recognized the land close to the village. Kaho slowed the dugout so that their approach would be more cautious. Selo, Teeka's mother, was by the river. She looked up and noticed the small canoe down the river. She stood erect, facing the oncoming canoe, trying to get a better look. She leaned out, looking farther down the river. There were no other canoes. This one came alone.

Kaho paddled closer, and Teeka stood in the bow. She recognized Selo, who still looked uncertain. The canoe came closer, and Teeka called out to her.

Finally she realized that it was her daughter in the canoe. Who had brought her home?

Teeka and Kaho sat in the still canoe some distance from the shore. Even though Teeka was with him, he thought the gesture of waiting for an invitation would be appropriate. Never had he waited before. In the past he had always marched onto the Tegesta shore, never requesting permission. But this time it was different.

A small group of Tegesta began to gather timidly near the shoreline. They looked curiously at Kaho, wondering if this was some deceitful plot. Teges finally arrived and motioned for Kaho to bring his craft ashore.

It was a tense moment for all when first Teeka and then Kaho stepped onto the Tegesta soil. Teeka embraced her mother as Kaho spoke.

"I return your visit to further explore your suggestions," Kaho said, addressing Teges.

Teges nodded at the Kahoosa king. "You are a wise cacique," he said, nodding to Kaho with respect. "Teeka, are you well?"

"Yes, Cacique. I am well and I bring good news. I am the wife of Kaho—by my choice."

"And are you happy and well treated?"

Teeka touched Kaho's hand. "I am very happy."

"The Kahoosa king has come in peace. I am convinced that this mission is the work of the spirits," he said to both.

Teeka scanned the background for Illa.

"Come and sit at my hearth," Teges requested.

Kaho followed the cacique. They would discuss many things today that would clear new paths in the future. The alliance would not be a sudden event but rather a slow and cautious transition.

Teeka followed her mother to the platform of Illa and Ata. Illa saw her as she approached. She had been inside the platform nursing the baby when Teeka arrived, and she had not heard. When she realized who was coming with her mother, she ran to meet her, holding the baby close to her.

"Teeka!" she called.

Teeka ran toward her until they were close enough to touch. Teeka wrapped her arms around her sister, the baby between them.

"Let me see her," Teeka finally said, letting go of Illa. "It is a girl, as you dreamed?"

"Yes, and she is called Teeka."

Teeka looked into the face of the infant. "She looks like Mother," Teeka commented, taking her mother's hand and pulling her close to look at the baby. "Mother, she has your eyes."

Selo smiled. "This is a happy moment for me to have my daughters together again."

The three women sat in the shade of the platform. "I

have good news to tell you," Teeka said.

Illa and Selo both hoped that the news was what they expected. Illa asked, "Are you coming home?"

"No," Teeka answered. "There is much to explain. Kaho is my husband."

"Oh, Teeka," Selo said sadly.

"No, Mother. As I told Teges, he is my husband by choice."

"No!" Selo said. "He cannot be."

"Please, Mother, let me explain. The spirits sent me to him. I love him, and it is good. We are the symbols that the spirits want the Tegesta and the Kahoosa to see. We are one, as both tribes will be one day."

Selo's face softened. "Does he love you? Is he a good husband?"

"He does love me and he is a good husband."

"That is all that really matters, I suppose," Selo admitted.

"I have more wonderful news. I carry a child."

Illa's arms immediately went around her sister.

"This child is Tegesta and Kahoosa. He is the blending of the two."

"That is a powerful sign," Selo added.

"Kaho and Teges discuss these things at this moment. Our shaman has had visions. Has Auro spoken of any visions?"

Illa's and Selo's faces drained of color, and their expressions changed dramatically.

It was so obvious that Teeka could not help but notice.

"What is it? What is wrong?"

"Teeka," Illa began. "Auro ..."

"Auro what?" Teeka asked. "Why are you stumbling over your words?"

"Auro is dead," Selo blurted.

Teeka's head dropped forward. "Auro is dead?" she asked softly, hoping she had misunderstood.

"Yes," Illa confirmed. "Olagale is the shaman."

"I want to see Shala. I need to see her alone," Teeka said, standing and starting to leave.

She walked away from her mother and sister and on to Shala's platform. She saw her sitting by her fire wrapped in hides, trying to keep her old body warm.

"Teeka?" the old woman asked as she saw the young woman coming to her.

"Yes, Shala, it is Teeka."

Shala struggled to get to her feet.

"Please do not stand." She put her hand on Shala's shoulder. "I want to sit with you."

"Auro is gone," Shala told her.

"Yes, I know. It saddens me so deeply."

"It had to be."

"I want to see his grave. There are things that I should say."

"He cannot hear you, Teeka."

"But I must say them anyway."

"Then I will show you where his body rests."

Shala stood with Teeka's help, but she did not head toward the burial mound.

"Where do you go?" Teeka asked.

"He is not buried with the People."

"I do not understand. Why is he—"

Shala interrupted. "He is dead by his own hand."

Teeka felt the pain of her breath being stolen. She followed Shala in silence until they reached the grave site. On her knees, Teeka brushed away the leaves and debris that had gathered on top of the marker.

"I will leave you alone," Shala told her as she walked

away.

Teeka sat back on her heels. "I am so sorry," she began. "We had no idea that it would end this way the night that we called the spirits and said our vows. I did love you, and I know that you loved me. But the spirits had a more important plan. The People bury you in dishonor when a proud marker should stand at your grave. They do not know the sacrifice you made as part of the spirits' plan. You did not even know. I tell you now so that you can rest in peace."

Teeka gazed down at the grave. "What happened to us will not happen again to one of our people. There is going to be a peace. The Tegesta and the Kahoosa will be one people. This is what you have suffered for. The spirits chose us to be a part of it."

Teeka placed her hand on her belly. "I know that in your heart you want my happiness. I am happy, Auro. I am where the spirits know it is best for me and for the People."

She sat silently for a few moments and then spoke again. "We were so young. Our marriage never could be. The spirits knew that from the start." Teeka's voice quavered with emotion. "But in my heart I have a special place, a place that belongs only to you, a space in me that only you can fill. That place is sealed, as it should be, so that it causes no more pain, so that I am able to give my love to another. I hope you were able to do the same at the end."

Teeka took a handful of loose soil and then spread her fingers apart, watching it trickle back to the ground. "Always," she whispered.

She felt Shala's hand on her shoulder. "We should return. Someone will ask where you are."

Teeka stood and put her arms around Shala, holding

her tightly.

"I am glad that you came," Shala said as they separated. "Auro knows that you were here."

Shala led Teeka back to the village. Kaho stood with Teges, Ata, and Illa. He smiled when he saw her returning. Shala had gone back to her platform, and Teeka reappeared alone.

Kaho walked to meet her. "It is time for us to leave."

He waited a moment before speaking again as if deliberating whether or not to say it. "Have you done everything that you wished to do while you were here?"

"Yes, everything," she answered, thanking him with her eyes. Her heart swelled with love for him.

Teges, Selo, Illa, Ata, Yagua, and Olagale walked them to the canoe. "As the caciques we have much to consider," Teges said as Teeka and Kaho prepared to leave.

Kaho pushed off the canoe and then poled into the deeper water. Teges and his party stood on the shore until they were out of sight.

"Sometimes it is hard to tell the difference between a beginning and an ending," Teeka said as they made the first turn in the river.

Kaho sat down next to her. "This is a beginning."

Epilogue

THE SMALL BOY DARTED in and out of the mist, intrigued with the fog. It looked as if he could walk into the clouds, but they were forever in front of and behind him, just out of his touch. His mother looked back to make certain that he followed. It brought joy to her to see him toddle through the haze, slapping his hands at the elusive wisps of air. He was robust, like the men of her people, but he was tall, like his father, and he would someday be the king of a new nation. That was the point of the journey her husband was about to make.

"Hurry," she said, encouraging the little one to catch up to her. "Your father is about to leave."

As they reached the water, the mist thickened. The young boy clung to his mother's leg.

In the canoe were the cacique and the shaman. This would perhaps be the most important journey they ever made.

Kaho stepped out of the canoe and walked to her. He pressed his lips to hers and then tousled his son's hair.

"Do you know who you are?" He laughed as he squatted next to his son.

The little boy giggled at his father's tickling. Teeka put her hand on Kaho's shoulder. "This is a good thing for us all."

The mother and son watched as Kaho and the shaman drifted into the fog. They would be gone for two moons. Not so long. A day to travel, a day to meet, and a day to return.

———

The site was neutral. Neither the Kahoosa nor the Tegesta claimed it. One moon cycle ago they had met here briefly. They had listened to the shamans, and they had designed a plan, which they took back to their people. Yagua and Kaho then met with their Councils of men. They discussed the plan, and now they met again.

Four men sat across from one another around a blazing fire. Two were Kahoosa, and two were Tegesta. They exchanged gifts of food for their dinner. Tonight they would make simple conversation. Tomorrow they would discuss the peace.

In the morning the men gathered, sharing their food again. When the morning meal was complete, they began.

Olagale was the first to speak, repeating what had initiated their first meeting.

"My visions have shown me that there is something coming, a bigger enemy than we are to each other. It can destroy us all. I have been told that we must unite, to be all one people."

The Kahoosa shaman agreed. "I have seen the same visions. I have been told that there is danger ahead for all of us and that we should not destroy one another, or we will be too weak to face this new threat."

The two caciques listened. If the shamans were right, and surely they were if they had both had the same vision, the survival of their tribes would be up to them as the leaders.

Kaho and Yagua were sober in their announcements.

Each told that his tribe had approved of the plan. The two tribes were to be at peace. They would share their wealth and the land. They would frequently visit each other, each learning the customs and beliefs of the other tribe so that they could understand and respect those values. The transition was to be slow but steady. When Kaho's son came of age, he would look to the Tegesta for a bride. With this last seal of peace, the two tribes would unite as one, becoming an incredibly powerful force. Kaho and Teeka's son would rule the new nation, selecting Tegesta and Kahoosa men to advise him.

When the discussions had ended, the four leaders shared some black tea.

When the night came, they looked at the fires that burned in the sky. The fires of the Tegesta spirits could not be told from those of the Kahoosa.

About the Author

Lynn Armistead McKee has worked as a writing trainer for Broward County Schools and Citrus County Schools in Florida. Her interest in archaeology and her work with the Broward County Archaeological Society led her to write historical fiction about the indigenous peoples of South Florida. Writing as Lynn Sholes she also co-writes thrillers with Joe Moore. Lynn is a member of International Thriller Writers, Mystery Writers of America, and The Authors Guild. She writes from her home in the Sunshine State.

Other Books by Lynn Armistead McKee

TOUCHES THE STARS

KEEPER OF DREAMS

WALKS IN STARDUST

SPIRIT OF THE TURTLE WOMAN

DAUGHTER OF THE FIFTH MOON

**Other Books by this author, writing as Lynn Sholes
with Joe Moore**

THE GRAIL CONPSIRACY

THE LAST SECRET

THE HADES PROJECT

THE 731 LEGACY

THE COTTEN STONE OMNIBUS

THE PHOENIX APOSTLES

THE BLADE

THE SHIELD

THE TOMB

THOR BUNKER, A Short Story

BAM! JUST LIKE THAT (short story)

Excerpt from

TOUCHES THE STARS

MIAKKA HAD BEEN WITH THIS MAN. She knew that he had been with many women. That was his prerogative as shaman. She studied his face for a moment.

Atula looked at Miakka, a young, small-boned woman. She knelt in front of him, her black hair spilling across her breasts, forming black satiny rivers that hid so much of her.

If he had been just a man, maybe he would have chosen her, Miakka thought. She looked away. The thought was not worth entertaining. He was more than a man. He was the shaman, and she was no more than a woman—a woman swollen with the fruit of his seed. As it should be.

"I am worried," she said. "The child I carry ..." she began, almost whispering, bowing her head in respect.

Being so close to him flooded her with sensations she barely understood. His clear, dark, gentle eyes reached deep inside her. How was she going to tell him? Though she had rehearsed it so many times, now that she knelt before him her mind tangled and her tongue became uncooperative. She would have to put aside those feelings, ignore the effect he had on her. She needed his help to resolve the horrendous thing that was happening to her and to the child that grew inside her.

"What is it that has you so concerned?" he asked, noticing the small tremors in her hands.

Miakka's head was bowed in respect and embarrassment. If she allowed herself to look at him, to realize how close she was to this man, she would lose sight of her mission. She would find herself too snared in emotion.

He could take no one woman to live at his hearth, no wife. Another presence could interfere in his communication with the spirits. Unlike the other men, he could have any woman anytime, and if she conceived she would hold an honored place with the People. The other men had to seek their women from other clans, other villages, not from the small circle of women who were members of their own clan. That was forbidden. The shaman sowed his seed in the bellies of the women of his village. It kept his line pure. One male child would be trained by the father, Atula, and that child would become the next shaman. Which male child it might be, only Atula would know for sure. There would be signs.

Miakka knew she would never live at Atula's hearth. There would never be any more between them than what had already been.

"Do you remember the night that you danced with me at the fire and how you led me to your platform? From that night a child has grown from your seed and has been nourished by my body."

"That is something good," he replied, reassuring her that she had not done anything wrong in the eyes of the clan. She need not worry. He would confirm that the child was his.

It should be something good, she thought. She could have lived with the clan's curiosity, but no one questioned that Atula was the father.

"You do not understand. No one doubts that the child is yours. I am not shunned for conceiving a child without a husband."

"Tell me, then, what has made you come to me? What makes your brow furrow with worry and your lovely mouth turn down?"

As he spoke, his voice conjured up memories of the tender things he had said to her that night. Miakka felt her face flush.

"Do you remember how long ago I was with you?" she asked, unsure that she was beginning correctly. "The night you danced with me and ... and do you see me now?"

Atula did indeed remember. It was after the return of the men from the Big Water. It was a jubilant occasion, and all had had their fill of cassite, an herbal decoction that was a mild intoxicant. From across the central fire he had seen her as she stepped to the music. The reflection of the fire made her hair look like strands of liquid black, charred coals melting down her soft back. Her head was tilted, the moonlight illuminating her delicate face. She swayed to the music like the night air when stirred by a gentle wind.

Atula had slowly walked across the crest of the hardwood hammock that so courageously rose up out of the wetland. He had passed the fire to be closer to her, to watch her as she lost herself in the music. As he had drawn closer, her dance awakened the need in him.

He was also being watched. Amakollee eased herself behind him and then to his side. She smiled as she danced in front of him, tossing her head provocatively and moistening her lips with her tongue. It was a gesture not missed by Atula, but it was Miakka who had his attention.

Atula had smiled kindly at Amakollee, continuing his walk, but she placed herself squarely in front of him and waited for a response. When he gave none, she took it that he had not read her gestures. She would not touch the shaman without invitation, but she did position herself closer.

"Have you enjoyed the evening?" he asked, hoping to distract her intentions. Through the throng and firelight he could still see Miakka moving alone to the music.

"The celebration is not over, Atula. The night has just begun."

Atula did not want to insult Amakollee. He had been with her before—a few times. The events had produced no child, and Amakollee still belonged to no man. It would not be long before her age would discourage a mate. Without a mate she would become a burden to the clan. Clans often sent young men to other villages to find mates, but no man from any other village had shown an interest in her. She had passed her youth, and the humiliation was becoming intolerable. Atula was her only hope. If she could conceive his child, the clan would always take care of her.

"I am hungry for only one thing this evening. Sleep. Too much cassite has made me groggy," he told her, trying to be polite.

Amakollee flushed with humiliation. Even though he had tried to be congenial, he was not interested. She had made a fool of herself. Her lips paled from their natural deep hue to a pasty gray. The color drained from her face and she was certain he could also see her humiliation. Quietly she moved away from him, realizing that he hardly noticed. She backed away from the fire and the rest of her people and ducked into the brush. When clear of the village and its sounds, she fell to the earth, pounded it with her fists, and screamed into the darkness.

Miakka abandoned herself to the music as Atula approached her. Her movements were fluid and graceful. Earlier, from a distance, she had watched him as she always did, but her shyness made her fear that he might notice. The cassite warmed her insides and unfettered her mind enough that she drifted with the fantasy.

The cassite had not dulled his senses, but it had compromised his inhibitions. He was not usually so forward and blunt. Atula stepped in front of her, began to move his body in unison with hers, and then reached out to wrap his palm and fingers gently around the nape of her neck.

Miakka opened her eyes and slowed her dance, startled by the company.

Though the shadows fell across his face, the sharp lines of his straight nose and strong jaw formed a clean silhouette.

"I like the way you dance. Do not stop," he said.

Miakka's small feet barely moved, losing the rhythm. She tensed. Her knees felt weak, and a shudder ran through her as his hand slid down her neck, brushing the hollow of her throat and then moving out to rest on her shoulder.

"Please continue," he said, pulling her a little closer. He could smell her now, sweet with the light fragrance of flower petals that she had steeped in water and then splashed on her body.

She knew immediately where this encounter would lead. She could not have refused him even if she had wanted to. He was the shaman, and he had the right to any woman of the tribe.

Atula took her to his platform. She was a maiden, never taken by a man before. She trembled at his touch, and her naïveté aroused him. In the protection of his platform, he brushed back her long black hair, exposing her body to his full view, his eyes reflecting his pleasure in what he saw. Slowly he slid her moss skirt to the floor, holding her hand as she stepped out of it. She had responded innocently to him, waiting for each touch, surprised at each new sensation. But she had not let out a sound, nor had she shuddered with the gift of joining. He regretted that. The ceremonial tea must have made him too impatient

Afterward he lay next to her, breathing deeply while she lay curled up next to him in a tiny frightened ball. He had not been proud of himself. Obviously she was a maiden; he had known that, and he had not taken time with her. Then, as he chastised himself, the cassite made him sleep.

Since then she had seen him at a distance a few times, and always she turned timidly away from him. Now she knelt in front of him, her belly enlarged with his child.

Atula's face showed his confusion. The evening he had spent with her had not been that long ago. Again it was about time for the men to make the journey to the Big Water, as they did on each fourth full moon. It was important that the moon be full. Without the light, they could lose sight of the other canoes and their direction. His memory must be tricking him, he thought. Either it had been longer ago that he had been with her or she had not been a maiden at all. Look at how large she was with the child.

Miakka looked up, registering his perplexed expression. Tenderly she touched her abdomen. "It is so large, and I have so much time left to go."

Atula continued to stare in amazement. "Does it cause you pain?"

"No, I would not call it pain. But it is so difficult for me to do many things. I fear that the child grows too fast, that I cannot carry it, that I cannot bring it into the world, that the child is deformed." Miakka looked down, hiding her face so that he could not see that at any moment she might cry.

Atula read her emotions well. He heard the anguish and fear in her voice and saw it in her eyes as she spoke. He got to his knees and rubbed the palms of his sensitive hands across her tight-skinned belly and then put his ear to it. With his head bent across her, Miakka leaned down to breathe in deeply, taking in the scent of his hair and skin. She closed her eyes, imagining his head turning, his lips falling on her stomach and then slowly making their way up to her lips, leaving a damp trail of warmth along the way.

"Miakka, I cannot feel or hear anything. It is too early. This is just a large child and your first. It will be a fine boy," he said, hoping to relieve her anxiety. "A strong boy that you will be proud of."

"I hope to honor you," she said softly, with worry still in her voice.

The honor was his, he thought. "Go then and speak with Wagahi. She has watched over many women during this time and has aided in the births. Certainly she will reassure you."

Miakka rose slowly to her feet, taking his strong hand for balance. As soon as she stood, she tried to release his hand, but he held it a moment longer.

"May I come again if Wagahi does not satisfy me?" she asked, breaking the heavy silence. "Will you consult the spirits?"

"If Wagahi does not relieve you satisfactorily, come to me again. But I predict only a strong, healthy hunter, a child of whom you will be proud," he said, letting go of her hand.

Though she was truly large for her time, she still moved with grace. After the child was born, perhaps he would entertain the thoughts she always stirred in him.

As she disappeared, he sucked in a heavy breath. She

was right. There was something different about this pregnancy. Maybe Wagahi would provide the answer. He would ask for her opinion after Miakka had seen her.

It troubled him that neither his hands nor his ear had perceived the normal vibrations, sensations. And indeed the child was large. Grotesquely large. He would not wait. In the private shelter of his platform, he would consult the spirits.

In the still darkness he searched his pouches for the stems, leaves, and bits of plant that would purify him so that he might call the spirits to bring him a vision. Alone by his fire, he ground the ingredients in his wooden mortar, poured the mixture into a ceramic bowl with a small amount of water, and then suspended it above the coals. As the tea came to a boil, he sprinkled the yellow flower petals of a spiny herb, the prickly pear, atop it. Gently he stirred the potion with a stick, taking care not to bruise the delicate brew. His father had taught him the motion of the wrist, the measurements of the herbs. He had gone with him on his first flight into the spirit world. Atula missed him.

Soon after sipping the elixir he began to feel its warmth spread through his arteries. His nostrils flared as he concentrated, letting an abundance of clean but warm, humid air into his lungs. There was a tingling at every hair shaft on his body. The fragmented long bones of an extinct beast, handed down from father to gifted son, lay at his side. He began with a barely audible humming noise, and as his voice lifted against the chorus of crickets and night animals, it became fuller. After taking three deep breaths through his nose and letting them out of his mouth, he reached for the bones. They were cool and smooth in his hands. Their history and significance flowed through him, connecting him to all the memories, all the magic, of those who had come before.

Lightly at first he tapped the floor of his platform, increasing the intensity of the percussion and hum of his voice until they rang out in harmony. The magic words, the holy words, rode on the night air, passing the leaves and grass that fluttered at the sound. Soon his voice could not be distinguished from the sudden breeze. A quick burst of wind crossed the mound, stirring debris and then letting it settle. The drumming hammered through the dimensions, opening the doors to the spirit world. The incantations completed, the spirit man's head rolled back, his eyes twitched, and he dropped the bone instruments. With a slow roll his head slumped forward, and the vision began.

CONNECT WITH LYNN ARMISTEAD MCKEE ONLINE:

FACEBOOK: SHOLESANDMOORE.COM

WEBSITE: WWW.SHOLESMOORE.COM